Abou

Claire Boston is a contemporary romance author who enjoys exploring real life issues on her way to the happily-ever-after. She writes heart-warming stories, with resilient heroines and heroes you'll love. In 2014 she was nominated for an Australian Romance Readers Award for Favourite New Romance Author.

When Claire's not writing she can be found creating her own handmade journals, swinging on a sidecar, or in the garden attempting to grow something other than weeds.

Claire lives in Western Australia with her husband, who loves even her most annoying quirks, and her grubby, but adorable Australian bulldog.

You can connect with Claire through Facebook (https://www.facebook.com/clairebostonauthor) and Twitter (https://www.twitter.com/clairebauthor), or join her reader group (http://www.claireboston.com/reader-group/).

Also by Claire Boston

Nothing to Hide

A Blackbridge Novel

Claire Boston

BANTILLY
PUBLISHING

First published by Bantilly Publishing in 2018

Nothing to Hide: The Blackbridge Series

EPUB format: 978-1-925696-21-9
Mobi format: 978-1-925696-20-2
Print: 978-1-925696-22-6

Cover design by Lana Pecherczyk
Edited by Ann Harth
Proofread by Teena Raffa-Mulligan

DEDICATION

To my friends at the Vintage Motocross Club of Western Australia.
Thank you for your support, encouragement and patience, especially when
I was still being lapped on the track.

And to my husband for introducing me to it all, especially the swinging —
sidecar swinging that is!

Chapter 1

Will's muscles tightened as he stepped from the white Parks and Wildlife Services four-wheel drive. The high-pitched whine of the motorbike engine set his teeth on edge, and the sharp smell of two-stroke fuel irritated his nose. Why the council had agreed to let a motocross track be built on the edge of the national park, he didn't know.

This was the last place Will wanted to be. He wasn't good with confrontations and the chance that the motocross rider tearing around the track would care about the endangered orchids he'd found, or his proposal was slim. The conversation would end up in a shouting match — no not a match, that meant he had to take part. Will would be shouted at while trying to convince the other person to at least listen to him. That's how it usually went.

But the orchids were important, and he wouldn't let this biker stop him from saving them. This was the perfect opportunity to discover who was in charge. He hadn't expected the gates to be open, or for someone to be riding around on a fifty-year-old motorbike.

He crossed his arms and leaned on the chest-high metal fence that separated the track from the spectator area. The rider wore a dirt-bike helmet, but little else in terms of safety gear — blue jeans, black boots, and a loose blue T-shirt. Sure, it was thirty-two degrees in the shade today, but safety was important, especially on bikes. If he fell off, he'd have a hell of a gravel rash. The bike disappeared as the track twisted away from the spectator area and was hidden by bush, but its whine still polluted the air.

Will took stock of the facility. To his left was a clearly marked pit area, though the bays were cobbled together out of sheet metal and recycled posts and looked like they would blow over in a strong breeze. A white Hyundai with a small trailer was parked in front of one of the bays. Behind him, towards the entrance gates sat a clubhouse — a large, deep green corrugated metal building, with its door open. It had a verandah of sorts, nothing more than a concrete slab and a couple of wooden posts that extended the roof a few metres. The whole building had to be a sweat box in summer.

The roar of the bike grew louder again. The rider took the final corner and barrelled towards the finish line. Will stood straight and raised a hand to get his attention.

The bike didn't slow.

Will coughed as the dust kicked up by the bike floated over him. The rider hadn't seen him or didn't care.

Maybe someone was in the clubhouse.

The heat inside hit him like a wave and he grimaced. It was the type of heat he was used to back home in Goldwyer which was two thousand kilometres north of the small coastal town of Blackbridge, Western Australia. No one was inside, but another door to the right was closed. "Anyone here?" His voice echoed.

Mismatched chairs and tables were stacked along one wall and on the other were kitchen facilities — a sink and oven, deep fryers, a couple of fridges and a kettle. Everything was second-hand and ancient, much like his own furniture.

An engine stuttered outside, and Will turned to the door as the rider pulled up outside the clubhouse.

Nerves prickled his skin.

This was it. He'd rehearsed his speech. He would simply outline the situation clearly and hope to get through the conversation without being called a tree-hugging hippy or worse.

The rider killed the engine and dismounted, and then leaned the bike against one of the wooden poles. He took off his helmet.

Correction — *her* helmet.

Fleur Lockhart.

Every thought, every prepared sentence was wiped from Will's mind. He took in her flushed cheeks, neat brown braid, and sparkling blue eyes. She pushed wayward strands of hair from her damp forehead as she smiled at him. "Hey, Will. What can I help you with?"

How could he have mistaken her for a man? The blue T-shirt clung to her small breasts, defining her lean figure and those denim jeans hugged her legs like Hardenbergia on a tree. Wow.

"Will?"

Crap, he was staring at her like a love-struck idiot.

He swallowed hard. "What are you doing here?"

"I'm the president of the motocross club," Fleur said. "I had to get a few things ready for our busy bee this weekend and thought I'd squeeze in a ride while I was here."

The president. Of course she was.

She tilted her head. "Can I help you with something?"

His mouth was drier than Goldwyer in summer. "Ah, yeah, the orchids." Damn it. Could he sound more like an idiot? This was not going to plan.

Her lips lifted. "Orchids?"

He cleared his throat and tapped his thigh. "I, uh, discovered some endangered orchids on the fence line between the national park and the track." And unfortunately they were more track side than park side.

Fleur frowned. "Do you want permission to dig them up?"

Will shook his head. This was the tricky part. "They're critically endangered because they're difficult to propagate. We need to protect any areas where we find them."

"Can you show me?"

He moved towards the track and Fleur fell in beside him, her stride matching his, the only sounds the scuff of their boots on the dirt and the distant tweet of a wren. She was so close, and despite the fact she'd been racing around the track, she smelled like roses. His fingers brushed her soft hand and he snatched his hand back, rather than hold on to hers like he

3

longed to. The urge was absolutely ridiculous. He barely knew her, had met her that one time in hospital when they'd both visited Mai and Nicholas who were recovering from the bush fire a few weeks back.

He didn't believe in love at first sight, but that one meeting had definitely hit him in the chest. He hadn't built up the nerve to ask her out. How could he? He'd not seen her since. No way would he waltz up to her front door, or into the emergency room where she worked and ask her out.

The very idea was nightmare-worthy.

He'd say the wrong thing, or she'd laugh at him for even daring to think she might be interested in him.

"Did the bush fire cause much damage to infrastructure in the park?" Fleur's voice was loud in the silence.

"Some." He could do better than that. If he ever did ask her out, his usual one-word answers weren't going to cut it. "A couple of picnic areas burned down. We're going to need to replace tables and signage."

"Is that something you do?"

He nodded. "A few trees will need to be lopped as well."

"Must be a lot of work."

"Not really." He didn't mind the work, it kept him out of the office and away from people, just the way he liked it.

As they crossed the track and strode into the ankle-high grasses on the other side, the tension in his shoulders lessened. This was his element. Snakes were unlikely with the vibrations Fleur had been making with the motorbike, but he kept a sharp eye out anyway. When the boundary fence came into view he put a hand on her arm to stop her. "Wait." Her skin was warm, and he snatched his hand back. Heat rushed to his cheeks and he avoided meeting her gaze, instead scanning the ground for the tell-tale thin leaves and the damp hollow he'd seen from the park.

There they were, five plants scattered over an area of about two square metres, almost indistinguishable amongst the grass. He moved closer, watching where he placed his feet to make sure he didn't accidentally squash one.

He squatted down and examined the orchid, its yellow flower almost spent. It could be the Tall Donkey Orchid. He pulled out his phone and took a couple of photos to send to the service's botanist.

"What is it?"

He startled at Fleur's voice and almost fell forward on to the plant. Swearing, he landed hard on a sharp stone, his wrist twisting at an awkward angle.

"Are you all right?" The thud of her footsteps was loud.

"Stay there!" he growled, pushing himself back to his feet, and grimacing at the throb in his wrist.

Fleur scowled.

Crap. He'd snapped at her. "Sorry, I'm fine." He gently rotated his hand, wincing a little at the tenderness, but it wasn't anything he couldn't handle.

"Let me take a look. I'm a nurse." She moved forward again.

"Not here!" Damn it, she could squash a plant. "Over on the track." He shooed her away.

Fleur turned, her movements stiff, her posture straight.

Way to go, Will, you sure know how to impress the ladies. "Ah, the orchids are difficult to spot." He followed her.

Fleur's hands were confident as they examined his wrist, her white skin a direct contrast to his own brown tones, and he gritted his teeth at the pleasure her touch sent through him.

"I don't think it's sprained, but keep it elevated for a bit just in case."

"It's fine." Still he placed his hand on the opposite shoulder.

She raised her eyebrows.

"Thank you." He needed to get away from her before he said or did anything else stupid. "Can I document the orchid population?"

Her nod was sharp. "Go right ahead. It's the off-season, so not many people are using the track. You shouldn't have anyone disturb you."

The first good news of the day. "Thanks. I'll fence off the area. I don't want a bike to runoff and squash them."

"Wait a second." She held up a hand. "What kind of area are you talking about?"

"About four metres, just to be sure — from the track to the boundary fence." He could picture it in his mind already. "I can do it today. I've got the hessian in the back of my car."

She shook her head. "We're not allowed any structures within three metres of the track. It's not safe."

Damn it. He was so close to getting what he needed. "You said it's the off-season."

She bit her bottom lip. "We're having a busy bee here this weekend and the only way we get people to turn up is to promise them a chance of tuning their bikes."

Fleur couldn't seriously think that letting some bikers use the track was more important than saving an endangered species. She'd seemed so nice. "Reroute the track."

"We can't. We don't have the equipment or manpower." She scanned the area. "Mark it out for me."

Will carefully paced out the area he wanted to enclose.

"It's on the outside of a corner so it's easy for the guys to overshoot here if they haven't slowed enough. I'm surprised no one has squashed the orchids yet."

That wasn't what he wanted to hear.

"Still," she continued, "the regulations allow us to build a tyre wall in front of permanent structures like trees, so we could do that in front of your fence."

"You're agreeing to it?"

"Yeah. I'll build the wall myself on the weekend, if you do the enclosure before then. Some of the guys might not appreciate the significance of the plants."

His lips twitched at her wry response.

"I can give you a hand setting up now if you want."

Maybe she'd forgiven him for yelling at her. This was a chance to get to know Fleur. His heart thumped in his chest. "That would be great."

A familiar shrill short bird call had him scanning the surrounding trees until he found an adult black cockatoo sitting on the branches of a gum tree. Nearby was a hollow and a chick, some of its feathers still fluffy, stood at its entrance. He touched Fleur's arm and pointed. "Look at that."

She grinned. "It's so cute."

"It's a Carnaby Cockatoo. They're endangered because they need hollows like that to nest in. A mating pair will generally go back to the same nest year after year." He'd have to check his records as to whether this nest had been documented.

The chick flapped its wings, testing them out, and the adult sat on a branch to its left encouraging it. This could be its first outing from the nest. "Come on, little mate. You can do it." The chick chirped at its parent and after fluttering its wings another couple of times, it launched itself from the nest and made an awkward flight to the branch. Will let out a breath. "He made it." He turned to find Fleur watching him, not the bird. Crap. Had he done something stupid?

"You care, don't you?"

He frowned.

"You really cared if the baby bird made it. You care whether these orchids survive."

"Yeah." Was that considered geeky?

She smiled. "I'm glad the world has people like you in it." She gestured him to follow her. "Come on. Let's get that fence set up."

She couldn't have given him a nicer compliment. With a lighter step, he returned to his four-wheel drive and Fleur held out her hand. "Give me your keys. I'll drive it over. The whole track needs grading and some of the jumps are a bit steep and uneven."

Will hesitated. He wasn't supposed to let anyone drive his work vehicle.

She raised her eyebrows at him. "I'm a capable driver and you should keep your wrist elevated a little longer."

Of course she was. He took the keys out of his pocket and tossed them in his hands. His brothers always teased him for abiding by the rules to the letter, but he'd seen how quickly skirting the rules could get someone with his dark skin into trouble. Still, this was her property, she was doing him a favour. He handed her the keys and got into the passenger side, winding down his window. She didn't say anything and he couldn't find the words to fill the silence.

He hadn't stopped thinking about Fleur since he'd met her

at the hospital. Something about her, maybe her friendliness, her appearance, her confidence, had stuck with him. He'd imagined a universe in which he actually had the courage to ask her out, a universe where she would say yes.

In his dreams.

"This is the fire break." She drove onto a sandy path which ran along the fence line of the property. "It will be easier to access your orchids from here."

"Thanks." He should ask her something about the club, anything to get her to talk. The warm breeze blowing through the window was nice but talking about the weather was lame. Suddenly he caught a whiff of something sharp, acrid. "What's that smell?"

Fleur's incredulous glance had him stammering. "No, I mean — stop the car. I can smell chemicals."

Fleur braked and he got out, sniffing the air.

Nothing.

But he hadn't imagined it.

He walked back the way they'd come and yeah, a definite sharp, acrid smell came from the bush between the fire break and the track. "What's through there?"

"Nothing." Fleur walked over and screwed up her nose.

"I don't believe you." He strode into the bush, following his nose, but being careful where he trod in case there were other rare plants around. As he walked around the shrubs blocking his view from the fire break he swore.

A dozen or more five-litre clear plastic chemical tubs had been dumped haphazardly in a depression in the ground. The labels identified drain cleaner, caustic soda and brake fluid and a couple of the lids had come off and the remains of their contents were draining into the soil, killing the grass around it. Anger welled up in him. How could people treat the land like this? It was bad enough that there were climate change deniers, but if people didn't even care on a local level, how the hell could they fix the world?

He spun around to Fleur, his eyes narrowed. "You call this nothing?"

Fleur stepped back at the fury in Will's dark eyes. She peered around him to see what he was so worked up about and her mouth dropped open.

Son of a bitch. Someone had used the track as a dumping ground.

"You might own this land, but that doesn't give you the right to use it as a rubbish tip." He was so animated, so angry. "The chemicals can seep through the ground, they could kill those orchids."

Fleur gaped at him for a moment while her brain caught up. "You think I had something to do with this?" What a jerk. She met his anger with some of her own. "I have enough trouble maintaining the track without having to deal with some idiot doing this. If it's one of the members, I'll ban them from the club." The rubbish tip was only a couple of kilometres further down the road. She took two steps down the incline to gather up the containers and Will grabbed her arm.

"Wait."

She shook him off. He didn't get to touch her. "They're leaking into the ground."

He took a deep breath. "If it wasn't you, we have to call Sergeant Zanetti."

"Lincoln? Why? It's just some dickhead who didn't want to pay the extra tip payment." She was mad, but she didn't need to go to the police about it. They hadn't been able to stop people breaking into the track to ride, so they wouldn't be able to stop this either. She'd just have to deal with it.

Will shook his head. "I've seen containers like this before."

Suddenly she remembered the chemical containers Mai had found a month back. She'd mentioned Parks and Wildlife had been called and it had been drug related. Her eyes widened. "Like by the river?"

"Yeah."

Fleur got out her phone, took a photo of the mess, and then called Lincoln.

"What can I do for you, Flower?"

His use of her nickname soothed some of her anger.

"Someone's dumped rubbish at the back of the track. Will said to call you."

"What kind of rubbish?" he snapped.

Talk about instant reaction. "Chemical containers — drain cleaner, brake fluid, caustic soda and a whole bunch of matchboxes."

Lincoln swore, loud and ripe. "Don't touch anything. I'll be there shortly."

This was serious. Fleur hung up. "He's on his way."

Will scowled at the scene, and shuffled his feet, not acknowledging her. She doubted she'd get an apology. His khaki uniform might mould to his dark skin, defining his broad chest, and perhaps he'd been kind of cute when he'd stuttered, but good looks definitely weren't everything.

"Why don't you go set up your fence and I'll walk back and wait for Lincoln?"

A nod. He turned to go, stopped and ran a hand through his hair. "Sorry." He grunted and walked away.

Talk about a split personality. She couldn't work him out, seemingly shy one minute and angry and cold the next. She scanned the area. The rubbish could have been there for months because the track was used infrequently during the summer. The depression was far enough away from the track that no one would see the bottom if they were on a bike anyway.

Walking back towards the fire break, she scanned the boundary fence. No signs of it having been cut, but that was no surprise. It was easy enough to drive through the unlocked front gates.

Could the same creepy guy who had threatened Mai last month be responsible for discarding the waste? Lincoln had said he was a guy for hire and he'd had a gun he wasn't afraid to use.

The bush next to her rustled and she whirled around. A blue wren, its bright blue plumage contrasting against the olive-green leaves.

All these thoughts of drugs and thugs were getting to her.

With a sigh, she headed back to the clubhouse.

It was a good half an hour before Lincoln arrived with Senior Constable Ryan Kilpatrick. Fleur had loaded her bike onto the trailer and filled the clubhouse fridge with drinks for the busy bee on the weekend.

"Where are they?" Lincoln asked as he got out of the police car.

"Nice to see you too, Slinky." She smiled. "Hi Ryan. How are Felix and Hannah?"

"They're great. Hannah's talking about doing a musketeers' night sometime soon."

Fleur beamed. "That would be great." She hadn't seen her best friends much lately, particularly since Hannah and Mai had found the loves of their lives. She walked over to the police car. "We might as well drive. This thing should handle the sand around the fire break." She hopped into the back seat. "It's towards the back hill."

Lincoln drove onto the track. "Did you say Will Travers told you to call?"

"Yeah. He discovered an endangered population of orchids near the track, and we were driving out to set up a fence for them when he smelled the chemicals."

"Lucky he was here. You didn't disturb anything, did you?" Lincoln asked.

"No. Stop here." She led them to the hollow and Lincoln swore.

"I'll call Albany." He took his phone out as Ryan snapped some photos.

Will had been right — it was serious.

When Lincoln was done he said, "Detectives are on the way and when they're finished, this will need to be professionally removed. I want to keep this discovery quiet. You can't tell anyone what you found here."

It was all very hush-hush. "What if it's a member and not related to drugs?"

"Who said anything about drugs?"

"Will did." She rolled her eyes. "I'm not stupid, Slinky. You wouldn't call Albany if this was a case of littering."

"I can't tell you anything," he said.

"Fine. If you want to keep it secret, you'll need to clean it up by the weekend. It's the busy bee and there will be people all around the track."

"Damn it." He ran a hand through his hair. "Can you postpone it?"

She laughed. "Not a chance. You know what everyone's like."

"All right." He sighed. "I'm going to need to ask you and Will some questions."

"Sure. Go ahead."

When she'd finished answering Lincoln and Ryan's questions, she went to check the fence Will had erected around his precious orchids. The hessian was attached to big star pickets and the fence was bigger than she'd anticipated, but she wouldn't make a fuss.

Will was at the end of the block searching for more specimens. She almost hoped he didn't find any. Then she wouldn't need to deal with his demands again.

Whether she wanted to or not, she needed to talk to him, tell him to shut the gates if he was the last to leave. She was done here and had to get to work.

She strode down the fire break, so she didn't get told off for potentially squashing any plants. He didn't so much as glance up as she approached.

"Will."

He whirled around, eyes wide.

Either his hearing sucked, or he was *really* focused on what he was doing. "I'm heading off," she said. "If you're last to leave, can you shut the front gates?"

"Does it need locking?"

"No point. People cut the chains if they really want to get in. Just slide the bolt shut." She turned to go.

"The fence is all right?"

"It's fine. I'll get some old tyres delivered later this week and build a wall in front of it over the weekend."

"I can help, if you'd like."

She raised her eyebrows. He wanted to be helpful?

He shifted his gaze to his toes. "I appreciate you letting me do this."

Did he think she was completely lacking in empathy? "I won't be responsible for the extinction of a species." While she was perfectly capable of building the wall, it would be one less thing on her mountainous to do list. "All right. I'll be out here from eight on Saturday and Sunday. Drop by whenever suits."

"Can I have your number?" The words were said in a rush. "Ah, in case something comes up."

"Sure." She rattled it off and he fumbled with his phone, almost dropping it before he managed to key it in.

"Thanks."

She nodded and walked away.

She gave him two days before he'd send her a text rescinding his offer to help.

But she could do it without him.

Chapter 2

The sun had yet to rise above the majestic gum trees shading the track, and the magpies chortled their morning greetings, bringing music to the stillness, lifting Fleur's spirits as she got out of her car. The crisp, sharp scent of the eucalypts filled her nose as she breathed deeply, enjoying the fresh, unpolluted air while she could. She loved being at the track, loved the quiet time before the bike engines roared to life, appreciated the stillness that only being in the country could bring.

She scanned her surroundings, adding items to her list of jobs for the day and then wandered over to the toilet block and unlocked the doors.

Would enough people turn up today to get the jobs done? She could count on the musketeers and a couple of regulars, but most of their members wanted to ride without putting in any work. Which left more work for her. She sighed. The track needed grading and extra sand dumped in the areas where the bikes and dirt had fought, and the bikes had won. The emergency access gate needed fixing, the hinges rusted and worn from the constant exposure to the elements.

The hessian fence around the orchids caught her attention. Would Will even show up today? She'd received no text, but she had her doubts. During the week, she'd asked around about him, but no one could tell her much. He'd only been in town for a few months, wasn't long out of university, and worked for PAWS. It wasn't much to go on.

A jaunty three beeps had her glancing towards the gate.

Kit drove her ute through with its tray full of solo bikes and a sidecar on the trailer. Her whole body tensed. Did Kit want to test the sidecar today? That wouldn't be good. She couldn't risk hurting her friend. She forced herself to smile and waved.

"What's on the agenda for today, Madam President?" Kit asked as she strolled over. As always she made work gear look fashionable, with the shorts maybe a little shorter than normal, and the white singlet covered by a red flannelette shirt hugging her body. The Akubra hat added to the female farmer look.

"I've got you down for drainage."

Kit grinned. "Have I done something to annoy you lately?"

Fleur laughed. "With your experience, you're the perfect person for it. If you can work out something for the pit area, I'll find someone else to dig out the drainage pipes."

"Deal." Together they walked over to the pits and discussed options. As they talked, more cars arrived — Mai and Nicholas in one, and Ryan, Hannah and Felix in the other.

"This place is so neat!" Felix's young voice carried clearly as he spun around. "Do you really race motorbikes out here?"

"We sure do," Kit told him. "When we're finished the work, we can take you for a ride on the sidecar if your dad says it's all right."

No. She wouldn't be riding the sidecar at all, but Kit could.

Felix whirled around to Ryan. "Can I, Dad?"

"If we can find you a helmet that fits," Ryan replied.

A red sedan drove into the track, but the wheelchair on the roof rack was what caught Fleur's attention. Her stomach clenched and her skin went hot and then cold. Surely Trevor wouldn't come out here. There was no need, nothing he could do.

"Where do you want us?" Mai asked.

Fleur blinked. Focus. "I need an inventory of the clubhouse and storage shed. Think you can handle that?"

Mai grinned. "Of course."

Fleur turned to Hannah. "How's your leg?" It had only just come out of plaster. "Do you want to help Mai?"

"I'd prefer some light exercise," she said. "I can cut down those saplings."

"Thanks. I also want to build a couple more pit bays, and I hear that's right up your alley, Nicholas."

"I'd love to. Where's the equipment?"

"I'll show you," Kit said. "I've got to get some things myself. Ryan you can help me or Nicholas."

"What are you doing?"

"Drainage."

Ryan grimaced. "I'll help Nicholas."

Fleur laughed as they all walked towards the equipment shed. It was nice that these two men had blended so well into their group. They'd both been in town for a short time and had quickly fallen in love with her best friends, Hannah and Mai.

"Morning, Fleur."

Every muscle in her body froze as she recognised the voice. She pasted a smile on her face as she turned.

Gavin, tall and broad with well-defined muscles, towered over his brother. Trevor sat in the wheelchair beside him, his face a little thinner than the last time she'd seen him. He used to be the bigger, more powerful of the two brothers but not anymore. From his waist up there was little difference; his black hair was tied back in a top knot on his head, his arms and chest maybe a little bit more muscled than before, but below that, his legs were no longer the powerful tree trunks they had been.

And it was all her fault.

"Trevor, it's nice to see you," she lied. What on earth could she say to the man she'd put into a wheelchair? Guilt threatened to swamp Fleur and she desperately wanted to run away, but her father had taught her to face up to her mistakes, so she looked him straight in the eye. "How have you been?"

Trevor shrugged, with a small smile. "I have good days and bad."

Rehabilitation was hard. Although his wife Nicole had forbidden Fleur to visit him, she should have done more. It had been her focus on winning the race that had paralysed him. "What are you doing here?"

"We've come to help," Trevor said. "I'm still a member after all."

She stared at him. "You want to help?" Why did he want to come anywhere near the place his accident had occurred?

"Yeah, I make a pretty good foreman, or can at least cook the sausages for lunch."

Fleur could hardly say no. "That would be great. Mai's doing a stocktake inside. Maybe you can help her."

"Sounds good." He hesitated. "There's something else." He glanced up at his brother. "I'd like to come back and race."

Was he kidding? Her eyes flicked to his wheelchair. "Why?"

"I miss it. I need to get back on the track. Racing is in my blood."

The man was crazy. Falling off a motorbike had stripped him of his mobility and left him without a job, not to mention irreparably changed his life. "Are you able to?"

"Yeah, should be. Gavin's modified my bike with a hand gear change and back brake. I thought I could test it today, before anyone else goes out on the track."

Bloody hell. She didn't want to make this decision. What if he hurt himself again? His wife would never forgive her. "Is Nicole fine with you riding again?"

He cringed. "I haven't told her yet. I figured I'd wait until I know for sure if the bike will work."

She closed her eyes. Nicole was not going to be happy.

"It'll be fine. Gavin's a genius with motorbikes."

He was, but still, "Won't it be dangerous?"

"No dangerous than it was before. I know what I'm getting into, but I want that rush again."

He was so earnest and damn it, she understood what he meant. She missed the rush of racing too. "Let me chat to the rest of the committee members."

"Thanks. I appreciate it." He wheeled around to go.

"Trevor, wait."

He circled around and Fleur's stomach clenched, her throat tight. "I'm so sorry for what happened."

"It wasn't your fault. We were both riding hard and your

throttle stuck. It was a freak accident. I don't blame you."

Except that was a lie. She should admit to it, tell him the truth.

"Shit happens, Fleur. Unfortunately it was my turn. Don't sweat it." He rolled away.

He was so matter-of-fact, so accepting of where he was. She couldn't be quite so flippant. She'd disabled him. She'd been so focused on the race, on making sure he couldn't pass her that she'd forgotten it was supposed to be fun, forgotten they weren't racing for sheep stations.

She should have let him pass.

If she had, he'd be walking not wheeling away.

With a shake of her head, she went to talk to the others.

The house seemed even more silent and empty than usual on Saturday morning as Will tried to eat his breakfast. The bundle of nerves in his stomach made it difficult to swallow.

He was supposed to see Fleur again today.

Dumping his spoon into his bowl, he surveyed the apple green Formica kitchen, and the living area. It wasn't much. He'd got pretty much everything he owned from the op shop. The kitchen table was a dark, almost red brown that was supposed to look like jarrah, but was made of a cheap pine or MDF. The two small sofas had a floral fabric reminiscent of a grandmother's house, and the pine coffee table was a dime a dozen. Not the fanciest place to bring a woman. Not that it would get to that stage with Fleur.

He sighed and checked the time. It was already nine o'clock and Fleur had said she'd be at the track by eight. If he was going to help build the tyre wall he needed to leave, needed to stop stressing about showing up where he knew next to no one and just go already.

His phone rang and he lunged for it, glad for the excuse.

"How's my baby?"

His mother's voice immediately made him smile. "I'm fine, Mum. How's everyone up there?"

"All good. I've had the grandies all week, and we're about to go camping."

His heart twinged. He loved when they went into the bush to camp out. The stars were always so bright and they were alone. It was so much more rugged up north, but the land was like his own backyard. And in a way it had been. His father or brothers had often taken him camping when he was a kid and on weekends he'd amused himself by playing in the bush near his house. His mother wasn't from the area, but he used to pretend this was his land and his ancestors had once hunted there.

"Sounds great." He tried to put some enthusiasm in his voice.

"Why are you so sad?"

He wandered over to the front windows to look out. A couple of kids rode their bicycles down the street, shrieking with laughter. "I'm not sad. I discovered a new population of an endangered species this week."

"Hmm, but there's something bothering you."

He didn't know how she did it. Maybe it was a mother super power, but she always knew when he wasn't telling her everything. He caved. "I miss home." Missed the red dirt and the big blue skies of the Pilbara. Missed the comfort of the community, of knowing his family was nearby.

"You can come home whenever you like, there's always a room here for you. I'm sure your father can get you a job at the mine."

He didn't want to have any old job at the mine. If that had been his goal he never would have left and wouldn't have endured close to six lonely years in Perth. He wasn't throwing that away. "I'd rather wait until an environmental job comes up."

"Are you sure? Your nieces and nephews miss you."

His mother suggested he come home every time he spoke with her, and the yearning to say yes was still as strong as the guilt of saying no. But he couldn't. Not like this. He wouldn't be a burden on his parents, or another unemployed Aboriginal statistic. "I'm sure."

"Have you made any friends yet?"

Will turned away from the window and walked through to the laundry and out the back door. His grass needed mowing and weeds were already popping up in the garden bed he'd mulched last week.

"Will?"

"Not yet." It wasn't that easy. He wasn't doing anything outside of work where he could meet people. He hadn't been brave enough to put his name down for a basketball or cricket team. That felt too much like high school and waiting to get picked.

"You should get a housemate."

He squatted down and plucked out the offending weeds. "A housemate?"

"Yes. You're in that house by yourself and you've got two spare rooms. Find someone to share with."

"I don't know." His time at university had shown him so many ways that could go wrong.

"You shouldn't be alone. A housemate would solve that. There must be plenty of nice people down there."

He didn't have the best track record with housemates. "I'll think about it."

"You need to do something, Will. You've been there for two months and still barely know anyone. You can't make a community by yourself."

She was right. He was lonely, and it was getting worse. But he'd never told her about his flat-mate who'd wrongly accused him of stealing. He'd said he should have known better than to share with an Abo — and then he'd found the item he'd lost as he'd been packing to move out. There had never been an apology. "Thanks, Mum."

After he hung up, he considered the idea. Perhaps this time would be different. Where did you advertise for a house mate — on Gumtree? He flicked through the classifieds website on his phone. Yep. Lots of ads. Maybe he could do this. If nothing else it would be a way of meeting at least one other person in Blackbridge. He could put together his requirements and choose whoever he wanted. If someone applied, he didn't have to accept them.

Nerves hummed over his skin as he pulled his laptop towards him and fired it up. He'd read through some of the other ads to check what he needed to include.

His cursor hovered above the post an ad button. Was he really going to do this?

All of the horrible options fluttered through his mind. He could easily get stuck with a psycho. Or someone who would actually charge him with theft.

No, he couldn't do it.

Not yet.

And he had to go help Fleur. That seemed the lesser of two evils right now.

He grabbed his keys and left the house.

The rest of the committee agreed to Trevor riding and ten minutes later everyone lined up at the start straight to watch him on his modified bike. Gavin kick-started it and then he and Nicholas helped Trevor on and strapped his legs to the pegs.

Fleur wanted to be sick. If he fell, the bike would fall on top of him, he wouldn't be flung loose of the machine. She didn't want to see this.

She couldn't walk away.

"Ready?" Gavin asked him.

Trevor nodded and gently twisted the throttle. And then he was off, riding slowly down the straight as he tested the gear changes. She'd told him he had to stay in the straight until he was certain the modifications worked, and as he reached the end, he did a U-turn and accelerated back. He was going far too fast for Fleur's liking. He whooped as he made another turn back along the straight, then as he reached the first corner, he kept going.

Fleur took a step forward, but she was helpless to stop him. He tore up the first hill and disappeared from sight.

Gavin laughed. "I guess it worked."

Anger flooded her body. "I told him to stick to the straight."

"Relax, Fleur. He's been riding since he was four. He'll be fine."

She gritted her teeth, her fists clenched as Trevor came back into view, tearing down the hill and into the S-bend. He looked like any other rider on a motocross track — confident and in charge.

Still, she wouldn't stay here. Couldn't deal with the tension in her chest. "Keep an eye on him." She stalked towards the clubhouse. She needed a minute to herself, couldn't let the others see how much this affected her, needed to pretend everything was fine.

Her hands shook as she took a glass out of the cupboard and she rested them on the cool metal sink, bending over and taking slow deep breaths.

"Want to talk about it?"

She closed her eyes at Kit's voice. Of course she wasn't going to fool her friends. They knew her too well.

Fleur pivoted slowly and found Kit, Mai and Hannah all at the entrance watching her.

The musketeers had come.

She swallowed hard, but the lump in her throat didn't budge.

"Trevor looks good out there," Kit said.

Mai nodded. "Gavin's right. He'll be fine."

They didn't see, couldn't know what was really wrong with her.

"It's not your fault, Flower." Hannah walked over to her and rested a hand on her arm.

"She doesn't blame herself." Kit squinted at her. "Do you?"

All of the words stuck in her throat. She couldn't vocalise how she felt, couldn't tell them how much it had kept her up at night, wouldn't tell them how she went out of her way to avoid Nicole or Trevor if she saw them around town.

"I think she does," Mai said, and she and Kit came closer.

"Why didn't you talk to us sooner?" Hannah asked.

Fleur shrugged helplessly. She'd talked to them when the accident had first happened, but she hadn't wanted to bring it up again, hadn't wanted to tell them the truth. Tears pricked her eyes. "My throttle didn't stick."

Mai frowned. "What are you talking about?"

"The day of the accident. I said my throttle had stuck open which is why I didn't give Trevor space. It's not true." She'd paralysed a man because she'd wanted to win.

"So you kept your line, Fleur," Kit said. "I would have done the same thing. Beating Trevor is a massive achievement."

Fleur looked up, eyes wide. "I paralysed him."

"No. The *accident* paralysed him," Kit said. "How many times have any of us fallen off in a similar way and jumped straight back on the bike to finish the race? It was dumb luck that this time Trevor couldn't get up."

"I can barely look him in the eye," she whispered.

Hannah put her arm around her. "It could have happened to any of us. It could have been you falling off and being paralysed — would you have blamed Trevor?"

"It's not the same."

"Of course it is," Kit said. "We all know the risks when we race — hell, the captain tells us them at the start of every race meeting. We take the risk anyway."

She still couldn't shift the guilt weighing on her shoulders. She was a nurse, she cared for people, she helped them get better, didn't make them worse.

"Does this mean you're not going to ride this season?" Mai asked.

"She has to — she's my sidecar partner," Kit answered.

Fleur spun back to the sink to pour a glass of water. She hadn't been brave enough to bring up the subject with any of the musketeers.

"Fleur?" Hannah's voice was soft.

"I can't." She couldn't meet their gaze.

"This is bullshit!" Kit was as forthright as always. "It was an accident. You can't give up racing because of it. You love it too much."

She did love it, loved the adrenalin at the start-line, the roar of the motors as the lackey disappeared and that race to the first corner, all the bikes bunched up together, close enough to touch, the heady exhilaration of soaring off a jump, or getting closer and closer to the rider in front of you, choosing a faster line. Even the dust or mud was part of the fun.

"Why don't you ride this afternoon?" Mai suggested.

"There won't be many people on the track. You can go at your own pace and keep your distance from the others, get back into the swing of things."

Kit nodded. "No way am I letting you out of being my sidecar rider."

She couldn't race. Couldn't be on the track with another rider, couldn't risk it happening again. Fleur braced herself for Kit's reaction. "I don't want to hurt you. The sidecar is worse than the solo."

"If by worse you mean more fun, then I'll agree with you. We're a team, Flower, and I know what I'm getting into."

The clubhouse was heating up and she didn't want to be cooped up in here with her friends. She pushed through them and outside into the shade of a gum tree. Trevor was pulling up in the pits and Ryan held the bike while Nicholas and Gavin helped him off. At least he hadn't fallen.

A tiny bit of the tension left her shoulders.

"It's not like you to run away," Kit said.

Why wouldn't Kit just let it go? She spun around and faced her. "I'm meant to heal not maim!"

Trevor's engine cut off and her words were loud in the fresh silence.

She cringed, not daring to check who had heard her. The crunch of tyres on the gravel announced someone new had arrived. Relief flooded her. "I'm going to talk to Will."

She stalked off.

Chapter 3

Fleur stood back from the car as Will got out, taking a couple of deep breaths to slow her racing heart. Right now his abrupt personality was far preferable to the mess she'd left behind. By the time he'd turned to her, she had her heart rate under control. "Good morning."

He was wearing workman's gear: long-sleeved fluoro yellow high-vis shirt, beige cargo pants and a wide-brimmed hat. His dark skin contrasted nicely against the light tones of his clothes, but the hat shaded his face so she couldn't see his expression.

He shoved his hands in his pockets. "Am I too late?"

"Not at all. I've just been giving out tasks." And needed an excuse to get out of here. "Do you want a coffee?"

"No."

Great. "Shall we get started? I've got the tyres on the trailer."

He followed her over to her car which she'd parked next to the emergency gate into the track. Thankfully she didn't need to go near Trevor and the others. Fleur climbed in and took another breath to calm the tension sizzling under her skin.

"Is everything all right?"

Will's question made her focus. "Yes, fine — club stuff. Don't worry about it." She put the car into gear and drove onto the track. She needed to think about something else. "Did you figure out if the orchid is an endangered species?"

"It is."

Fleur waited for him to expand, but he didn't. "What does that mean? Do you collect seeds, or move them somewhere secure?"

"I'll add them to my monitoring list."

"So I need to keep the fence up indefinitely?"

"Yes."

She raised her eyebrows. Geez, no discussion at all. Who did this guy think he was? She manoeuvred her car around the track towing a trailer full of used tyres. It shouldn't take long to build the wall in front of his orchids. She parked with the trailer as close as possible to the fenced area, without actually leaving the track. As she got out, she asked, "Have you ever built a tyre wall before?"

"No."

"It's fairly simple. We lay them flat and tech screw the tyres next to each other together. Then you offset the next layer and screw them to the layer below and the one next to them." She heaved two tyres off the trailer and carried them over to the fence, laying them out how she wanted them. When she turned, Will was behind her with two more, carrying them as if they weighed nothing. There had to be some strong muscles under that shirt. "Great. If you're happy carrying them, I'll screw them."

He nodded.

Getting conversation out of him was harder than finding a good vein on a drug addict.

She lifted her cordless drill and the box of tech screws from the boot of the car. The wall didn't need to be more than a couple of metres long and a metre high so they should be done in no time. She followed him back to the fence. Those cargo pants did mould to his butt nicely. Not that it mattered. A guy had to have more than good looks for her to be interested.

A shout had her glancing up to find Lincoln and his brother Jamie had arrived. Fleur handed Will the drill and her hand brushed his. "Can you handle screwing while I go and give them instructions?"

He nodded again, snatching the drill from her.

She frowned. "Thanks." What was his problem?

Fleur spent the next half an hour giving tasks to other members who arrived and then wandered back to check how Will was doing. He was screwing the last tyre together.

"Looks like I've got good timing," she said.

"It wasn't hard."

She pushed the wall and it didn't budge. "Good job. Thanks for your help."

He cleared his throat. "Thanks for letting me." He took his hat off and pushed his hair back. The day was warming up and he had a sheen of sweat on his brow.

So the man could be polite. "No worries. I'll give you a lift back to your car."

"I, ah, didn't finish my survey the other day." He tapped his hand rapidly on his thigh.

Was he nervous? Was that why he was so abrupt?

"Go ahead. Help yourself to the drinks in the clubroom, and the toilets are unlocked."

"I've got water in my car." His voice was smooth like honey, but he shuffled his feet, not looking at her.

Definite nerves, rather than arrogance. All at once his behaviour made sense. It had to be hard being new in town. "There are some cold bottles in the clubroom. I'll bring one out."

"Thanks."

The slight upturn of his mouth could have been a nervous tic, but she chose to believe it was an attempt at a smile.

She should go easy on him.

Maybe she could crack his quiet, uncommunicative shell.

And see what kind of guy he was underneath.

The sun beat down directly overhead before Will finished surveying the back of the track. He'd also checked the hollow where the chemicals had been dumped and discovered they had been cleared away. Whoever had done it had done a good job.

"Want to break for lunch?" Fleur's low, friendly voice cut through the silence, startling him again. She had an innate ability to sneak up on him, to catch him unawares. His pulse beating rapidly, he found her on the track behind him, her jeans covered in dirt and her face flushed.

"I'm done here."

"Does that mean you want food? We're having a sausage sizzle at the clubhouse. It's our way of saying thanks for helping."

"I haven't helped." Damn it! Why did he continually say the first thing that came into his head? She was asking him to lunch and he was arguing semantics. Get a grip man.

Fleur's smile faltered. "You built the tyre wall. I think that deserves food."

"All right." Way to sound ungrateful. "That's nice of you." Inwardly he rolled his eyes. He couldn't string a decent sentence together when she was around. He was hopeless around pretty women at the best of times, but he was worse around women he was attracted to and admired, and Fleur was both. He'd watched her directing members around the track, had seen her pitching in and digging trenches in the hard earth.

"Come on, then." She waved him over and he fell into step beside her. "Did you find anything else?"

"No orchids." He swallowed and brushed his hand over the rough bark of a tree. The texture centred him. He could do this. "I did find a couple of other species which need to be watched."

"Is my track going to be covered in your fencing?"

"No need. They're far enough off the track."

"Good."

Will inhaled deeply as the aroma of fried onions and sausages hit his nose. People were already gathered outside the clubroom in the shade of the verandah, talking and eating. He recognised Lincoln and Ryan, as well as Mai and Nicholas, but the rest of the half dozen people were strangers.

He sucked at crowds.

Sticking close to Fleur, he accepted a hot dog from a guy

in a wheelchair. "Thanks."

"No worries, mate."

He stepped back, out of the way as a woman said, "Hi Fleur."

Fleur stiffened beside him, but smiled and replied, "Nicole, how are you?"

"Incredibly busy as always. It's tough to juggle two jobs and the kids." Nicole shrugged. "Did you know about my husband's crazy plan to ride again?"

Tension was coming off Fleur in waves. He had no idea what was going on, wasn't sure if he should go so they could talk privately, but the idea of leaving Fleur when she was upset didn't sit well with him.

Fleur shook her head. "Not until today."

Nicole sighed and shook her head, gazing at the man in the wheelchair with affection. "I knew when I married him that I married his bike obsession as well. I shouldn't be surprised." She ran a hand over his shoulder and he grinned up at her.

Some of the tension eased from Fleur until a car pulled up outside the clubhouse. She groaned. "What's Paul doing here? He knows he's been banned." Without waiting for an answer, she strode over to speak with the tall redhead getting out of the car.

Suddenly alone, Will bit into his sausage looking for someone he could talk to. Ryan and Lincoln were speaking to a couple of women, and Mai and Nicholas were chatting to a couple of guys.

His stomach swirled. He hated this. He didn't know anyone well enough to interrupt their conversation and say hi. What if they were talking about something private, or if they completely ignored him? He had nothing to add to a conversation about motocross anyway.

Taking another bite of his lunch, he wandered into the clubroom. It would be as good a place as any to hide out. But holy crap the heat was like an oven, with no air movement whatsoever. He'd get a drink and get out of there. The only reason to stick around was to ask Fleur out, but who was he kidding? The likelihood of that happening was as high as the likelihood of Fleur saying yes — zilch.

Unable to find a glass, he splashed some water on his face from the tap.

"There you are."

He spun around, face dripping with water, and Fleur was there.

He wiped his face with his hands. He must look a complete mess.

"It's like a sauna in here." She walked over to the fridge and held it open, her eyes closed, head lifted as the cool wafted over her. Her groan sent shock waves through his system and his mouth went dry.

"Do you want a drink?"

She was looking at him, but his mouth wouldn't work. He nodded.

"Coke?"

He nodded again and she pressed an icy cold can into his hand. "You're a man of few words, aren't you?"

What was he supposed to say to that?

She laughed. "Come outside where it's moderately cooler. I'll introduce you to the others."

Still mute, he followed her out. She walked as if she owned the place, her pony-tail swinging imperiously behind her. She wasn't someone who would ever have difficulty talking to anyone, she was too confident for that. He doubted she'd have any problem asking someone out on a date either, which meant she wasn't interested in him. Why would she be? He'd barely said two words to her.

Outside the clubroom a gentle breeze had kicked up, drying the sweat on his arms. Fleur picked up a water bottle from the table and led him over to where Nicholas and Mai were now talking with the other two women.

"Have you met all of the musketeers?" Fleur asked.

What was she talking about?

"That's the town nickname for Mai, Fleur, Hannah and Kit," Nicholas said.

Great, the guy had been in town for less time than he had and he knew more. Though he was dating Mai so perhaps that explained it.

"I'm Hannah." The short-haired blonde held out her hand and he shook it.

"Will." At least he'd got his name right.

"Kit van Ross. You'll want to come out to my farm to check the Good's Banksia population at some stage," Kit said. "Let me know when."

He straightened. "Thanks. How big's the population?" He hadn't memorised all of the monitoring requirements yet.

"A few plants last I checked."

That was great.

Fleur sipped from her water and they all stood silently for a moment, while Will tried desperately to think of something intelligent to say. "The fire didn't do any lasting damage?"

Mai gaped at him, the disbelief on her face clear and he suddenly remembered she'd lost both her apartment and bakery in a fire. Crap. "I, uh, meant the bush fire."

"We're both fine," Nicholas said. "I appreciate you getting us to hospital so quickly."

"It was part of the job." He cringed. Now it sounded like he wouldn't have done it otherwise. Was there a cure for foot in mouth disease? He needed it fast.

"Seriously?" Kit's tone was incredulous.

"He didn't mean it like that," Fleur said.

He shook his head fast and his hand trembled. Coke leapt out of the can and over his pale shirt, the dark stain spreading quickly. No one could save him. "I'd better go."

He bolted for his car.

"Will, wait!" Fleur hurried after him, leaving her bottle on the table. He was definitely shy. The mortification on his face just now had confirmed it.

"Don't go." She sucked in a breath. She shouldn't be breathless after such a short jog. She gasped for air and her tongue tingled. The hand she raised to her chest was covered in a rash.

Shit. She was having an allergic reaction.

She slapped Will. "Can't breathe. Need EpiPen." How could she be having a reaction? The only aspirin she'd touched was when she'd cleared out the first aid kit earlier and she'd washed her hands well afterwards.

Will swore, scooped her up and carried her back to the clubhouse yelling, "She needs her EpiPen!" Gently he placed her on a bench seat and cradled her against him.

"Car." It was hard to get the word out. Her whole mouth was swollen and each breath was harder than the last. Her head spun.

"I'll get it!" Kit called.

Across from her, Hannah was on the phone, calling the ambulance.

She couldn't breathe. She would die if she didn't get the pen fast. Die even younger than her mother had been. Her father would be so pissed with her. She gasped, trying to get some precious air into her lungs. It wasn't enough. She unbuttoned her jeans, and tried to shove them down. She had no strength. Luckily Mai realised what she was trying to do and pulled them, exposing her thigh.

Kit pounded up the verandah and Fleur reached for the pen. Together they administered the adrenaline, her hand shaking. Almost immediately the pressure on her throat lessened. Still it was like she was sucking in air through a straw.

"Ambulance is on its way," Hannah reported. "Should be here in ten minutes."

Lincoln ran up with the track's first aid kit and oxygen cylinder.

He placed the mask over her mouth and she inhaled as deeply as she was able. Slowly the dizziness eased.

"What brought that on?" Lincoln asked.

She shook her head and it spun. She leaned into Will and his arms tightened around her, stopping her from falling. He smelled good. "The only thing I've had is water."

Lincoln picked up the water bottle on the table. "Is this yours?"

She nodded. The oxygen was helping and her head cleared. Taking the mask away from her face, she said, "I checked the first aid kit earlier. I must have had some aspirin residue on my hands."

The ambulance sirens wailed in the distance.

"Damn it, Fleur. Next time let someone else do that." The worry was clear on Kit's face.

It had been such a long time since she'd had an allergic reaction, she'd forgotten how bad it was, but she never would have expected such a violent reaction from so little of the drug.

Her arms itched, still covered in a splotchy red rash. She rubbed them, and Will's hand covered hers, firm but gentle, stopping her. He was right. She shouldn't scratch.

She should take an antihistamine, but the ambulance would be here soon. They would want to administer the required drugs. And she could breathe almost freely now.

As her field of focus widened, she noticed a crowd had gathered. Great. Her pink cotton undies were on show.

She reached for her jeans and Will lifted her as if she weighed nothing, so she could slide them back on.

"Thanks."

He cleared his throat, not looking at her. "No problem."

He was sweet, and the way he'd taken charge, picking her up and carrying her was totally hot. And the fact she could think that meant she was feeling better.

The paramedics, Cynthia and Guy greeted her as they came over. "How are you, Fleur?"

This was going to suck. She had to go into work as a patient. "A lot better." It wasn't a complete lie. The lightness in her head had faded. As much as she didn't want to go, one look at Kit told her she wouldn't be allowed to stay here. "Can we get out of here?"

"In a minute," Cynthia said. "You know the deal."

She did. "Can you get rid of everyone?" she asked Mai who was crouched nearby. "And drive my car back to town?"

"Of course. I'll call your dad as well."

"Don't!" At Mai's raised eyebrows, she added, "I'm fine and it will only worry him." And he'd lecture her about being more careful.

"I've already called him," Hannah said. "He'll meet you at the hospital."

Fleur groaned. He would stress and she hated causing him

concern. He only had her.

She answered the paramedics' questions and then Guy administered some antihistamine and the itchiness faded.

Will shifted and Fleur was aware of his warm body, the hardness of his chest. He must be uncomfortable, but she didn't want to move away. His quiet strength was reassuring.

"Sorry." She shuffled away and immediately missed his warmth.

"It's not a problem." He gave her a half-smile, but before Fleur could say anything further, Guy was helping her to her feet.

"We need to get you to the hospital," he said. "Can you walk?"

She nodded. She was halfway to the ambulance when she turned. She hadn't said thank you to Will.

He was already heading to his car, head down, hand tapping his thigh.

She willed him to turn around, but he didn't.

She'd have to catch up with him later.

Now she knew he was shy, she wanted to get to know him better.

Chapter 4

As Fleur was helped to the ambulance, Will moved over to his car. He wanted to get out of here, needed the time to process what happened. His heart raced as he remembered how quickly the rash had appeared on Fleur's face, how fast she'd swelled up. He'd panicked, picked her up ready to save her without knowing how.

Thank God her friends knew where her EpiPen was.

"Hey, Will!"

Will turned to Lincoln, who was holding a water bottle.

"Thanks for your help."

He glanced over to the ambulance, but Fleur was already inside. "She's going to be all right, isn't she?"

"I'd say so. You acted quickly."

Relief swept through him. He opened his car door.

"You can hang around if you want."

Hell no. He forced a smile. "No, I was leaving anyway." He needed to change his shirt and hopefully forget that whole unfortunate incident.

"All right, I'll see you around."

Will put his car into gear and drove away. He shuddered, his chest tightening. Fleur had nearly died.

And he'd been too scared to even ask her out on a date. He could have missed the opportunity to get to know her.

Life wasn't guaranteed.

He was tired of the miserable existence he'd been living. Having Fleur leaning against him as she'd recovered was one of the nicest feelings he'd ever had.

He wanted more of it.

So he needed a plan. He had to get better at socialising.

He parked outside his fibro beach shack and stripped off his sticky, stained shirt the moment he got inside.

His mother was right. Step one was finding a house mate, someone he could at least talk to about something other than work. It would be good practice. And he'd be more careful this time.

Step two would be asking Fleur out, but if he thought about it now, his nerves would get the better of him.

He showered and changed into board shorts and a singlet. The house didn't have air con, but he didn't mind the heat. It reminded him of home. He grabbed his laptop and went outside to sit under the gum tree. He read through ads for people looking for a house mate. He could do this. He had control of the whole situation, he didn't need to say yes to someone just because they applied. With that at the forefront of his mind, he clicked 'post an ad'.

About half an hour later, his phone rang. It wasn't a number he recognised. "Hello?"

"Hi, my name's Elijah. I'm calling about the room." The voice was upbeat, cheerful and male.

That was quick.

"Is it still available?"

Will cleared his throat. "Yeah."

"Can I come and take a look?"

Crap. This was actually happening. He could do this. "Sure." He gave Elijah his address and hung up. What did he do now? The house was tidy, the spare room empty and as far as he could see there was nothing that would put a prospective house mate off. But this was such a bad idea.

He paced the living room. It was all right. He didn't have to agree to it. This was testing the waters. Everything would be fine.

A loud rat-a-tat-tat on the door set his heart racing again.

Striding to the front of the house, he opened the door and stared.

The man standing there had the most perfect hair Will had ever seen, dark brown and styled in a wave on top that defied gravity. The black eyeliner and glaringly bright rainbow tie-dyed T-shirt next caught his attention. He was probably in his mid-twenties, shorter than Will at about six feet, and slim, without many muscles. Here was someone who would stand out in a crowd.

"I'm Elijah." The guy held out his hand. "Sorry, I didn't catch your name on the phone."

"Will." He shook his hand and gestured for Elijah to enter.

"Nice place." Elijah scanned the living room. "Do you live alone?"

"Yes."

Elijah wandered down the hallway, poked his head into the bathroom and laughed. "Wow, seventies retro orange, I love it! Is there just the one bathroom?"

"Yeah." Which meant they would be sharing. He hadn't thought of those logistics.

Elijah opened the cupboard under the sink that contained Will's toothbrush, shaver and a comb. He raised his eyebrows. "Looks like there's plenty of room for my products. You're lucky you're naturally gorgeous."

Will's eyes widened. What did he say to that?

Elijah brushed past him and into the spare room. "Is this my room?"

He nodded automatically and then clarified. "Ah, it's the room I'm renting."

Elijah assessed it, hand on his chin and paced out the distance. "It's a good size." He returned to the living room and Will trailed after him, slightly bemused by his confidence. Elijah could teach him a thing or two about interacting with people.

Elijah peered out the kitchen window at the backyard. "I don't garden. Is that going to be a problem?"

"No."

"OK, so what are the house rules?"

"Rules?"

Elijah grinned at him. "I can tell you're new at this house mate thing. Are we going to share the cooking or keep our food separate, how anal are you about keeping things clean, will we have a timetable for using the living room, what's your policy on sleepovers?" He ticked off the items on his hand and winked at the last one. "Oh, you do realise I'm gay, don't you?"

He'd suspected as much. Will nodded, his mind whirling. He hadn't considered any of this. He slid into a chair at the table.

"You have a problem with my sexuality?" Elijah tensed, shoulders high and it kind of reminded Will of a frilled-neck lizard with its frill up.

"No, no." He held up a hand. He had to get the words out. "I'm not good with people."

"Then why do you want a roommate?" Elijah pulled out a chair and sat opposite him.

Will winced. "To improve."

"Improve?" Elijah frowned. "What, improve your social skills?"

"Yeah."

"Well that's a new one. Listen, I'm so desperate to move out of my parents' place, that I'll take just about anywhere, but we should get to know each other. Mind if I get a glass of water?" He went into the kitchen.

"Top cupboard."

Pouring them both a glass, Elijah sat back down and pushed a glass towards Will. "I grew up in Blackbridge, but I've been travelling the world since I graduated high school. I'm working out at the Vale winery doing odd jobs and I'm after more permanent work on a farm. I'm fairly neat, like to read and listen to music and love to cook." He took a sip of his water and looked expectantly at Will.

Right. He could do this. "I've been in Blackbridge for a couple of months, work at Parks and Wildlife Services as a park ranger." What else had Elijah said? "I like to garden, read and learn things on YouTube."

"What sort of things?"

He shouldn't have mentioned it. "Ah, well I learnt how to draw, how to pick locks and how to bind journals."

Elijah frowned. "Why did you want to learn to pick locks?"

Will winced. "I locked myself out of the house once, just before a major exam. There wasn't enough time to call the locksmith, so I broke a window." Stupid idea. "The neighbours called the police and I almost got arrested."

"And you thought picking a lock would draw less attention?"

He nodded. "I carry my lock-picking kit in my backpack now."

"Awesome. You'll have to teach me. It's so James Bond." Elijah grinned. "I don't have a lot of furniture so are you cool with me using your television?"

He nodded.

"Anything you can't stand?"

"Smoking."

"Me too, so we're good with that. Anything else you want to ask me about?"

He seemed nice. He was definitely far more energetic and vibrant than Will, but that was what he was looking for, wasn't he? He needed to clear up one thing though. "I'm Aboriginal. Do you have a problem with that?"

"Of course not."

The tension in his shoulders eased. What other questions had Elijah asked? Sleepovers. "The walls are thin."

"Huh?"

Will cleared his throat. "If you have a sleepover, know that the walls are thin." His face heated.

Elijah grinned. "Gotcha. Does this mean I've got the room?"

"Yeah."

"Brilliant! Thanks so much. I'll go get my stuff right now." He left Will sitting at the table shaking his head.

What had he done?

Hannah accompanied Fleur in the ambulance to the hospital

and Kit, Mai and Jamie weren't far behind. When Guy opened the ambulance doors, her father was waiting outside, his tanned, weathered face abnormally pale. He let out a deep breath and ran his hands through his hair. "She's all right?"

"I'm right here, Dad," Fleur said, climbing out of the back. Though she was still weak, they weren't going to wheel her into the emergency department on a gurney.

The triage nurse, Tim, came out with a wheelchair. "Don't even think about arguing."

Her father nodded and she sat in the chair. At least it was marginally better.

"What caused it?" Tim asked.

"I handled some aspirin when going through the first aid kit," Fleur told him. "I washed my hands afterwards, but there must have been some residual powder left. The attack came on about an hour later."

He frowned. "That's a severe reaction. Are you sure there wasn't anything in what you ate or drank?"

She shook her head. "I'd had a sip of my water, but I didn't put anything in it."

"Could you have drunk someone else's water?" Hannah asked.

It was possible, but people didn't generally take aspirin in an almost full bottle of water. "No."

"No more drinking out of anything you haven't kept with you at all times," her father ordered.

It was a freak occurrence, but she'd definitely be more careful in the future. She wanted to live a long life, grow old with someone.

It was almost early evening before the doctor gave her the all clear to leave. Fleur had a new prescription for an EpiPen which she filled, and her father drove her home.

Jamie had left her car in the driveway and the keys were on the kitchen table when she walked in. All she wanted to do was sleep off the woozy feeling in her stomach and pretend she hadn't nearly died. Her chest tightened. She wanted to do so much more with her life. She turned to her father. "Dad, you don't need to stay. I'm fine." He didn't need to know how freaked out she was.

"I'm not leaving you tonight." He filled her kettle. "Cup of tea?"

She recognised the set expression on his face. It had been a while since she'd seen it, probably not since she'd been living at home, but it meant there was no changing his mind. "That would be great."

Fleur sat on the couch and let him potter around the kitchen, making the drinks and getting a couple of Mai's biscuits out of her biscuit tin.

When he put the cups of tea on the coffee table, she smiled. "Thanks, Dad."

He sat next to her and pulled her into his arms. "You scared the shit out of me today. When Hannah called and told me the ambulance was on the way..." He shook his head. "I won't lose you like I lost your mother. Christ, you're about the same age."

Her heart clenched as she hugged him back. "I'm OK." She closed her eyes. She was very conscious that she was only a year short of the age her mother had died, but she hadn't realised he had been too. It was hard not to be. Whenever she looked at the framed photo on top of her dresser, she saw someone who could have been her sister now.

"I'll be more careful in future. I should have worn gloves when I went through the first aid kit. I won't make the same mistake again."

"You'd better not. This is serious, Fleur." He glared at her.

She couldn't be angry at him. He was worried, he loved her. He'd lost his wife from breast cancer when he was in his twenties. They had been each other's rocks during that time, and then she'd had the musketeers.

Her dad had no one else.

"I know, Dad." She reached for her tea, curled her hands around the mug and blew into it to cool it.

"Weren't you playing golf today?" She hated that her father missed out because of her mistake.

"Yeah. Don't you worry about that."

She would still worry, just like he'd worry about her. Aside from her father's sister in nearby Walpole, they didn't have any other family. They had to take care of each other.

They were a team.

Fleur woke later than usual the next morning. The sun was already high in the sky and Kit had told her not to hurry to the track for the rest of the busy bee — the musketeers had it sorted. Her body was still lethargic and heavy, a side-effect of the anaphylaxis. When she left her bedroom, she found her father sitting at the kitchen table with a cup of coffee, reading the newspaper.

"Been down the street already?"

He nodded. "Don't know how you can sleep so late."

She smiled as she put on the kettle. "I don't normally."

"Are you all right?" He was half out of his chair before she stopped him with a hand on his arm.

"I'm fine, Dad. A little tired is all. I'm going to cut some flowers."

He sank back into his chair. "Enjoy."

Fleur stepped outside her front door and drew in a deep breath. The air was cool and fresh, the heavy fragrance of her mother's roses blooming in the front yard settling over her. The flowers were a constant reminder of her mother. Normally they cheered her up, made her feel closer to her, reminded her of times when she'd sat by her mother's side while she'd pruned and taught Fleur how to make sure they thrived.

Gone so young.

And Fleur had nearly been the same.

No, she wouldn't think like that. She would focus on the positive, those precious moments in the garden, rather than the memories of sitting by her mother's bedside when she'd been too ill to get up.

Taking the basket with the secateurs off the small table, she then trotted down the steps and into her front yard. She brushed a finger lightly over the soft petals and chose a mixture of colours, deep red, pale apricot, vibrant yellow, cutting long stems so they would look nice in a vase. While she was there, she dead-headed spent blooms and trimmed

CLAIRE BOSTON

unruly stems. They would continue to bloom for the rest of summer and into autumn. Satisfied, she turned to go back inside and found her father on the verandah, a sad smile on his face.

"You're so much like your mother," he said as she joined him. "She used to go out to pick flowers and I'd find her still there half an hour later tending to some other part of the garden."

Had she been out there that long? "She taught me everything I know."

He put an arm around her shoulders and they went back inside together. "She would be so proud of you."

Fleur swallowed the lump in her throat. She hoped so. The older she got, the more she realised she would never really know her mother. All she had were memories shaped by an eight-year-old child. Her mother would forever be the perfect mother, but she would never be friend, or confidant, or adult. She'd never have a mature relationship with her, like she had with her father.

But she'd accepted that.

Now she needed to take care of herself, so she didn't die young either.

Chapter 5

Will shut the front door behind him and winced at the ABBA song assaulting his ears. Elijah was home and probably cooking in the kitchen. In the three days since he'd moved in, there had been more noise than Will was used to. But he'd also eaten better than he ever had. Elijah was a hell of a cook.

Still today he'd been in the office for meetings and he was almost all peopled out. The music should be a good cover for him to sneak into his room without being heard. Then he could have some peace, if not the quiet. He peered through the living room into the kitchen where Elijah's back was to him as he washed some dishes and bopped to the music, singing to the upbeat tune.

Will strode across the living room, aiming for the hallway that ran to his bedroom.

"There you are!"

He almost didn't hear Elijah over the music, but then it switched off and the silence was sweet. He stopped and pasted a smile on his face. "Hey, Elijah."

"Want to go to the pub tonight?"

"On a Tuesday?"

"Yeah. They're doing a singles Valentine's Day special. We can get a meal and maybe meet some people." He winked.

Kill me now.

"I don't think so." He turned to go.

"Wait. Why not? You said you wanted to get better at socialising."

"I'm not good in crowds."

"It'll be fine. We'll find a table, have a meal, and if others are looking for a table, we can ask them to join us."

Will's whole body tensed, from his toes curled up in his boots, to the ache in the back of his neck. It was ridiculous, *he* was ridiculous. It was a simple dinner and Elijah was right. He wasn't ever going to improve if he didn't make the effort. "All right." Would Fleur go to a singles event? He'd rung the hospital on the weekend to check how she was, but she'd already been discharged.

"Great. Tell me, what kind of woman do you want? I can be your wing man."

His heart raced as he backed away. "No way."

Elijah raised a hand in a placating gesture. "All right. I won't force you."

He let out a breath. Don't panic.

He could do this.

The pub was an old colonial style building right next to the river. The deep burgundy bricks gave it a regal feel and the balustrades on the first floor were a pretty decorative iron. Walking through the heavy wooden doors put an end to any thoughts of history though. The music was contemporary rock and just on the too loud side, blaring out from a juke box in the corner. The posters stuck around the place advertised different types of alcohol and the bartenders all wore black. The place was packed with people everywhere — at each of the booths that lined the walls, at the tables scattered over the scuffed wooden floor and hanging out by the long wooden bar that stretched the entire length of the room. The smell of beer was only a little stronger than the woman's perfume who pushed past him to get further inside.

Will took a step back. No way was he staying here. There was too much noise, too many people, too many ways he could make a fool of himself. "We should go," he shouted to Elijah.

Elijah shook his head. "We'll find a table." He scanned the

room and a huge grin lit up his face. "There's Kit! I haven't seen her since I left high school. Come on." He strode across the room without waiting for Will's answer.

Will's stomach dropped as he saw who Elijah was making a bee-line towards. Fleur's friend Kit who'd been disgusted by him on the weekend. Then Elijah moved to the side and the person he'd been blocking came into view.

Fleur.

She had curled her long brown hair so it hung prettily along her jawline and she'd done something with her eyes to make them darker, more intense. The red top she wore drew his eye straight towards her perfectly pert breasts.

All his good intentions fled. He couldn't possibly go over there. He should leave before Elijah realised he was missing. He could go home, eat one of his microwave meals and be safe in the knowledge that he hadn't made a fool of himself today.

"Will, come on."

His eyes lifted from Fleur's cleavage to find them all looking at him. Blood rushed to his face. Too late to avoid being a fool. Every nerve in his body wanted to run, but he was almost certain Elijah would come after him and drag him back. And that would be ten times worse.

He forced himself forward. By the time he reached the table, Elijah was sliding into one of the spare seats.

"Found us a table," Elijah said. "Kit and I went to the agricultural school together and this is her friend, Fleur."

"We've met Will," Fleur said. She smiled and gestured to the spare seat next to her. "I didn't get a chance to thank you for your help the other day."

"It was no problem." He pulled out the chair with jerky movements. "I'm glad you're all right." She was so close and he could smell the faint hint of roses. Her nearness frazzled his brain, making it hard to concentrate on the conversation.

"How do you two know each other?" Kit asked.

"We're roomies," Elijah said. "I've been desperately looking for somewhere to stay that wasn't my parents' place, and Will advertised a spare room on the weekend."

"The odd couple," Kit said.

"Nothing odd about us," Elijah replied. "Can I get anyone a drink? My shout."

Oh, no. Elijah couldn't leave him here alone with these two. He'd have to say something, and right now his mind was batting zero. "I'll help." He shifted back his seat to get up, but Elijah put a hand out to stop him.

"No need. I've got this. Do you want a beer?"

He hated the taste of beer, but how would it look if he ordered a soft drink? His mind whirled as he tried to decide and then just nodded. He didn't have to drink it.

Left alone with Fleur and Kit, he played with the paper coaster on the table in front of him. Come on, there had to be something he could say. "How did the busy bee go on Sunday?"

"Really great," Fleur said. "We got everything done that we needed to."

Silence.

What else? He glanced over at the bar where Elijah was still waiting in line to be served. He wasn't going to get any help from him any time soon.

"Did the fencing around the orchids hold up?" He winced. Way to go, talk about plants like a crazy guy.

She smiled. "It was still there the last I checked."

He focused on Kit. She and Fleur were similar in appearance, both tall, slim and fit with long brown hair. But Will didn't feel any pull of attraction to her. Her skin-tight fitted white top left little to the imagination, defining her breasts, and the muscles in her arms showed she worked hard for a living, but his heart didn't race when he looked at her. Perhaps he should talk to her. He cleared his throat. "I read my notes," he said. "If it suits, I'll come out on Friday to review the banksia population."

"Sure. Let me know what time, and I'll be at the house to show you the way."

That was the limit of what he had to say to them. But what had the person on YouTube said? Ask questions. "Do you ride motorbikes too?"

"Yeah, and I swing for Fleur."

His eyes widened. What did she mean by that? Was it her

way of telling him they were gay? That would be his luck.

Fleur laughed. "What she means is she's my sidecar passenger. They're called swingers."

Right. Of course. There'd been a sidecar on the back of a trailer when he'd been at the track on the weekend. "Where do you sit?"

"I don't," Kit said. "I move sides depending on the direction of the corner we're going around. I'm ballast."

He had no idea what she meant but was saved from answering when Elijah returned carrying four drinks. "Here we go."

"Thanks." He took a sip of the cold beer, forced himself to swallow the bitter, yeasty drink. Ugh. He should have said no.

"No good?" Fleur's voice was right next to his ear and he turned, heart pounding, to find her leaning towards him, her face only centimetres away.

"Huh?"

"Don't you like the beer? You kind of grimaced when you took a sip."

Great, he was racking up the nerd points. "It's fine." He took another sip to prove it and managed not to pull a face — just.

"You should get Fleur to take you out on the sidecar one day," Kit said to him.

"No!"

Fleur's firm denial was a sharp stab to his heart.

"I mean, not right now," Fleur amended, glaring at Kit.

He shrugged as if he didn't care. What was he doing here? He had no business pretending he could socialise like a normal person. He pushed back his chair and stood. "I've gotta go." He didn't look at any of them as he strode out of the pub.

Outside, he took a deep breath in and paused to let his ears adjust to the reduction of noise and then crossed the road, heading towards the river foreshore. He needed some quiet, some time with nature and no one was on the grassed area this evening.

"Will, wait!" It was Fleur's voice, but he had to be

imagining it. She wouldn't come after him.

"Will." A soft, feminine hand on his forearm had him freezing. Fleur was right next to him, touching him. There was a God.

"I'm sorry. I didn't mean to offend you." She removed her hand from his arm. "I didn't say no to you about the sidecar because of you, but because I don't want to take anyone out on it." Her eyes were hooded and full of misery. And in that moment she stopped being Fleur, Goddess of Beauty and became Fleur, real person.

"Why not?"

She pressed her lips together and then sighed. "Let's walk." She wandered towards the gently flowing river and when she was at the edge, she bent down to pick up some gum nuts which she threw into the water, one at a time.

He waited, recognising her need to get her thoughts in order before speaking.

"Last year there was an accident at the track." She stared out across the river, but he could tell she wasn't seeing what was in front of her. "One of our members was paralysed. It was my fault." Her voice broke.

What was he supposed to say to that? "What happened?" Was he the guy who'd been handing out sausages at the track?

"We were racing, Trevor fell off..."

And for some reason she blamed herself. "Did you crash into him?"

"No."

"Then how was it your fault?" Guilt was never a rational emotion.

"I said my throttle stuck, but it didn't. I wanted to win, so I didn't let him pass."

Will frowned and scooped up a couple of gum nuts, rubbing his thumb over the rough surface and handing one to her to throw. "Isn't that the point of racing?"

Her laugh was brittle. "We don't do competitive racing, no points are scored, it's all for the love of the machines and the race. I should have let him pass."

He knew nothing about motor sports. "Would he have let you?"

She shook her head. "That's beside the point."

"I think that's exactly the point," he said. "It sounds like it was an accident."

Her eyes glistened with unshed tears. "When I race, it's like this mist falls over me and I forget about everything except the race. I can't risk it happening again."

His heart clenched at the pain in her eyes and he pulled her into his arms. She was warm and soft, and her curves fit his body like they were designed for it.

Fleur hesitated and then her arms came around him and she was hugging him back, her body shaking.

She was in so much pain. He stroked her back, brushing her curls away from his face and trying to figure out the right words. But there weren't any. This was something Fleur would need to work through.

After a couple of minutes, she pulled back, sniffing, her cheeks red. "I'm sorry. You must think I'm crazy."

"Never." He smiled at her as he ran a finger over her cheek to wipe the last tear away.

"You should smile more often," she said. "It's beautiful."

Heat rushed to his face and he reverted to his tongue-tied former self. "Uh…"

She laughed. "You don't need to say anything." She let out a long sigh. "Thank you. The guilt and doubt has been building up over the off-season and seeing Trevor at the track on the weekend brought it all to the surface."

He nodded.

"I don't feel like going back to the pub. Do you want to walk me home?"

Fleur was asking to spend more time with him? He'd stepped into some kind of alternate reality and he liked it. "Sure."

He fell into step beside her after she'd sent a text to Kit, and they headed down the main street. It was a beautiful warm evening and a few families were at the nearby ice cream shop, but mostly the street was empty.

The awkwardness whenever he was near Fleur was gone, replaced with a companionable comfort. He never would have imagined it.

"You haven't been in town very long, have you?" Fleur asked.

"A couple of months."

"It's the first time I've seen you at the pub."

"I don't get out much." Or at all.

"Is it because you're shy, or because you don't like people?"

He met her gaze. She wasn't judging him, she was curious. "I, uh, don't normally know what to say to people."

"You're doing fine with me."

"You're special." Shit, he shouldn't have said that. He faked intense interest in the clothing shop they were walking past.

She slipped her hand into his and his heart almost stopped. "Thank you. I think you're pretty special too."

He stared at her, full of disbelief. Were they seriously having this conversation?

"There aren't many guys who wouldn't run at the first sign of a weepy woman."

"You were hurting."

She nodded. "You're a good listener."

He chuckled. "Listening is easy."

"Not for everyone," she disagreed. "A lot of people only want to hear themselves talk."

Yeah, he'd been around a lot of people like that.

They turned at the fire station and headed up a hill. It was a nice part of the town, with old houses on big quarter acre blocks. Many of the gardens were full of bloom, flowers of every colour and some wonderful fragrances teased his nose.

He wanted to find out more about Fleur, but what question could he ask that wouldn't make him sound like a moron?

"This is me." Fleur stopped in front of a miller's cottage, the wooden cladding a sunny light beige colour and the porch posts a deep, rich green that contrasted nicely with the colourful flowers blooming in the front yard.

"Beautiful roses."

She smiled. "Thanks. They were my mum's."

"You grew up here?"

"No. Dad let me transplant them when I bought the place. He's not much of a gardener."

Should he ask about her mother? Was that none of his business? What if she expected him to ask? "Your mum didn't mind you taking them?"

Her smile was sad. "She died when I was eight. But I got my love of roses from her."

"I'm sorry." It was nice she had this connection though.

"Yeah, me too."

Now what? Did he kiss her? Did he ask her out for dinner? What if she'd already put him in the friend zone because she'd cried over him?

Though they were still holding hands.

"Do you want to have dinner with me tomorrow night?" Fleur asked.

Did she really just say that? She was waiting for an answer, so she must have. "Ah, yes, please. I mean, OK."

Her lips quirked upwards. "Great. What's your address?"

He managed to tell her.

"I'll pick you up at six-thirty." She leaned forward and kissed his cheek, her lips warm, and they lingered a while. His breath caught and he couldn't move as she walked up the gravel driveway to her front door.

He was still standing there when she turned and waved, before closing the door behind herself.

Fleur had kissed him.

OK, so it was a kiss on the cheek, but it was more than the type you'd give to your aunt or mother.

He stood smiling, the joy radiating out of him, for probably longer than he should. If she looked out her front window, she'd think him an idiot.

He headed down the hill, his steps lighter than they'd been in a long time.

He had a date with Fleur Lockhart. His steps faltered.

Shit.

He had a date with Fleur Lockhart. What was he going to say for the hour or two he was with her, just the two of them?

The nerves skittled back and he stomped on them. He'd already spent time alone with Fleur and he'd managed fine.

He would be all right tomorrow.

And when he got home, he'd make a list of potential conversation topics, to make certain.

He wasn't going to mess this up.

Chapter 6

Will was glad he had a heap of standard monitoring tasks to keep him busy. If he allowed his mind to wander, he'd start panicking about his date with Fleur. Instead he obsessively checked his grid map against his coordinates and made notes. He'd not been into this part of the park before. It bordered the area where the bush fire had been and only one road accessed it. That was where he'd left his car and begun his search. He was looking for traces of quenda or chuditch in the area as well as keeping his eye out for endangered plants or any weeds that might have arrived in the park.

The Albany bottlebrush was in full bloom, its bright red flowers like baubles on a Christmas tree, outshining the smaller lanoline bush's little yellow flowers. It was a joy to discover each of the different plants here.

The showy male blue wrens were doing their best to attract a mate, chittering and flitting about the branches of the dense shrubs, and above in the eucalypts were the more common rosellas and lorikeets, squawking away.

Occasionally a rustle in the grasses identified a blue-tongue or some other lizard, but aside from the fauna he was alone. He didn't have to worry about what he was wearing, or how he behaved, he could be himself.

He breathed deeply and his shoulders relaxed. The bush was home, whether it was down here on the southern coast, or up in the dry Pilbara, nature always welcomed him.

His search took him deeper into the park. The scrub between the trees was low and not difficult to move around. But not long after he'd stopped for lunch he came across a trail of broken and squashed plants. Correct that, two trails, wide enough to be tyre tracks.

He frowned. Nothing was supposed to be in this area. Someone must be using the park as their recreational playground. This was how diseases like dieback spread. Mumbling under his breath, he marked his map and followed the trail.

About five minutes later he came to a stop.

What the hell was a garden shed doing in the middle of the national park? It was almost brand new, its dark green metal sides still glossy despite being exposed to the weather. He moved closer, checking the area for any clue why it might be there. It wasn't on his map, and he hadn't read anything in his notes about a new development. The bush was silent aside from the rustle of the wind through the trees and the occasional bird call.

The area had been cleared though, a small rectangular space between the trees, large enough for the shed and for a vehicle to turn around. The space had been made larger by cutting down two big jarrah trees. He growled as he traced his finger around the rings in the stump. This was old growth forest; those trees were hundreds of years old. And someone had chopped them down like they were nothing, without a care for all the vegetation they squashed underneath.

He reached the shed. The door had a padlock on it and an acrid smell permeated from it. Was something leaking inside? He circled the structure, swearing as he moved around the back and discovered empty containers of chemicals and general waste behind it.

He froze.

A shed not on his map, a whole bunch of chemicals, and a lock on the door. He should call the police. He walked back around to the door. The padlock was new and chunky, but similar to the one he'd used when he'd learnt how to pick locks last year. He shrugged his backpack off his shoulders and pulled out his lock-picking kit. Before he brought the police out here, he wanted to confirm there was a reason, and ensure nothing was leaking.

Still he scanned the area. The last thing he wanted was for someone to come across him picking the lock. If whoever owned this came while he was there... he'd run that way. It had the most trees and would be difficult to follow him in a car. Plus if they drove in, he'd hear them coming.

Carefully he worked at the lock until one by one the springs fell into place and the lock clicked open. He put the kit back in his backpack and opened the door.

The wave of fumes had his eyes watering and he stepped back. He had to check what was causing the smell. If it was something combustible, it could cause another bush fire.

He held his breath as he walked through the door, blinking rapidly as he took in the trestle tables, the beakers and glass tubes, the open containers of some clear chemical.

He coughed, the smell overwhelming him, and his head spun.

He had to get out of here. Spinning around, he lost his balance and crashed into a shelf next to him. Glass crashed together and another sharp scent was added to the mix, his shirt wet.

He was going to be sick.

He stumbled outside and moved as fast as he could away from the shed. He needed to call the police... and maybe an ambulance. Head thumping and nausea rising in his stomach, he leaned against a nearby tree and fumbled getting his phone out of his pocket. He dialled triple zero and waited for the operator to pick up.

No, he needed to keep moving, needed to get back to his car. It would be too hard to find him here.

He answered the operator's questions and used his map to give her the coordinates of where he was.

It was hard to concentrate on what she was saying. Her voice grew faint.

Will sucked in more air, but all he could smell was the sharp scent of a chemical he didn't recognise. He dumped his backpack on the ground and stripped off his shirt.

The car park was just up ahead.

He tripped over a low shrub and fell to his knees, pain shooting through his leg. Damn. His arms were too weak to lift him. He was close enough for the paramedics to hear him call when they arrived.

Now if only his head would stop thumping and spinning.

He closed his eyes.

Fleur couldn't wait for the day to be over. The emergency department had been quiet. The lack of patients was a good thing, obviously, but it did make the day drag.

Or maybe she was just looking forward to her date tonight.

In less than half an hour, she'd be free. She'd go for a run with Mai and spend a couple of hours pampering herself before her date. It had been a while since she'd been out with a guy.

She smiled.

Will was a real sweetheart, shy and endearing and the way he fidgeted when he was nervous was cute. But the one genuine smile he'd given her had spiked the cute all the way up to stunning.

She wanted to get to know him, find out what made him tick. He'd been so kind when she'd been upset, and she'd let her guard down. It wasn't something she did with many people and particularly not someone she barely knew.

"We've got incoming," Tim called, and Fleur snapped to attention.

"What have we got?" She strode towards the front of the department, and the wail of an ambulance siren reached her.

"Potential meth lab exposure," he said.

She had no time to ask for further details as the ambulance pulled up and she hurried outside to help.

The paramedics opened the doors to the ambulance and pushed the gurney out.

Her heart stopped.

Will.

His eyes were closed, one hand flopping by his side while

the other was on his stomach, an I/V already in his arm.

She moved with the bed as the paramedic gave the handover.

"He called before he passed out. We found him near his vehicle, unconscious. Managed to revive him, rinse him off and he's responded well to the I/V."

They moved the gurney into one of the cubicles and Fleur checked his pulse. His eyes opened and they weren't quite alert.

"Hey, couldn't wait to see me, huh?" she said. "You could have just dropped by the hospital rather than going to all this trouble."

His lips twitched.

She put a blood pressure cuff on and read the results. "How are you feeling?"

"Crappy."

"Any nausea? Headaches? Dizziness?"

"Lightheaded, nauseous, eyes hurt." He closed them.

"Keep your eyes open for me, Will."

He didn't respond.

"Will." She gently shook his arm. "Don't tell me you're sick of looking at me already. That won't help our date tonight."

His eyelids fluttered open.

"That's better. I need to see those gorgeous chocolate eyes of yours." She checked his pupil dilation. "Did you touch anything at the lab?"

"Crashed into a shelf. Spilt something on me."

"OK, I'm going to rinse your eyes again." Fleur continued to talk as she worked, giving him instructions, asking him for more detail about what happened. His responses became faster, though not much longer than before. It would have concerned her if she hadn't known that he wasn't much of a talker. When she was satisfied he was improving, her shoulders relaxed. "We're going to keep you here for a couple of hours for observation and I need to get your details."

He nodded, and she took him through the admissions sheet, noting he was younger than her and it was his birthday on the weekend. When she was done, she asked, "Do you need to call work?"

His eyes widened, and he tried to sit up. She put a hand on his bare chest. "Relax. Tell me what you need."

He stilled and then cleared his throat. "My car's still out there."

"We'll get someone to fetch it." She handed him the bag of personal possessions the paramedics had given her. "Your phone might be in there. Give work a call. If they can't get your car, I'll get it myself." Her shift was about to finish anyway. "And here's a gown for you to put on. You should get Elijah to bring you a change of clothes."

"Thank you."

She left him to get dressed and went to talk to Tim. "Has someone called the police?"

"Yeah. The sergeant was en route when the paramedics picked Will up."

"Where was he?"

"In the national park, about twenty minutes from here."

That was too close to town for her liking. And wasn't meth more of a city drug?

"It's time for handover." Tim motioned to where the new shift was waiting.

Fleur took her colleague, Sarah through the two patients they had in the emergency room and then went to check Will. He was sitting up, his phone in his hand. "Did you contact the office?"

"Yeah. They can't get anyone out to get my car until tomorrow."

"Let me see what I can do." She moved away and called Lincoln.

"What's up, Flower?" he asked as he answered.

"Are you still out at the meth lab?"

"What do you know about it?" His tone was abrupt.

"Will came into emergency. He's worried about his car being left out there."

"I'll lock it up when we're finished here," Lincoln said.

"Can I come and pick it up?"

"That's going above and beyond for a patient."

He was poking, which was kind of unusual. "He's also my

date tonight."

"That's not a good idea, Fleur."

She frowned and walked away from the nurse's desk to get a little more privacy. "Why?"

There was a long pause before he said, "We don't know whether Will discovered the lab or was working in it."

Fleur glanced at the bed where Will still lay. "You think he might have set it up?"

"I don't know, but it's an option we need to investigate further."

Her gut told her he wasn't responsible, but how much did she know about Will anyway? He kept to himself, he was shy, he worked long hours by himself in the park — which gave him plenty of opportunity.

But he could equally be completely innocent — and that's what she'd go with — innocent until proven guilty. He'd been angry when he'd seen the waste at the track. "Thanks for the warning, Lincoln. Can I come and pick up his car?"

Lincoln swore. "No. We've got to search it. I've got his backpack with the keys in it, so I'll get someone to drive it into town when we're done."

"Thanks, Slinky. I'll let him know."

"Fleur don't tell anyone about the lab."

He was using his worry voice. "I won't, Lincoln. Take care of yourself. I don't want to see you in here."

"I always do." He hung up.

Fleur sighed. She didn't often worry about Lincoln. He might be a police officer, but here in Blackbridge they didn't have any major crimes. At least not until recently. The drugs had them all a little worried after what had happened to Mai last month.

She returned to Will's cubicle and pulled up a chair. "Lincoln's going to arrange for your car to be returned," she told him. "But it will be later this evening."

"Thank you."

She took hold of his wrist and counted his pulse beats. It was strong. "How are you?"

"Head feels a little weird still, but everything else is all right."

"Good." She didn't want to leave him here by himself. "Is there anyone you need me to call? Family? Elijah?"

He shook his head. "Family is all up north. I'll call them when I get home."

It was sad he had no one who would visit him in hospital. Even if her dad was out fishing, she had any number of friends she could call.

Sarah entered the cubicle. "Oh, I thought you'd gone home."

"I'm keeping Will company."

Will shot her a confused look as he answered Sarah's questions and let her take his blood pressure and pulse. When she left he said, "Have you finished your shift?"

"Yeah."

"You don't have to stay."

"I can go if you'd prefer to rest."

"No, I'm fine." He shifted in the bed and the silence grew.

It wasn't going to be the chattiest of dates tonight, of that she was certain. "Where does your family live?"

"Goldwyer. I grew up there."

Right in the middle of Western Australia where temperatures averaged forty degrees in summer. Not somewhere she could imagine living. "Blackbridge must be some change for you."

"I've been at university in Perth for the last few years, but the summer is definitely colder than what I'm used to."

"Not many days above forty degrees here," Fleur agreed.

"Not many days above thirty," he corrected.

She chuckled. "Wait until you get to winter."

"I'm already dreading it." He shuddered, his smile cautious. Fleur wanted more of that. Wanted him to relax and show her who he really was. She was certain there was an interesting man underneath. With that in mind she asked, "Do you still want to go out to dinner tonight?"

His face fell. "Would you prefer not to?"

"I've been looking forward to it, but after this, you might want to go straight home."

"I'm fine. I don't need to be here." He swung his legs off the bed and then swayed.

Fleur leapt to her feet and steadied him. "Slow down. You need to rest a little longer." She waited by his side as he moved back on to the bed. "I've booked us into the Vietnamese restaurant, but we could always get takeaway and go to my house."

He blinked at her, the now familiar surprise on his face.

"We'll play it by ear," she said, not wanting him to freak out any further.

"All right."

Her phone rang and she excused herself to answer it.

"Are you working late?" Mai asked.

Damn. She'd forgotten about Mai. While she wanted to stay and talk to Will, she couldn't fob off her friend for a guy. "A little. I'm leaving now."

"No worries."

Fleur went back to Will. "I have to go. I promised Mai I'd go jogging this afternoon. Give me a call when they release you and I'll pick you up."

"It's fine. I'll walk."

"You probably want to save your energy for our date."

Will's mouth dropped open and Fleur laughed.

"That came out a lot more suggestive than I intended. Call me if you need me."

He nodded and she walked away.

Tonight was going to be fun.

Chapter 7

Will had another two hours in the hospital to imagine all the ways his date with Fleur could go wrong. It didn't help that he was still weak, light-headed and was wearing a hospital gown that didn't cover much.

Sarah came into his cubicle to take his blood pressure again.

"When can I go?"

"The doctor's due in the next half an hour. After she's seen you, you should be right to leave."

After she left, he called Elijah and explained the situation.

"You should have called me sooner," Elijah said. "I'll come and keep you company."

It was nice he cared. "Can you bring me a change of clothes?"

"Yeah. I'll be there soon." He hung up before Will could tell him what clothes to get.

It should be fine.

Hopefully.

He didn't have long to wait to discover what Elijah had chosen. He heard him enter the emergency department, greeting everyone as he made his way towards Will.

Elijah handed him a plastic bag. "We're going to have to go shopping," he said. "There's no variety to your wardrobe at all. It's sad."

Will rolled his eyes. Fashion, like women, was another thing that baffled him. Jeans and T-shirts were suitable for almost every occasion, why would he need more?

Elijah plonked himself down in the chair where Fleur had sat a few hours earlier. "Are you good to go?"

"Not until I dress and the doctor's checked me." He gave Elijah a pointed look.

"Oh, right. You want some privacy?"

"Please."

Elijah pulled the curtains of the cubicle around Will and left. Will quickly dressed in the jeans and black T-shirt, and then opened the curtain to let his roommate back in and almost crashed into Sarah.

"Oh, you're up. The doctor's here." She gestured behind her at an older woman.

"Sit down, Will," the doctor said.

He did as he was told and a few minutes later he had his discharge notes and was ready to go. He walked out into the sunlight with Elijah and squinted at the glare, his eyes still tender.

"What do you want to do tonight?" Elijah asked as they got into his car.

"I'm, ah, going out."

Elijah raised an eyebrow. "Who with?"

Will looked out the window, his stomach swirling with nerves. "Fleur."

"You two really hit it off last night, huh?"

"I guess." The fact Fleur had asked him out was still a shock. And though he wasn't a hundred percent better, there was no way he was going to cancel on her.

He might never get the chance again.

Back at home he had a long shower. He could smell ammonia still, so he scrubbed himself several times, using some of Elijah's fancy smelling body wash as an extra layer of defence. He swayed a little as he got out, a bit lightheaded. He probably needed something to eat. Wrapping a towel around his waist he hurried to his bedroom. He wasn't quite used to having Elijah in the house and had made the mistake of leaving the bathroom naked one day and running into him in the hallway.

It wasn't an experience he wanted to repeat.

Standing in front of his wardrobe, Will knew he was screwed.

He had nothing decent to wear.

When he'd bought takeaway from the Vietnamese restaurant in the past, he'd never paid any attention to how the patrons were dressed. Was it casual, or posh?

The black jeans would have to do. The only other pants he had were his suit pants, which would feel like he was going to an interview.

Which he kind of was. Interviewing for the role of boyfriend.

Nerd. He shook his head at himself.

As he sorted through his shirts to find one which wasn't too faded, or too dorky, Elijah yelled, "Will, you've got visitors."

His heart raced as he checked the time. It was only five o'clock. It couldn't be Fleur yet.

No, Elijah had said visitor*s*.

Will threw on a T-shirt, before heading down the hallway to the living room where Ryan and Lincoln were waiting.

"G'day." He should have been expecting them.

"We've brought your car back." Lincoln handed him the keys and his backpack. "We wanted to ask you some questions about today."

"Have a seat." He gestured to the sofas.

"Can I get you guys a drink?" Elijah asked.

"A glass of water would be great," Ryan said.

Will waited while Elijah got them all drinks and then at Lincoln's pointed look, left the room.

"Can you tell us about your movements today?" Lincoln asked.

"I was doing a monitoring sweep, looking for rare plants and evidence of any rare fauna."

"What made you search that particular place?"

"According to my maps, it had the right kind of conditions and I hadn't been into that section of the park before."

"You were very specific in your coordinates to the

paramedics."

What was Ryan implying? "I was doing a grid pattern search," he told them. "Marking it off on my map as I went." He got to his feet and dug through his backpack. It wasn't there. "I must have dropped it when I fell."

Ryan and Lincoln exchanged a glance and Lincoln asked, "When did you find the shed?"

"After I'd stopped for lunch."

Lincoln was silent, so Will expanded. "It wasn't on my map and it looked fairly new, so I figured it hadn't been added yet. I could smell chemicals and was worried something might have spilt."

"There was a padlock on the door. Did you have a key?"

They thought he was involved. He sat back, crossed his arms. He should be used to the assumption he was guilty that he usually got from the police, but he'd thought Lincoln and Ryan were better than that. "I picked the lock. I figured it was either PAWS property and they hadn't given me a key, or something relating to drugs, and I wanted to be sure before I wasted police time."

"Where did you learn how to pick locks?" Lincoln asked.

"YouTube." He didn't want to explain, but it would be better if he did. "I locked myself out of the house one day and had to break a window to get in. Afterwards I bought a lock-picking set and learnt how to use it."

Ryan looked up from his notepad. "Handy."

"Cheaper too. I like learning new things."

"Like what?"

His face flushed. "Ah, bookbinding and drawing." All things that didn't cost a lot of money and meant he didn't need to interact with anyone.

"Got any examples of your work here?"

They didn't believe him. It stung. "Maybe." He'd given most of what he'd made to op shops, or his family. He scanned the bookshelf before finding what he needed. "I made this." He handed the hardcover sketchbook to Ryan. "The cover's made from a recycled wall calendar."

Ryan flipped through it. "The drawings are really great."

"Thanks."

"What happened after you picked the lock?" Lincoln asked.

It was all a little hazy. "I opened the door and the stench of chemicals made me dizzy. There was some kind of lab set up and it wasn't a PAWS structure, but I thought something was leaking so I went in. Then the fumes overwhelmed me. I crashed into some shelving before I left. I was going to call you, but then I was sick, so I called triple zero instead."

"How long since you'd been in the area?" Lincoln asked.

"I drove all the roads of the park to familiarise myself when I first started, but I hadn't been off the path in that area before." At Lincoln's frown he added, "It's a big park."

Ryan tapped his pen against his notepad. "Have you seen any unfamiliar vehicles in the area?"

"At this time of year there are lots of tourists driving through, going to the picnic spots." He considered it. "I don't recall any cars in particular." His head was throbbing again and he wanted to be all right for his date with Fleur. He walked into the kitchen to get some painkillers from his first aid kit.

"Are you OK?" Ryan asked.

"Just a headache." Maybe that made him look guilty. "Still feeling a bit off from the meth lab."

Lincoln pursed his lips. "What makes you think it was a meth lab?"

Crap. "Wasn't it? I assumed with the chemicals, the lab set up, and the fact we've been finding discarded chemical containers around town for the past month, that it's all connected." They couldn't seriously believe he was responsible. He'd seen firsthand the damage addictive substances could do to a community, and he wouldn't condone the dumping of chemicals in the environment. When neither of them said anything, he asked, "Do you have any other questions? I need to get ready for my date."

"With Fleur," Lincoln said.

Surprise had his eyebrows raising. "Yeah." How did he know?

"Have fun." Ryan got to his feet. "If you think of anything else, or see anything suspicious while you're working, give us a call."

"I will." He shook both men's hands and walked them to the door.

The moment the door shut behind them, Elijah came out. "You're not making drugs, are you?"

Will's mouth dropped open as incredulity spread through him. Was he serious?

"What? We don't know each other very well, so I figured I'd ask straight out, instead of wondering whether I was living with a drug overlord."

Will couldn't fault his logic. "No, I'm not."

"Great. I'm glad we got that cleared up. Now we need to talk about what you're wearing for your date tonight."

Will glanced down. "This isn't all right?"

Elijah tsked and shook his head. "The jeans yes, if you dress them up with some nice leather shoes — you've got something other than work boots, haven't you?"

"Yeah." He had his interview shoes, but they pinched his toes something fierce.

"The T-shirt is a flat-out no. You want to impress Fleur, don't you? Have you got something with a collar? Do you know where you're going?"

"The Vietnamese."

"Oh, nice." Elijah led the way down the hallway to Will's bedroom and flung open the wardrobe. He took a long hard look, his arms crossed. Then he dragged out a pair of Converse sneakers Will had forgotten he owned. "Try these on." He flicked through the couple of items Will had hanging up. "Is this it?"

"Yeah." He didn't have much reason to dress up.

"We're going shopping if you continue to date," Elijah said. "Let me check my wardrobe to see if I've got anything that will fit you."

Will was left standing staring at the meagre contents of his wardrobe and moments later Elijah was back. "I've got it." He thrust a navy blue, short-sleeved, collared shirt at Will. "Mum gave this to me for Christmas and it's the wrong size, and totally not my colour. It's her way of showing she doesn't like the way I dress." He grimaced. "It's yours if you want it."

Will took the shirt and hesitated. Should he get undressed now, in front of Elijah?

Elijah was waiting, tapping his foot.

It didn't matter. Elijah had already seen him naked. Will stripped off his T-shirt and Elijah grinned. Heat rushing to his face, Will slipped the shirt on.

"Sorry, Honey. I didn't mean to embarrass you," Elijah said. "I can't help admiring a beautiful specimen of man."

Will cleared his throat. "I'm not."

"Honey, if I looked like you, I'd never put a shirt on. Those shoulders are divine, but I won't go on. Let's take a look at you." Elijah stood back and nodded. "Perfect. What do you think?"

Will examined his reflection in the mirror on his wardrobe door. The shirt fit nicely, clinging to his chest. "It's not too tight?" He picked at the fabric.

"Not at all. Fleur's not going to be able to take her eyes off you."

There was a knock on the door.

It was six thirty.

Will swore.

"Don't panic. You look great. I'll get the door and you can brush your hair before coming out." Elijah was gone before Will could agree.

This was it. He was going on a date with Fleur. He examined himself in the mirror as he brushed his hair, so it sat flat.

Ask her questions about herself.

Relax.

Talk about work if you have to.

Just don't say anything stupid.

Elijah was chatting to Fleur when Will walked into the living room. Her back was to him and he took a moment to gaze at her.

She'd gone casual too, wearing blue jeans that clung to the luscious curve of her butt, and an emerald green top without sleeves that was kind of floaty and clingy at the same time. It showed off her lovely long arms and her smooth shoulders. Like him, she wore a pair of Converse sneakers, hers covered in flowers.

"Here he is now," Elijah said.

Fleur twisted, and he discovered her floaty, clingy top also had a deep neckline that teased without quite showing the roundness of her breasts. She really was stunning.

"Hi, Will. How are you?"

He swallowed to get some moisture back in his mouth. "Fine." He forced a smile, hoping he didn't look like he was grimacing. He had to relax. He'd managed to talk to Fleur like a normal human being last night when he'd walked her home, and today at the hospital. He could do this. "Shall we go?"

"Have fun you two!" Elijah called as they walked out of the house.

Fleur's small, white Hyundai hatchback was a few years old, but clean and tidy inside. He moved the passenger seat back a little, so he could fit his legs in.

"Sorry about that," Fleur said. "Mai was the last person to sit in the front and she's got much shorter legs than you."

"No problem." Maybe he should have asked before adjusting the seat.

It was a short drive to the Vietnamese restaurant located on the main drag in town, but the silence was loud. He had to say something. "How was your jog?"

"Really great." She grinned. "We did about five kilometres. It's the first time Mai's been able to do any distance since she sprained her ankle."

"I'm glad it healed all right."

"It was brave of you to go in and get them."

He shrugged. There hadn't been many options. When the fire had started, he'd been on the other side of the park and the only one in any position to reach them, because the bush fire had cut off the emergency services from town.

Inside the restaurant Fleur greeted the Asian maître d', who was about his age, with a hug. "How are you, Kim?"

Will shuffled his feet. He shouldn't be jealous. Fleur was friendly to everyone.

"Fleur, I noticed you had a booking." Kim glanced at Will.

"Who's your friend?"

"This is Will. He's the guy who rescued your sister and Nicholas last month."

Kim held out his hand and when Will took it, he shook it vigorously. "Thanks, mate. That was some serious stuff. I'm glad you were there."

Will's face flushed. "It was nothing."

"That's not how Mai tells it," Kim said. He led them over to a table in the corner. "Hey, do you play cricket?"

Will frowned. "A little." He wasn't very good.

"Great! My team's down a man. Want to join us Sunday afternoon? It's just a bit of fun, so it doesn't matter how good you are."

He hesitated. Could he do this? He wouldn't know any of the guys on the team. But that was the point. He would get to know them. "OK. What time?"

"One o'clock at the town oval." He handed them the menus. "I'll be back to get your order soon." He walked away.

Will blinked.

Fleur chuckled. "You look surprised."

"I, uh, haven't had any invites like that since I arrived."

"When did you move to town?"

"Beginning of December." Did that make him seem pathetic? "I've been busy settling into work." And now it sounded like he was making excuses.

"Fair enough. Do you ride motorbikes?"

Her open, friendly smile set his heart pattering faster. He shook his head.

"I could teach you if you wanted to join the vintage club."

"Thanks. I'll think about it." Now wasn't the best time to mention he hated the pollution they put out. He swallowed as he read the extensive menu though the text was a little blurred. That was weird. He blinked a couple of times, but it didn't help. He swore inwardly.

No. Not now.

It wasn't the text. The blurred words were the first sign he was getting a migraine.

It could be an hour or more before the actual migraine hit. He didn't get them often, but when he did, he usually took a couple of strong painkillers and went to bed, hoping to sleep through it.

He looked at Fleur.

No way was he bailing now. Not when he was finally on a date with her.

He'd tough it out and hope this time the migraine wouldn't hit until he was at home after the date. He poured them both a glass of water and took a sip from his.

"I always have trouble deciding what to eat," Fleur said. "Do you want to get a couple of meals and share?"

"All right. You can choose." That way he wouldn't order anything she didn't like.

"Are you sure?"

He nodded as Kim came over to take their order and Fleur named a couple of dishes.

Small twinkling lights appeared at the edges of his vision. Sign two. That wasn't good.

His chest tightened and he sipped more water. Relax. Stress would only add to the problem. He needed to find something to talk to Fleur about, ignore the signs.

"When does the motocross season start?"

"Not until April, but we're doing a night race at the end of the month."

"Night race?"

"Yeah, we'll shorten the track, set up lights and have a night time event. It's too hot during the day in summer to race."

"Is it a lot to organise?"

"I've got a pretty good committee. We've already sourced the lights, so it's mostly set up on the day."

Will wanted to offer to help, if only to give himself an excuse to see her again, but he didn't know the slightest thing about motorbikes and racing, except it was noisy, dusty and smelly. He wasn't the best candidate for a new member.

"What do you do in your free time?" Fleur asked.

He didn't want to go there, not if it meant admitting he was learning how to bind books. That was a direct path into the geek zone, or worst yet, the friend zone. "I like swimming."

After living most of his life in the middle of Australia, the ocean was an endless fascination to him. He wasn't the best swimmer, but he enjoyed walking down to the beach at the end of the day and going for a swim.

Kim brought over their dinner and as Will served himself the twinkling in his eye stopped.

Damn.

Almost instantly, his head began to throb — thud, thud, thud. He squeezed his eyes closed. He would *not* let a migraine ruin his date. He'd eat quickly and leave. He could do this.

"Are you all right?" Fleur asked.

He opened his eyes and forced a smile. "Fine." He ate a mouthful of the stir-fry to prove it.

"Have you discovered all the beaches in the area yet?" Fleur asked. "My favourite is Green's Pool."

He shook his head and winced at the pain. "No. I'll have to check it out."

"Are you really OK?" She took his hand, her fingers warm on his skin and it took him a second to notice she was taking his pulse. He pulled away.

"It's a little fast."

It could very well be because she'd touched him, not because of the migraine, but he wasn't going to admit to that. "A headache," he said as if it was no big deal. "I'm fine."

She pulled her handbag out from under the table and passed him a packet of tablets. "Take two."

"I had some earlier."

"Paracetamol?"

"Yeah."

She passed him another packet. "Take two of these then."

Dating a nurse had its advantages. He wasn't going to knock back the offer. Quickly he swallowed the tablets. Now if they would only kick in fast, he'd be all right.

"Did the doctor give you any instructions, or medications when you were discharged?" She'd clearly switched into nurse mode.

"No, just to take it easy."

She frowned. "You should have rescheduled. You should be in bed now, not here with me."

He'd like to be both—with her in bed—but he'd never voice that. "I'm good," he lied.

She studied him, so he concentrated on his plate, eating more of the stir-fry although his stomach swirled, that awful nausea which accompanied the killer migraines. The universe was definitely out to get him today.

He needed to think of something to get her talking, so that all he had to do was listen. "You've lived in Blackbridge your whole life?"

"Yeah. Born and bred, though I went to the city for uni."

"Which one?"

"Curtin."

"Me too." They might have been there about the same time.

She smiled. "Hannah and I used to hang out at the Tav all the time. What was your favourite haunt?"

He couldn't tell her he hadn't had one, that he'd gone to class and then gone to work more often than not. The few times he'd tried, he'd either been singled out by the police, or drunk patrons and he'd narrowly missed being in a number of fights.

Pain stabbed the middle of his brain, making him gasp. He clutched his head with his hands, eyes squeezed shut and willed it away. This could not be happening.

"Will, what's wrong?" Fleur was out of her seat and crouching beside him.

He cracked open an eye. The restaurant was silent and everyone was looking at him.

Shit.

The pain stabbed again, and he admitted defeat. He had to. It was beating him. "Migraine," he said, his jaw tight. The nausea in his gut rose and fell like the ocean swell.

This was not going to end well.

"Let's get you home." She glanced up to Kim who had come over. "Can you get our bill?"

He left as Fleur stood and helped Will to his feet.

Every step was pure hell as he fought back the swell in his stomach and the stabbing pain. He was stupid.

So stupid.

Fleur was right. He should have rescheduled. This was far worse. If he didn't get home soon, he would vomit all over his shoes and that would make a far worse impression on Fleur than rescheduling ever would have.

They reached the counter and Fleur gave Kim her card.

"Wait." He wasn't letting her pay. He reached for his wallet and she tapped his hand away.

"Leave it. You can pay next time."

As if there'd be a next time. She wasn't going to want to see him again. But he was in too much pain to argue.

Once outside, the cool breeze gave him a moment's respite. He sucked in the air and his stomach jolted.

He was going to be sick.

He pushed Fleur away, only vaguely noticing she tripped on the pavement, and retched, his head almost splitting in two as the contents of his stomach made its appearance all over the bitumen and both of their shoes.

Hell.

Chapter 8

Fleur winced and scooted out of the way as Will retched, his face a picture of misery. She wasn't fast enough to avoid some splatter. The poor dear. It was lucky he hadn't had much to eat today, but there was still a mess to clean up. She glanced over to the restaurant doorway where Kim stood.

"I'll clean it up," he said. "You take him home. I'll get you a container in case he vomits again, and a bag for your shoes."

She smiled her thanks as he went back inside, and then gently led Will away from the vomit to her car. She opened the passenger door. "Sit." It was testament to how weak he was that it only took a minute amount of pressure for his legs to buckle and for him to sit, his legs still outside of the car.

She knelt and unlaced his shoes, ignoring the remains of his dinner. She dealt with far worse at work.

Kim returned with a takeaway container and a plastic bag and she dumped their shoes inside and put them in the car. "Think you'll be all right on the drive back?"

He grunted, which she took as a yes, and she helped him get his legs into the car, handing him the container when she was done. This was not how she'd envisioned her date to go.

She drove back to Will's place, pulling into his dirt driveway in record time. It was lucky Lincoln hadn't been on the roads to pick her up.

Pop music blared out of the house. "I'll ask Elijah to turn

it down. Stay there."

Will didn't answer. She left him in the car and hurried to the front door, pounding loudly on it.

No response.

She tried again, and when no one answered, she tried the handle. The door was unlocked, so she pushed inside and yelled, "Elijah, are you there?" Following the music into the living room she found Elijah, barefoot, dancing around the room. He came to a sudden stop when he saw her.

"Fleur?"

She went over to the stereo and switched it off.

"Where's Will?" Elijah asked.

"In the car. He's got a migraine and the music's way too loud for him."

Elijah winced. "Poor thing. Do you need a hand?"

"Is there a first aid kit? I want to see what pain medication he's got."

"I'll look."

Back outside, Will had opened the door, but hadn't made a move to get out. "Let's get you inside." She helped him stand and kept an arm around his waist as she walked him into the house.

"I'm sorry," Will murmured.

"Not your fault," she said. "We'll get you into bed and you'll feel better in no time." At least she hoped he would.

Elijah met them in the living room. "I found this." He waved a packet of pills at her.

"What's the active ingredient?" she asked.

"Oxycodone."

He must have broken something in the past. "Good. Can you get a glass of water? And a bucket if you've got one." She led Will down the hallway. "Which room's yours?"

"The end."

She'd never seen a sparser or tidier room. The double bed was neatly made with a blue bedspread, and next to it was a square pine table with a phone charger on it. The only other furniture was a dark wooden wardrobe. With no lamp in the room she'd make do with the light coming from the hallway.

Quickly she unbuttoned his shirt and slid it off his

shoulders, then she reached for his belt buckle.

"I've got it." His hand gripped hers so fast that she stepped back.

Oh, yeah. He probably didn't want his date stripping him naked in order to put him to bed. At least not in this way. She flushed and turned away. "I'll check what Elijah has found while you get into bed." Hurrying down the hallway she met Elijah coming the other way.

"This is the best I can find." He waved a plastic mixing bowl.

"That'll work." She glanced over her shoulder. "Will's getting undressed. Do you have a flannel?"

"Maybe." He went into the bathroom and soaked a hand towel, giving it to her.

She squeezed it out. It might help. "Can you make sure he's in bed?"

Elijah nodded and came back a minute later. "He's decent."

Fleur went back into Will's bedroom. He was lying with the sheet pulled up to his chin. "Hey, how are you?"

"Head, splitting." The words were forced out.

"OK. I want you to take some more tablets, but first, have you taken anything aside from the ibuprofen I gave you earlier and the paracetamol?"

"No."

"Are you allergic to anything?"

"No."

She popped two tablets out and helped Will lift his head to take them. Then when he lay back down, she placed the damp towel over his forehead. "Try to sleep. The tablets will kick in soon."

"Thank you."

Fleur pressed a kiss against his cheek. "You're welcome," she whispered. "I'll call you tomorrow." She closed his bedroom door.

Elijah hovered outside. "Is he OK?"

"He should be. He hasn't had a great day." It was a shame. She'd been really looking forward to spending some time with him.

"He'll be gutted this happened on your date." Elijah walked her out into the living room. "Don't hold it against him."

She frowned. "Why would I? It wasn't his fault."

"I don't know." Elijah shrugged. "Give him a chance to make it up to you."

What kind of person did he think she was? "I'll call him tomorrow," she said. "Does that suit you?"

He had enough grace to blush. "Yeah. Sorry. I'm butting in where it's none of my business. Will's a nice guy is all — he's shy."

"Noted." She paused at the front door. "Do me a favour and keep an eye on him tonight. If he gets worse, give me a call." She reached into her bag and scribbled her number on a piece of paper.

"Will do. Thanks, Fleur."

She drove home, lost in thought. She should have rescheduled the date. Will had been in hospital all afternoon, of course he wasn't up for going out. She should have been thoughtful, rather than being so eager she hadn't considered his welfare.

She wasn't normally that selfish.

Or that interested in a guy.

Maybe it was because he hadn't judged her when she'd told him about Trevor.

Fleur sighed. She'd call him tomorrow, check how he was and ask him out again.

And this time she'd be more considerate.

The next day, Fleur rang Will as soon as her shift ended. Her call went straight to voice mail. Perhaps he was out of signal range. She left a breezy message. "Hi Will, it's Fleur. Just wondering how you're feeling. I hope we can catch up soon." She hung up. Hopefully that sounded casual and yet still keen. She wanted to dig through his shyness and draw him out.

On her way home, she stopped at the grocery store to buy something for dinner. Her father was coming over and she wanted to make him something nice. She perused the selections in the meat section to find something that wouldn't take an age to cook and was easy. Her father had always been partial to her marinated steaks. She reached for the last packet and bumped into the person next to her.

"Oh, sorry." Her smile faded, and her pulse raced. "Hi, Nicole."

"Fleur." The greeting was warm. "How are you? That was a nasty reaction you had the other day."

Fleur blinked. She'd expected Nicole to be unhappier about Trevor racing. "I'm fine. I should have been more careful when I went through the first aid kit."

"Have you got the musketeers coming to dinner?" Nicole asked, nodding to the large pack of steak in Fleur's hand.

"No, my dad."

Nicole hesitated and then asked, "Will you need all of that? It's just that Trevor specifically asked for steak tonight and that's the last packet."

"You take it." She handed the steak to Nicole. No way was she going to take food away from their family. "I can find something else."

"Thanks so much," Nicole gushed. "How is your dad? I heard he had an accident on the boat not long ago. Is he all right now?"

"Yeah. It was a minor sprain. He was back on his feet within the week." Unlike Trevor. She cringed. How insensitive could she be? "How's your family?"

"Really good," she enthused. "Trevor's been so excited about riding again and they've given me more hours work at the rubbish tip."

The guilt was sharp. Nicole hadn't needed to work before. "I'd better go. Nice seeing you." She grabbed a packet of mince and hurried away.

Once at the checkout, she took a deep breath and her heart rate slowed. She couldn't help her reaction to Nicole, couldn't stop the guilt from welling up inside her. The day after the accident, when Fleur had driven all the way to Perth to visit Trevor in hospital, Nicole had refused to let her see him, had told her she'd ruined their lives. The doctors had given Trevor little chance of walking again even then. Things had been strained between them ever since, but maybe now they'd turned a corner.

Fleur drove home, the day of the accident running over and over again in her mind. If she'd accelerated there, or slowed on that corner, if she'd given a little more room, it could have been a very different story.

Her stomach tied into knots and her chest tightened.

Ugh, the musketeers were right. She couldn't keep going through this. She needed to work through it, but first she had to get out of the house, needed to distract herself. She rang Mai.

"Want to go for a jog?" she asked.

"Sure. I'll meet you at the beach in ten."

Fleur hung up, already feeling a little lighter. She changed, slid her phone into her exercise armband, grabbed her keys and left the house. She'd drive the short distance to the beach today.

The sea breeze was in, the southerly blowing cold, and waves crashed against the sand, too sloppy for any surfers to be out. There weren't even any families on the beach, the summer holidays were over, and the tourists had headed back to wherever they'd come from. The beach was almost deserted except for Mr Corson walking his dog.

Fleur stretched to warm up and it wasn't long before Mai pulled up in her little red Mazda. Her long black hair was pulled back in a ponytail and she was wearing her new pink sneakers and jogging clothes.

"Hey, Fleur."

Mai joined her and began to stretch.

"How are things going with the mobile bakery?"

"Fantastic. Demand is so high that Penny is getting her house licensed, so she can bake from there."

"I'm so glad."

Mai had lost everything when her bakery had burned down last month, but she'd bounced back quickly, setting up a mobile bakery with delivery options that would see her through until the building was rebuilt.

They jogged down the beach to the hard sand and then along it.

The spray from the waves was salty and cool. Fleur breathed deeply, enjoying the sensation. She needed to exercise the remaining guilt out of her system. Not that it wouldn't come back.

She sighed.

"Rough day?" Mai glanced at her.

"Work was fine."

"But…?"

Fleur smiled. There was no fooling her friend. "But I ran into Nicole at the grocery store."

"How did it go?"

"She was nice to me. Friendly even. She seemed happy that Trevor is riding again." Her chest tightened again, and she made an effort to relax.

"I spoke to her about it on the weekend. She knows it was an accident. She said she was sorry she'd been so angry with you."

That made it so much more difficult. Fleur would have preferred if Nicole had yelled some more, blamed her, got angry.

It would have been easier to cope with.

They continued up the beach not talking, the only sound the rumble of the waves against the shore.

"I think we need a musketeer meeting," Mai said as they hit the halfway point and headed back along the beach.

Fleur loved getting together with her friends, but they would want to talk about Trevor. Still she wasn't one to say no. "OK. When are you free?"

"How about this Saturday?

"All right. I'll call the others. At my place?"

"If you're up for it."

She preferred her place to driving out to Kit's farm, or Hannah's converted shed, and Mai was currently living with her parents.

Rain clouds gathered in the sky and Fleur pushed a little harder, Mai keeping pace with her. She wanted to get home before they both got wet.

The first big fat drop of water hit only a minute later. It was quickly followed by another, and then another, and then the heavens opened, and rain fell in sheets around them.

Fleur laughed as the water ran over the brim of her hat and down her neck.

"We're not going to need a cool down at the end." Mai grinned.

In minutes Fleur was drenched, the cold beginning to seep into her skin as the wind picked up. Luckily the car park was just ahead.

They ran up the beach path and stopped outside their cars, both dripping.

"Have you got a towel?" she asked Mai.

"Yeah, not that it's going to do much good."

She was right. The water would soak right through. Fleur gave her friend a hug. "I'll see you Saturday."

She did a couple of quick leg stretches while Mai backed out and then her gaze caught on her flat back tyre. "Damn it!" The water dripped down the back of her top, in a never-ending shower. With a sigh, she got the spare out of the boot and jacked up the car. She shivered and hunched as low as she could to protect herself from the freezing wind. At least the rain would be good for the motocross track and their upcoming meet. It would fill the water tank too. She should swing by the track and check if the drainage Kit had put in was working. Make sure nothing had gone wrong. If she was quick, she'd have time.

She tightened the last nut, and wound down the jack, before examining the flat tyre for nails, but couldn't see what might have made it go flat. She'd have to take it in to be fixed.

Squeezing out as much water from her shirt as she could, she got into her car, soaking the front seat immediately. Oh well, it couldn't get much wetter. She turned the heat on full and when it finally kicked in, her windows fogged up, making it difficult to see. Driving through town, she headed out to the track and through the open gates. People would never learn. She'd lost count of the number of times she'd told the members to latch it before they left.

Stopping in the pits, she got out. The diversions Kit had put in were working well, moving the water around the pits so it didn't cut deep grooves into the ground. She'd have to let

Kit know.

But now it was time to get home and dry. She gave the area one last slow scan and swore.

The clubhouse door was wide open, and chairs had been strewn around outside.

Why were people so damned inconsiderate?

Fleur was halfway across to the building when she stopped. Only a couple of people had keys to the clubhouse, and none of them would have left the building open. They certainly wouldn't leave furniture outside in the weather.

Her skin prickled, and she scanned the area more slowly this time. No cars, no motorbikes leaning up against a tree, no people that she could see.

The rain trickled down the back of her neck.

First the chemicals being dumped and now this. She needed to be careful. She flicked to Lincoln's number on her phone as she crept over, keeping her steps quiet as she moved to the open door.

Bloody hell.

The place was trashed. The neatly stacked chairs and tables were on their sides, shards of glass and soft drink cans from the broken drink fridge were all over the floor. Several cans had been opened, the sticky sweet liquid attracting a trail of ants, and the door to the truck shed was dented like someone had kicked it.

Black spray paint was scrawled across the walls and the cupboard doors with no discernible words.

She swore again and dialled the police.

Lincoln answered. "Don't tell me you've found more chemicals."

"No. Some bastard has broken into the clubhouse and trashed the place."

He sighed. "Don't touch anything. Are you sure they've gone?"

"Yeah, there's no one else here."

"Good. I'll send Ryan and Adam out shortly."

She hung up. The steady beat of rain on the metal roof was loud and normally a comfort, but Lincoln's comment had her worried. Maybe the person who did this was still around.

The gates *had* been open.

Fleur walked out onto the verandah and positioned herself at the corner, so she could see in both directions. After what had happened to Mai and Hannah in the past couple of months, and with Creepy Guy still out there running the drug ring, she wasn't taking any chances. Maybe she should fetch her car from the pits, bring it closer.

She called her dad and explained what had happened. "I might need to postpone dinner."

"How about I bring some takeaway out to the track?" he said. "You'll need to clean up after the police have been and I can help."

"That would be great." With him here she wouldn't be so creeped out. "Thanks, Dad."

"Anything for my baby girl."

"Could you bring me a change of clothes too?"

"Sure."

Fleur hung up, the tension melting away. Both the police and her father would be here soon. She would be fine. She was getting worked up over nothing. It was probably just bored teenagers.

Nevertheless, she headed back out into the rain and drove her car over to the clubhouse. She'd rather be paranoid than dead.

She sat on the verandah while she waited for the police. Despite the no trespassing signs, people often sneaked onto the property to use the track, but no one had ever broken into the clubhouse before. Fleur shivered; her pony-tail dripped steadily, and the wet fabric of her T-shirt clung to her skin. She stripped her shirt off and wrung it out, before putting it back on and then did the same with her socks. Jogging on the spot, her hands tucked under her arms, she tried to get warm. Her dad wouldn't be long and she didn't want to drain her battery by using the heater in her car.

As the rain let off to a steady drizzle, the rumble of a vehicle reached her. Ryan and Adam drove up, and the last vestige of tension left her.

"Thanks for coming," she said as they got out of the car.

Ryan smiled at her. "What have we got?

She showed them into the clubhouse. "I came out to check how Kit's drainage was working and noticed the door open. I haven't been out since the weekend."

"You locked up when you left?"

She nodded. "Always do."

"Have you touched anything?"

"I picked up this chair that had been knocked over, but that's it."

"All right. We'll take a look." Ryan spoke to Adam and he went to get something out of the police car.

Fleur shivered.

"I've got a jacket in the boot." Ryan called to Adam to get it out.

"Thanks." She followed them, standing at the doorway of the clubhouse while they examined the area, frustration welling up in her. Why did some people think it was fun to trash another person's property? The drink fridge had been donated by a local business and they didn't have the money to replace it.

Her father arrived not long after with a bag of dry clothes and a couple of large pizzas. His grin was the same wide smile that always made her feel safe and warm. "How's my Rose?"

"I'm fine, Dad. I'm sorry about this." Fleur took the bag of clothes and towel and kissed his cheek.

"Not your fault. You get dry and I'll ask if the boys want some pizza." He went into the clubhouse.

It was still drizzling so she changed on the verandah rather than making the dash across the dirt to the toilet block. She was drying her hair as the men returned.

"Find anything?" she asked.

"A bit of blood on the broken glass, and some fingerprints. We'll see if we get any matches," Ryan said.

"But you don't think you will." She could read between the lines.

"If it's bored kids we won't."

Something in his tone made Fleur examine him more closely. He was worried.

"You might want to put some cameras out here," he continued.

"Why? This is the first break in we've had at the clubhouse."

Ryan cleared his throat. "Hannah and Mai's troubles started with a break in," he said. "I think it's worth taking this seriously."

He'd made the same connection to the creepy guy as she had. That wasn't good. She'd been certain she was overreacting.

"Is my girl in danger?" her father asked.

"Not at this stage, Gary, but it's better to take some precautions."

Her father nodded.

Great, this was just what she needed. Her father going into overprotective mode. "I'll look into cameras tomorrow," she promised.

After Ryan and Adam left, she and her father sat on the verandah to eat the pizza. The rain had stopped, and the air was fresh with the scent of damp earth and eucalypts. It was starting to get dark, and birds called to each other as they flitted through the trees.

"You'll be careful, won't you, Rose?" Her father's voice was loud in the stillness.

"Of course, Dad. I don't take unnecessary risks." It had taken her many years to train him out of being a worrier. After her mother died, he'd wrapped her in cotton wool, not letting her do anything he considered dangerous. It had taken patience, time and some help from Hannah's grandparents for him to see that life came with risks, but that she was sensible. It had helped that she'd been able to use his job as a fisherman to show he took more risks than she did every day.

"So, what's new with you?" She needed to distract him.

"Not much."

She worried her father didn't have enough hobbies. Aside from his work, he rarely went anywhere, and she hadn't been able to convince him to join the motocross club.

"What about you?"

"I went on a date last night." Will still hadn't called her back.

Her father snorted. "Anyone I know?"

"Not sure. Will works for Parks and Wildlife."

"A greenie." The words were more of a curse and she smothered a smile as she put the remaining slices of pizza into a single box.

"He's nice enough."

"The problem with greenies is they aren't practical. They don't think about people, only the environment. Without commercial fishermen, we wouldn't be able to feed the world's population."

She held up a hand. "I know, Dad."

"Well make sure he knows too," he grumbled.

She'd have to ask Will where he stood on the matter of commercial fishing. She would hate for them to be at loggerheads with each other.

But that would only be a problem if things went anywhere with Will.

"I'm going to clean up inside."

"I'm right behind you, Rose."

She smiled. With her father's help they'd be done in no time.

Chapter 9

Will drove along the karri tree-lined gravel drive, noting the black and white cows in the paddock to his right. This was dairy country, but in the distance was native bushland which had to be part of the property as well. That was probably where the banksias were.

His muscles tensed as he drove past the quaint wooden farmhouse with its wrap-around verandah and headed towards the large silver sheds where Kit said she'd be.

A couple of blue heelers raced towards him, barking madly.

He slowed. Kit said they were friendly, but the last thing he needed was to run one over.

He needed to make a good impression. Kit and Fleur were good friends and although he hadn't called Fleur back yet, he wanted to. The message she'd left yesterday seemed like she wasn't mad about him vomiting on her, but he still felt sick thinking about it.

The sun was warm on his face as he got out, ignoring the dogs prancing around him. Kit wandered out from one of the sheds and whistled. They immediately went to heel.

"Hi, Will, how's things?"

She was friendly enough. He could do this. "Great. Can you show me the banksia?"

Kit shook her head. "I've got a sick cow and I'm waiting

89

for the vet. My farmhand, Paul, has gone AWOL again."

Damn it. She could have called him, instead of wasting his time.

"I've arranged for someone else to take you," she continued and shaded her eyes, looking behind him. "She's right on time."

Will's stomach clenched at the small white car coming down the drive. Surely it wasn't Fleur.

The car pulled up next to his and Fleur got out, the white singlet she wore stretched tightly across her breasts and the denim shorts barely covering the essentials. Her legs were long, so damned long, and Will forced himself to stop staring.

"How's it going, Will?" Fleur asked.

He should have called her back. This was all kinds of awkward. "Fine. Thanks." Perhaps he could clear things up now, but not in front of Kit. "Kit said you can show me the banksia population?"

"That's right." Fleur reached into her back seat and brought out a picnic basket. "Have you had lunch yet?"

Will stared at her. "No."

"Great. I thought we could eat together." Without waiting for his answer, she put the basket in his four-wheel drive and climbed in.

Kit walked over to her window. "Stop by when you're done. I want to talk to you about something."

"Sure."

She'd brought him lunch. That had to mean she wasn't annoyed at him, that she wanted to spend more time with him. Amazing. He started the car. "Which way?"

She pointed and he headed down one of the dirt roads that led further into the property.

"Did you recover from your migraine all right? Some people feel crappy for days afterwards."

"I'm really sorry about that." He kept his eyes on the road.

"Not your fault. They hit without warning sometimes."

He had to be honest. "I knew it was coming."

"Why didn't you tell me?"

He shrugged. He'd ruined the night anyway, so it didn't really matter. He stopped at a farm gate.

"I'll get it," Fleur said. "Drive through and I'll close it behind us." She jumped out and strode over, her bottom jiggling nicely, and those legs… he wanted to touch every inch of her skin.

He shifted in his seat, adjusted himself and closed his eyes briefly. No. He couldn't have those thoughts now. She was about to get back in the car with him. He needed to think about something else. Like vomiting on her shoes.

Yep. That helped.

He drove through the gate and waited for Fleur. She jumped in, a vibrant breath of rose-scented air. "Follow this road."

He did as she asked and the silence stretched between them. "Thank you for taking care of me." His voice was loud, rough.

"You're welcome. You had me worried for a while. Do you get them often?"

He shook his head. What else could he say? "You've got the day off?"

"Afternoon shift. I've got to be back in town by two."

He should be done by then.

They were driving towards the wall of trees.

"I haven't been out this way in a long time." Fleur smiled.

"What were you doing out here?"

"The musketeers all used to come out here regularly when we were kids. We'd run amok for hours until it was time to go home." She pointed to a spot ahead of them where the wire fence separated the trees from the paddock. "Pull up there."

He braked and she jumped out, taking the basket from the back seat. He followed, grabbing his backpack. "We'll need to climb through the fence." She placed the basket on the ground and carefully held the barbed wire open so he could climb through, and he returned the favour. He didn't want the wire to cut her unblemished skin.

"It's this way."

She strode confidently down a barely there path, the scrubby undergrowth only slightly squashed in places. Something rustled to his left.

"Wait!" He grabbed her wrist and she stumbled into his

arms.

She smelled so pretty. Her eyes were on his and he was staring, still holding her so she could get her balance. "What is it?"

What it was, was that he was so attracted to her he couldn't think straight. But somehow he managed to grunt, "Snakes. Let me go first."

"But I know the way."

"Direct me." He stepped in front of her to stop any argument. His steel-capped boots and long cargo pants would do a lot more to deflect a snake bite then her tiny sneakers and smooth, bare skin.

Don't think about it.

He walked slowly, scanning for the banksia he was there to monitor. They reached the river and the scrubby undergrowth changed to long grass and paperbarks. The river was about ten metres wide and flowing slowly, its clear brown water babbling gently against the shore.

"Kit says the easiest access point is up here." Fleur pushed past him and stomped along the long grass.

"Stay here," he barked and she whirled around.

"We used to play here when we were kids," she said. "We never saw a snake." The little bit of snark in her tone halted him. He'd been brash, abrupt. She knew the area a lot better than he did.

"I don't want you to get hurt."

"I won't. This is where the musketeers had our first official ceremony," she said, a smile in her voice. "It's sacred ground for us."

And here he was telling her what to do. "Sorry. I'll be careful." He moved past a paperbark and saw one of the low prostrate banksias behind it at a bit of a distance from the river. He held up a hand for her to stop.

"Is that it?"

He nodded.

"We used the flowers in our ceremony to make Lincoln our protector. If we'd known it was endangered... I'm glad we only picked one flower for the crown."

"Protector?" He didn't like the twinge of jealousy.

"We must have been about twelve and had decided we wanted a knight protector like in some old movie we'd been watching. Lincoln was the natural choice because he lived next door with his brother Jamie, and he was six years older. So he kindly went through the ceremony and promised to take care of us always. It's a bit of a double-edged sword, because these days he can be a pain in the ass if he doesn't agree with something we want to do."

It was so nice she had friends like that. He'd been a loner for so long he'd forgotten what that was like. He'd preferred the solitude of the bush rather than deal with ignorant comments about his heritage. "I guess now he's a cop, he has more right."

She chuckled. "Or so he thinks."

They arrived at the low shrub, stretched out over the ground like a thick, prickly carpet. He retrieved his clipboard from his backpack and made notes. The population was thriving here. When he returned his clipboard to his bag, Fleur said, "Is that all you do?"

He glanced up at her, raised an eyebrow.

"When you're monitoring endangered species, do you just keep an eye on them, write a few notes?"

"I give the botanist all the details and she'll decide what to do. I'll probably need to collect seeds later in the year."

"You don't need to fence this one off?"

"Do the musketeers still come here?"

She shook her head.

"Then there's no need. We avoid disturbing the natural environment as much as possible." He got to his feet and followed her back to the shore, where she'd left her basket.

"Are you ready for lunch?" She waited for his nod before taking a picnic rug from the top of the basket and spreading it over the ground. Then she proceeded to take containers of salad, meats and bread out of the basket.

Wow. His stomach grumbled.

She smiled at him. "Have a seat. I wasn't sure what you liked so I brought a bit of everything."

Far better than the sandwich he'd thrown together this morning which was probably getting soggy in his car.

"Help yourself." She passed him a plate and then cut a small loaf of crusty bread.

"Thank you." No one had ever brought him lunch before. His insides tingled. He took the bread she handed him and put some meat and cheese on top.

"I'd forgotten how nice it was out here," she said. "I used to borrow Dad's dinghy and bring Mai and Hannah out to visit Kit and Jamie. They'd meet us here and we'd spend hours swimming. There used to be a rope swing there." She pointed to the nearby gum tree.

He could imagine it. The five of them hanging out here, splashing and laughing. It felt as if there was no one else for miles. The bush behind them blocked the view of the paddocks and in front of them, over the river was a thick grove of paperbark trees. The cicadas were loud but unseen and the gentle swoosh of the river as it flowed past was calming. "It's a place for dreams and secrets."

She beamed at him. "You get it. Did you have a place like this in Goldwyer?"

"There was one place I used to go, far enough away from town that people didn't know about it."

"By yourself?"

His skin tightened. "Yeah."

She put a hand on his arm. "Were you lonely?"

How would it come across if he told the truth? Only one way to find out. "Sometimes, but the bush has its own secrets, its own life." He ran two fingers up a stalk of grass, the texture dry as it fought to hold on to the last specks of moisture.

"So how did you end up so far away?"

"There was a job here."

She handed him a bottle of hibiscus tea. "Do you want to go home? Some of my high school friends went to the city for university and never want to come back."

He shook his head. "I don't like the city. It's too noisy and busy. There's no community." And in Goldwyer at least he had family.

"I get that. I couldn't wait to come home."

They shared a smile.

He never would have imagined having a picnic with Fleur and making conversation. Maybe he was finally getting the hang of it. "I'd go home in an instant if there was a job there."

A frown flittered across Fleur's face and she checked the time. "I need to get back." She packed up and Will helped, putting lids on containers. He didn't want the picnic to end, but maybe they could do this again.

"Are you free tomorrow?" he asked.

"I've got the musketeers coming over in the evening." Then her eyes widened. "Hang on, it's your birthday isn't it?"

His mouth dropped open. "How did you know?"

She grinned. "You told me when you were admitted into the hospital the other day. I made note of it. Do you want to do brunch?"

She knew his birthday. She wanted to do something with him. This day was getting better and better. "OK. Where do you want to go?" He had no idea where to go for brunch in Blackbridge.

She pursed her lips as she got to her feet. "Let me organise it. I'll pick you up at nine?"

She'd already done a lot of the organising and picking up so far. "Do you want me to drive?"

"No. I'm good. If I pick you up I can keep it a surprise." She winked.

God she was beautiful. Her smile, her enthusiasm, her joy at life was infectious. He smiled back, and she put a hand on her chest.

"That's some weapon you've got there."

He frowned.

"No, don't frown." She stepped forward and helped him to his feet. "Your smile is amazing. You should do it more often."

She was standing so close to him, only inches apart, and her eyes captured his with their earnestness. He wanted to kiss her. He was almost certain she wanted to kiss him.

Almost.

He needed to do something fast, before the moment was lost.

Slowly he lowered his head and Fleur closed the distance

between them. His lips met hers.

They were soft and sweet, and her hands slid around the back of his neck, pulling him closer.

Holy yes.

He wrapped his arms around her waist and tasted her, his whole body tight. She parted her lips and his tongue brushed hers, the sweetness of the hibiscus tea still lingering. He wanted more and he deepened the kiss. Her breathy moan made him harden.

She brought her hands to his chest and stepped back. He took an involuntary step towards her.

Her eyes were intense. "You're going to make me forget I have to go to work."

His face heated, but a grin slipped out. "Sorry."

"Don't be." She folded the picnic rug and picked up the basket, then held out her hand so he could take it. "Come on."

Will followed her back to the car in a slight daze. The sun was somehow brighter, the barbed wire fence not so sharp.

And Fleur wanted to see him again.

Living in Blackbridge suddenly seemed like a damned good thing.

Chapter 10

The weather was perfect for a picnic. Fleur sighed in relief as she looked out at the blue skies, the sun shining above. She poured hot water into the final thermos and checked she had everything for brunch. She'd briefly debated against another picnic, but it really was the perfect option because Will had totally relaxed without other people around.

Glancing at her reflection in the oven door, she adjusted her royal blue shirt, so she didn't show too much cleavage and twisted to check if her white three-quarter pants had picked up any dirt. All good. She'd enjoyed his hungry gaze yesterday when he'd seen her booty shorts and couldn't wait for his reaction when she revealed her barely there bikini. Grinning, she slipped on her flat strappy sandals with the diamantes, grabbed the basket and her beach towel, and walked out the door.

On the way, she picked up Will's present from the garden centre. She'd agonised over what to get him. It couldn't be some token gift. Their kiss the day before had been something to tell the musketeers about, if she was the type to kiss and tell. She'd meant to keep it light, have a taste, but he'd reacted so fast, had swept her up in the moment that she'd forgotten where they were and what she was supposed to be doing until her phone alarm had vibrated in her back pocket.

The passion had been a welcome surprise. She hadn't had a kiss she'd felt all the way down to her toes like that ever.

She pulled into his drive and got his present out of the car, a few nerves prickling her skin as she did so. Would he like it?

Will opened the door almost as soon as she knocked. This was the most casual she'd seen him, dressed in green board shorts and a black T-shirt that emphasised his broad, muscular physique.

"Happy birthday." She handed him the kangaroo paw and brushed a kiss against his cheek.

He stared at the plant.

Maybe it hadn't been a good idea. He'd have to take care of it. "I can exchange it for something else if you'd like."

He shook his head and ran a finger over a glossy leaf. "No. It's perfect. I wasn't expecting anything." He smiled at her. "Thank you."

So, he wasn't disappointed, he was surprised. She had to get better at reading his reactions. "Are you ready to go?"

"Yeah, let me get my towel. Come in." He placed the plant on the living room coffee table.

Elijah was sitting on the couch having breakfast. "Hey, Elijah."

"Hi. You guys going to the beach?" he asked.

She nodded. "I've got a birthday picnic planned."

"Happy birthday."

Fleur shook her head. "It's not mine, it's Will's."

Will came back into the room and Elijah spun to him, his eyes wide. "You didn't tell me it was your birthday!"

Will cleared his throat. "It's not a big deal."

"Sure it is. I feel like an inconsiderate prick." Hurt shone in his eyes.

It was nice he cared. "I'll have him back by about three if you guys want to do something."

"No, it's fine," Will said.

"The strippers it is," Elijah declared and the horror on Will's face made her laugh.

"Just kidding, mate," Elijah said. "We'll do something low key. You two go have fun."

She took Will's hand and led him out to the car.

"Where are we going?" Will asked as she drove out of town.

"Green's Pool," she said. "You mentioned you liked to swim and at this time of the morning we might be lucky to have the place to ourselves."

"That sounds great."

"You don't like being around people, do you?"

He glanced out the window for a moment. "I got used to playing by myself," he said. "I was the youngest of my family and all of my brothers are much older and didn't want me hanging around."

"What about at school?"

He shrugged. "Goldwyer is a small town and kids moved away regularly when their parents got other jobs. Then in high school I had to take the bus to a neighbouring town and I didn't really fit in. I never knew what to say."

It sounded like a lonely existence. "Well, you don't have to worry about what you say to me."

He snorted. "That's my constant worry."

She frowned. "Why?"

"Because you're gorgeous." His eyes widened. "I mean, I really like you." He groaned. "Because I keep saying the wrong thing like that."

She laughed. He was incredibly cute when he was flustered. "I really like you too."

He stared at her.

"Don't look so surprised. I've been thinking about that kiss since it happened."

He looked away but smiled. "Me too."

If only they were closer to their destination so she could kiss him again. "Good." She squeezed his hand and then let go. "I'm not going to jump down your throat if you say the wrong thing."

"Thanks."

The silence between them was comfortable as she drove the remaining distance to the beach. Only a couple of cars were parked in the large car park and she took Will's hand as they walked down the sloping path to the water. The air was cool and still but hinted at a warmer day to come.

"This place is lovely," Will said.

Two people walked along the far end of the curved beach, and someone swam laps in the water. It was quiet, not yet filled with the shrieks of children playing. They'd have more privacy on the gently sloping, smooth granite rocks that formed one side of the bay. Fleur left the white sand and walked up the rocks and when she was satisfied they were out of view of the others, she spread out the picnic rug. "Take a seat."

Before she could sit down, Will took her hand and tugged her towards him.

Surprise had her eyes widening. She was so close to him, as close as when they kissed yesterday.

His eyes were dark, intensely focused on her. "I, ah, I'd like to kiss you again."

She grinned at him, anticipation humming through her veins. "What a great idea." She closed the distance between them, wrapping her arms around his neck and then pressed her lips to his.

Man, he was a good kisser. He took his time, exploring her lips, tasting and touching. Her pulse rate skyrocketed. She slid her hands under his T-shirt, felt the warmth of his solid abs and moved closer, feeling him harden.

He stepped back, cleared his throat. "We should eat."

Was he embarrassed about his reaction? "You're right." It would be easy to get carried away.

Mai had dropped off fresh croissants and muffins and Fleur had brought a selection of fruit. "Coffee or tea?" She'd made a thermos of both.

"Tea, please." He sat next to her on the rug. "You didn't need to go to so much trouble."

"It was no trouble," she said. "Besides, it's your birthday and you're worth it."

He glanced away in a move she now recognised as embarrassment.

She poured him a mug of tea and passed him the milk and sugar, before spreading out the food she'd brought. "Help yourself."

"Did Mai make these?" Will asked as he spread a croissant with jam.

"Of course. I wouldn't get them from anywhere else."

"How's she doing since the bakery burned down?"

A lot of people had asked her that during the month since Mai had lost everything. Most of them were eager for juicy gossip, but Will appeared genuinely concerned. "She's coping well. The delivery van she bought is perfect and she's selling everything she makes."

"I miss not dropping in there on my way to work each day."

"They poured the slab for the new development last week, so it won't be long until the bakery opens again."

She poured herself a coffee and then spread cream cheese and jam over her croissant.

They chatted while they ate, and the sun's rays heated up the rocks around them adding extra warmth to the day. "Do you want to go for a swim?"

"Sure."

They packed up the food and Fleur stripped off her top, adjusting the brightly coloured floral bikini top she had on underneath. Will's sharp intake of breath was so loud that she looked up.

He was staring at her breasts.

The blatant appreciation made her feel attractive, powerful.

"Could you rub sun cream into my back?" She passed him the bottle and he took it, tearing his gaze away and smiling at her a little sheepishly.

"Sorry."

"No worries." She was tempted to tease him, to strip slowly out of her three-quarter length pants, but she didn't want him to be uncomfortable. Instead she sat still as his strong hands worked the cream into her back, his fingers delicately lifting one strap and then the other, so he could rub cream underneath them.

Every stroke left a trail of delicious warm shivers over her skin, and she wanted him to explore further, lower. It had been a while since she'd dated anyone, and maybe that was why she was having such an intense reaction to him.

Will cleared his throat. "Done."

She took a second before she turned to him with a smile. "Do you want me to do your back?"

He nodded, and hesitating, he stripped off his T-shirt.

My, my. She hadn't paid attention to his body the other night when she'd been in nurse mode, putting him to bed. Now though...

His back was broad across the shoulders, narrowing as it came to his waist, his skin a rich brown, and his muscles tightened as she spread the cream over him. He was warm and smooth, and she itched not only to rub his back, but to run her hands over his chest as well.

Instead, she stepped back. "You're done." She undid her pants, sliding them off and quickly added sun cream to her legs.

"I'll meet you in the water."

Before she had a chance to say anything, Will moved down the rock face to the sand.

That was odd.

She followed him more slowly, watching as he strode into the water and then dived under. When he surfaced, water cascaded down his body. He was the epitome of man — strong, powerful, sexy.

The water was a little cold as she walked in, but she kept moving, her gaze fixed on him. Will stood there, half of his body in the water, half above, his eyes locked on her.

The intensity, the focus was nothing she'd experienced before. It was as if they were the only two people on the planet.

She finally reached him, stopping no more than a foot away. "Hi."

His lips quirked upwards. "Hi."

She slid her hands up his chest to his shoulders and he pulled her closer, his hands resting on her lower back.

"What are we going to do about this spark between us?"

He lowered his head, so his lips were only centimetres away from hers. "This."

His lips met hers and instead of the gentleness she was

expecting, they were firm, demanding.

Yes, please.

Delighted by the change, she clung to him, meeting his demands and enjoying the ride. Her groin ached, and she wanted to be closer to him, so she jumped up and wrapped her legs around his waist.

He fell backwards and all of a sudden they were both underwater.

She surfaced, laughing. "Whoops. Sorry about that."

His small grin set her heart racing again. "Was that meant to cool me down?"

She wanted him hot, steaming. She shook her head, loving his playful side.

A child's shriek pierced her consciousness. They weren't far from a couple of families who had arrived, and what she wanted to do with Will wasn't appropriate in public. "Follow me."

She swam towards the large boulders in the middle of the pool. If they were on the far side it would block them from view. When she stopped, he was right behind her.

"This is better." She reached for him and he picked her up, so she could wrap her legs around his waist. She squeezed him closer as he kissed her again, and his hardness rubbed against her. He was as into this as she was.

And she wanted him badly.

His hands roamed her body, over her back, squeezing her butt, then his thumbs brushed her breasts.

The water should be boiling around them.

Will pressed her against the smooth rock and moved away just a fraction, his breath coming fast.

"Don't stop."

He stared at her, his gaze a little uncertain.

Was he worried about being in the water? "I want you to touch me." She took his hand and brought it up to her breast, resting his palm against her skin.

"Jesus, Fleur," he whispered before he rubbed her nipple through the fabric of her bikini.

It wasn't nearly enough. She needed to touch his skin. She pushed the fabric aside and his sharp intake of air sent a rush of power through her until his mouth replaced his fingertips and he took control.

And oh, my God, he took control with a possessiveness that melted her with its intensity. His tongue teased her nipple and his warm breath on her skin contrasted sharply with the coolness of the water. He sucked and licked, and Fleur moaned, her head thrown back as she squeezed him with her legs.

She wanted more.

Needed more.

But Will seemed content with her breasts. She wriggled, pressing her groin against his hard crotch and he groaned, pulling her butt closer and rubbing her along his length.

Yes.

This was what she wanted.

She slipped her hands between them, feeling for the drawstring of his shorts, needing to get them off him. She slipped her hand down the front of his pants and Will stopped her, breathing heavily.

She glanced at him.

"Slow down," he panted, squeezing his eyes shut.

She didn't want slow, she wanted fast and now, but she had to listen to him. Nibbling on his neck below his ear, she said, "I want you inside of me."

His whole body tensed. Had she gone too far? Before she could ask he pressed her back against the rock, kissing her desperately. When he broke free he asked, "What about a condom?"

At this moment she didn't care. "I'm on birth control and clear."

"Me too." He winced. "About the clear thing, not the birth control thing."

She chuckled and squeezed him tight against her. "Good."

She slid his shorts off and his penis came free. She stroked its hard, warm length.

Will gritted his teeth as he moaned and pushed her bikini bottoms down. She unhooked her legs from his waist only long enough to get one leg free of her bathers and then she wrapped them around him again, guiding him into her.

Yes.

There.

Will gripped her hips tightly for a second before a groan tore from his lips and he moved, thrusting into her, each stroke rocking her to her core. She tilted her hips, so he rubbed the right spot and clung to him, nibbling his neck, his chest, his lips.

Sensations built inside her as he thrust faster and faster.

More.

"Oh, God," he moaned, and he thrust deeper and Fleur exploded around him, clinging to him as he clung to her and they both cried out in ecstasy.

Holy shit.

No other words could even come close to describing the experience.

Will had just had sex.

With Fleur

In the ocean.

He held her tightly against him as his legs threatened to weaken, and he desperately tried to slow his pulse rate.

"Wow." Fleur's breathy chuckle had him hardening again. She loosened her legs around him and he let her go, sliding out of her and the shock of the cold water had him quickly tucking himself back into his shorts.

Fleur ducked under the water to slip her bather bottoms back on and when she surfaced, face flushed, hair wet, Will had no idea what to say.

What did one say to the woman who'd rocked his world, who had shown him what he'd been missing?

"Thank you."

Fleur raised her eyebrows and smirked. "You're welcome."

Shit. He'd said it aloud. Heat rushed to his cheeks and he looked away.

Fleur's cool hand on his cheek brought his head back to her and she kissed him. "Don't be embarrassed. I'm feeling pretty thankful myself."

"You are?" Seriously was there *any* filter on his mouth?

"Yeah. It wasn't what I was planning when I invited you to brunch, but that was incredible."

Pleasure swelled up inside him. He'd been good. He'd always feared he'd make a fool of himself.

She kissed him again and he drew her closer, unable to stop himself. He wanted to keep kissing her, keep touching her, wanted to keep her right where she was.

She was his for this moment.

Fleur leaned back and sighed. "You keep that up and I'm not going to be able to resist you again."

He was totally OK with that.

"But as those kids' shouts are getting closer, maybe we should head to my place."

He tuned into the surroundings and the splashing coming from the other side of the rock. It was just as well Fleur was paying attention. The thought of kids catching him with Fleur…

He cringed.

"Hey, are you all right?" She stroked his arm. "We don't have to go to my place."

"No. I mean, yes, I'd like to go to your place." Don't get flustered. Fleur isn't going to judge you. "The idea of those kids arriving sooner…"

She laughed. "Yeah, I know what you mean." She let go of him and they swam side by side until they reached the shore.

Fleur climbed up the rock to where they'd left their stuff, her floral bikini clinging to her breasts and her butt and leaving a whole lot of gorgeous tanned skin naked.

She bent over to pick up her towel and he smothered a groan. Her butt was sublime.

A towel hit him in the face and he took a step back, lunging for it before it fell.

"Sorry, I thought you were looking." She winked.

He chuckled. A chunk of nerves fell away as he dried himself. "So, you want to go back to your place?"

"Only if you want to. It's your birthday. We can do what you want."

What he wanted was more of Fleur, naked, under him. "Your place sounds great."

The nerves came back as Fleur pulled up into her driveway and they got out of the car.

"I need a shower." Fleur dropped her towel and the picnic basket on the kitchen table.

Right. What did he do now? Did he go with her? Did he watch TV until she was done?

"Want to join me?" She held out a hand and he took it, allowing her to lead him into her small bathroom. Turning on the shower, she dropped his hand and then took off her top and slid off her pants. That bikini left him lost for words.

She reached behind herself and suddenly her bikini top was loose and on the floor. The bottoms quickly followed.

Now he was not only lost for words but lost for breath.

She was beautiful.

"Are you all right, Will?" A tiny crease crumpled her forehead.

He nodded quickly and stripped off his top and shorts. He hesitated at his underwear. He'd never been fully naked in front of a woman before, had never been entirely comfortable with his body. Plus his erection was hard and would spring out with an announcement as loud as 'look at me'.

Fleur stepped closer, ran a hand up his chest to his shoulder. "You don't have to get naked if you don't want."

Oh, he wanted to all right. He just needed to get past his fears.

"I'll let you decide." She stepped into the shower and drew the shower curtain closed, blocking his view of her gorgeous body.

Get a grip, mate.

Quickly he stripped off his underpants and then slowly he pulled across the curtain.

Fleur had her head tilted backwards, her eyes closed as he slipped into the shower. When she opened them, she smiled at him. "Glad you could join me."

So was he.

She slid her hands up his chest and over his shoulders.

He ached for her. He ran his hands slowly down her back, controlling his desire to press her against the wall and have his way with her again.

"Can I ask you something?" Fleur pressed a kiss on his neck and then his cheek, before finally kissing his lips.

"Yes." She could do anything she wanted.

She stepped back from him, her eyes concerned. "It's personal, and I don't want to offend you."

As long as she kept running her hands over his body like she was doing now, she could ask him anything. "It's fine."

"To be clear, you were amazing earlier, in the ocean."

She was delaying what she wanted to say, and he suddenly had an inkling of what she was going to ask him. Crap. "Go ahead."

"It's just you seem a little unsure and I don't know whether it's because you're shy, or whether you, you know, haven't done much before." Her face was flushed a pretty pink.

His face would have been beetroot red if it changed colour like that. He swallowed hard. He didn't want to lie to her, even if it might make him appear like a loser. "Well, ah, that was my first time."

Fleur stepped away. "I'm sorry. I should have made the moment special."

He didn't want her retreating. He pulled her back towards him. "It was special," he said. "It was the best damned moment of my life. You were so sexy, and you wanted me and it happened so fast that I didn't have to worry about what I was doing, and how many guys can say they lost their virginity in the ocean with the sexiest woman on the planet?" He was talking too much now.

She laughed. "OK, you've convinced me." A glint came into her eye. "So, you've never showered with a woman before?"

He shook his head.

Slowly she slid down his body until she was on her knees. She took hold of his throbbing cock and grinned up at him. "Let me show you some of the benefits."

Her mouth took him in and Will's brain turned to mush.

Chapter 11

After the shower, they moved to the bed, and Will had been keen to explore Fleur's body. And she had no complaints. Her whole body had a lovely satisfied glow. She brushed a hand over Will's chest as she lay with her head in the crook of his shoulder, the sheets only covering their lower bodies.

"This is the best birthday ever." Will's voice was low, not far from her ear.

She chuckled. "I'm glad. What do you normally do for your birthday?"

He was silent for a while. "Not much. Back at home, Mum would bake a cake, but since I've been at university, I haven't done anything."

Her heart hurt for him. "I'm pleased I could change that."

"Me too." He kissed the top of her head.

"What do you miss most about Goldwyer?"

"My mum, and the country. The dirt is a really rich red, and there's a harsh beauty to it."

"Is that why you became a park ranger? Because of the country?"

"Yeah. I want to protect the environment, ensure it's here for the next generations. And I figured it was a job where I didn't need to be around people."

He was the most introverted person she'd ever met. "So, if a job comes up there, you'll move back?"

His hand slid over her side and pleasure hummed along her skin. "That's always been my plan."

So where did that leave them?

A loud bang sounded through the house and then a voice called, "Fleur, are you home?"

Kit.

Fleur sat bolt upright in bed. It was only two o'clock. The musketeers weren't due for another couple of hours.

Will scrambled to a seated position beside her.

"Stay here. I won't be a minute." She flung the sheets back. Kit would search the house until she found them, and she didn't want to put Will through that. Grabbing a dress from her wardrobe, she slid it on and then hurried out, almost crashing into Kit in the doorway. She shut the bedroom door firmly behind her.

"Hi, Kit. What are you doing here so early?"

"Paul was doing my head in, and if I stayed at the farm I was going to kill him." She frowned. "Were you having a nap?"

Fleur ran a hand through her hair and led her friend back into the living room. "Ah, not so much."

"What then?" Kit's eyes widened. "Oh, did I interrupt something?"

"Your timing could have been worse."

"Shit, sorry." She tilted her head. "Who?"

"Will."

"Well, I didn't expect that." Kit flashed her a grin as she paced through the room. "It's always the quiet ones."

Fleur smiled. "He's a little shy."

"Obviously not too shy." Her friend kept pacing.

Something was bothering her. "Is everything all right?"

"No. I'm so frustrated!" Kit tugged on her ponytail.

Concerned, Fleur took her arm and pressed her down onto the couch. "What's wrong?"

"Paul flaked on me again today. I'm so behind on the fencing it's not funny and he doesn't care. I think I'm going to have to sack him."

Kit had been friends with Paul for longer than he'd been working for her as a farmhand. It wasn't going to be easy for her to fire him. Fleur hesitated. She had a sexy, naked man in her bed, but she had one of her best friends in the world in need of her help.

The musketeers always had each other's backs. "Give me a second and we can talk about it."

Will was sitting on the edge of the bed, the sheet covering his groin, but his broad, muscular chest on display. Yum.

"Could you get my clothes?"

She blinked. Of course, they were still on the floor of the bathroom. "Be right back." When she returned, she handed them to him and kissed him slowly. "I'd love for you to stay longer, but Kit needs my help."

"OK. I heard a little of what she said." He dressed quickly. "I've had more time with you today than I'd hoped for."

He should have higher expectations. "Thank you for understanding."

She kissed him again and then took his hand and led him into the living room. Kit looked up. "Hey, Will. Sorry for disturbing you."

"It's fine." He squeezed Fleur's hand and she walked him to the door.

"Damn. You don't have a car."

"I can walk." He drew her close to him. "Don't worry about it."

She would, despite what he said. "I had fun today."

His grin was fast. "Me too. Are you free tomorrow?"

"Aren't you playing cricket with Kim?"

He swore. "I forgot. What about tomorrow night?"

"I'm working. I've got a whole week of afternoon shifts. How about Saturday?"

"Yeah. I'll call you." He kissed her again and then trotted down her front steps and down the street.

Saturday couldn't come soon enough.

Heading back inside, she found Kit in the kitchen making cups of tea.

"I am sorry, Fleur. I didn't mean to cramp your style."

"Don't sweat it." Her friends had always had free reign in her house, had always been there for her. She wasn't going to dump them now she had Will in her life, she'd just need to make a couple of adjustments. "Tell me what Paul's done this time."

"It's what he hasn't done that's the problem." She carried both cups of tea over to the coffee table and sat on the couch. "Yesterday he called in sick, which would have been fine if Jamie hadn't seen him surfing at Lowland's Beach in the afternoon." She growled. "Then today I asked him to check the fences by the river, and found him out towards Foley's farm, sitting in the ute having a cigarette, flying his damn drone."

"What did he say?"

"He claims he thought I asked for aerial shots of the farm, but that's bullshit. He's been so unreliable since Gordon died last month. I know they were good friends but acting up like this isn't his normal style."

But thinking he knew better than others was. Fleur had been forced to ban him from the track for a year when he and some friends had been caught with their modern bikes there. He'd been using his drone then too. "Maybe you should talk to him about it."

Her friend nodded. "I'm so annoyed, I'm struggling to be civil. His attitude makes me steam." She got up and paced again.

"You're entitled to give him a warning." Fleur sipped her tea as Kit paced. Kit had to get her frustrations out in a physical way — no yoga or meditation for her. "That might be enough to make him realise you're serious. Then if you do have to sack him, you've got proof he's had a chance to change his ways."

"You might be right, but I hate all of that HR stuff, all the stupid paperwork." She sat back down again. "I'll do it this week." And just like that, she was calm again, sipping her tea. "So, tell me, what's going on with you and Will?"

Fleur smiled, used to her friend's rapid mood changes. "You could say we're dating."

"Looks like you're doing more than that." Kit winked.

"Maybe."

"Come on, tell me all about it."

She and her friends often discussed men, but this time she

didn't want to. She didn't want to betray Will's confidence. "It's early days."

Kit raised an eyebrow. "So, no gossip?"

"Not about Will."

"Hmm, maybe there is more to the mysterious Will than meets the eye," she said. "When are you seeing him again?"

"As soon as we can work out a time. I've got afternoons this week."

"Shame. So, what's happening about the night race? The long weekend is only a couple of weeks away."

It was another thing she had to sort out. "I'm waiting for the permits to arrive, but the lights have been booked." She placed her mug on the coffee table. "I didn't tell you, the clubhouse was broken into the other day."

"Damn. Anything stolen?"

"Not that I can tell. They damaged a couple of tables and spray painted the walls. I need to try to get it off, otherwise I'll have to arrange to paint over it."

"People suck sometimes," Kit said. "If you need a hand, call me."

Another knock at the front door and before Fleur could get up, Mai and Hannah walked in. "You girls get started without us?" Mai asked.

"I'm just complaining to Fleur," Kit said. "Though Fleur might want to complain about me. I interrupted her with Will Travers."

Hannah's and Mai's eyes widened. "Do tell," Hannah said.

Fleur laughed. It was good to have her girls around.

Will hesitated with his finger over the call button. Was it too early to ring? Fleur had been out with her friends last night, so they could still be sleeping.

"Call her already." Elijah plonked down on the couch next to him with his bowl of cereal. "You both had fun, right?"

Fun wasn't the word Will would use. Mind blowing, amazing, and also somehow comforting. He hit the call button and got up, wandering over to the back window to look out at his garden. He'd buy a pot for the kangaroo paw today and transplant it. That way he could take it with him when he left.

"Hey, this is Fleur, leave a message." His heart skipped a beat and then the beep made him freeze. What should he say?

"Ah, hi. It's Will. Just calling to…" To what? "Say hi." He cringed. "Talk to you later." He hung up, shaking his head at himself.

"Don't sweat it," Elijah called. "It's not a big deal."

When Will had got home yesterday, Elijah had wanted to hear all about the date. And Will had wanted to talk about it — not all of it — but the bits where he and Fleur had really talked, where he'd been comfortable with her. It was amazing how much being naked in bed together removed his inhibitions.

It had been a day of firsts: first sex, first real connection with a woman, and first time he'd had a friend to talk things over with. It was so great.

His phone rang in his hand and he jumped. Fleur. He grinned, his chest already lighter. "Hi."

"Hey, sorry I didn't get to my phone in time." She was a little bit breathless.

"Where are you?"

"Home. I was outside saying goodbye to the girls."

She was alone, and he still had three hours before he had to be at the oval for cricket. "Do you feel like company?" What was he saying? Her friends had just left. She probably wanted peace and quiet.

"Only if it's you."

Oh. That was nice.

"Why don't you bring your cricket gear over and you can leave from my house? That will give us some more time together."

Cricket gear. He hadn't thought about that. They usually played in white pants and shirt. "I don't have any gear." Was that going to matter? He couldn't even call Kim to find out.

"Don't worry. Wear loose pants and a T-shirt — white if you've got it. I drive past the oval on my way to the hospital and there's often one or two guys without it."

"OK. I'll see you soon." He hung up. He could do this.

He wasn't going to stress about the cricket match. It didn't matter.

"Told you." Elijah winked. "What gear don't you have?"

"Someone invited me to play cricket this afternoon."

"Cool. What time? I'll come and watch."

It would be easier with Elijah there. "One. I'll pick you up."

"All right. Now go and see your girlfriend."

Girlfriend. Was that what this was? The word was foreign to him. But he wasn't going to worry about it. He had a beautiful woman to visit.

The second Fleur opened the door, she was in his arms, her lips on his. Lust shot through him as he kissed her back, pulling her closer. He'd never experienced such want before. He wanted to devour her at the same time as take care of her.

She broke the kiss, her breath fast. "Hi."

He chuckled. "Hi." He could handle that kind of welcome every time he saw her.

"If you're interested, we could go for a walk, maybe get an early lunch?" she said. "I suspect, if you come inside, we'll head straight for my bedroom and I'd like to talk."

"It doesn't have to be the bedroom."

Fleur laughed. "You know what I mean. I can't keep my hands off you, and I want to find out what makes you tick."

He was probably better at sex than talking, but he wanted to get to know Fleur as well. "OK."

"Be right back." She dashed inside and came back a moment later with her handbag. Taking his hand, they walked down the street towards the centre of town.

"Did you have fun last night?" Will asked.

"Yeah. A musketeers' night is always fun. Mai is already planning her wedding and Hannah announced she's moving in with Ryan and Felix, who have a new place in town." She sighed. "It's so great they're happy, but it's harder to organise time together now they both have significant others."

Hopefully Fleur would soon consider him as her significant other. "What do you do at a musketeers meeting?"

"That's a closely guarded secret. I'd have to kill you if I

told you." She winked at him.

"What can you tell me then?"

She pursed her lips. "We support and protect each other, keep each other sane."

It would be nice to have that kind of support. "Is your family jealous that you're so close?"

"Not at all. Dad loves the musketeers as much as I do. They were there for me when Mum died, and Hannah's grandparents used to take care of me after school when Dad was at work."

His heart squeezed. "How did your mum die?"

"She had breast cancer." Fleur was silent for a while. "We had a Silver Chain nurse come to visit every day in the last weeks of her life before she was hospitalised, and she made such a difference, really helped Mum. That's when I decided I wanted to be a nurse."

"That's brave."

She had a slight frown on her face. "Why do you say that?"

"As a nurse you'd see people at their worst. It's got to be hard."

"It can be, but when you help them, it's such a thrill."

He hadn't thought about it that way. "I couldn't do it."

They turned down towards the river. "I like people, but my dad doesn't get it, he hates going near hospitals, I think because it reminds him of the time he spent in them when Mum was sick."

"Do you remember much of her?"

"Yeah. She was always laughing and singing. We used to bake cakes for Dad or do craft projects, and I'd help her tend her roses."

"That sounds nice." His mother had worked a lot when he was younger.

"It was. When she got sick things changed."

He frowned. He couldn't imagine what it would be like to lose a parent so young. "It must have been hard for you."

She sighed. "It was. I thought if I did everything I could to help, she'd get better." She shook her head. "But life doesn't work like that."

It was a harsh lesson to learn at any age. He changed the subject. "What does your father do?"

"He's a commercial fisherman, catches mostly pilchards."

Will grimaced. At university commercial fishermen and mining companies were public enemy number one as far as his lecturers and many of his peers were concerned.

"Do you have a problem with that?" Fleur asked.

He hesitated. "What type of nets does he use?"

"Purse seine."

"That's not too bad." There would never be an ideal solution to commercial fishing. Their nets often caught protected species, but the alternative was they wouldn't be able to earn a living and he didn't want to get into an argument with Fleur about it.

"So, what was growing up in Goldwyer like?"

He considered his answer. "My neighbour, Aggie, was a wildlife carer and she taught me how to take care of injured wildlife." It was something he'd loved to do, so perhaps he was a little like Fleur in his desire to care for the injured.

"Sounds lovely. Do you get to do that here?"

"Not so much. There are other wildlife carers already set up. Maybe once I'm more settled I'll look into it."

"So what else did you get up to?"

"On the weekend I'd take my bike and go out bush." It had been easy to amuse himself for hours.

They walked past an ice cream shop and he paused. "Do you want an ice cream?"

She smiled at him. "Yes, please."

They ordered and when he took his from the server he almost crashed into a guy in a wheelchair behind him. The same guy who had given him a hot dog at the track. "Sorry."

"No worries, mate. I should have given you space. I wanted to talk to Fleur for a second."

Fleur's face paled and the smile on her face was forced. "Hi Trevor, Nicole."

The tall woman standing next to Trevor smiled. "Hey." She put a hand on Fleur's arm. "Are you all right? You're a little pale."

"A minor headache."

Will was pretty sure Fleur was lying.

"Oh, I've got tablets if you want." She fished into her handbag and brought out a collection of pill packets. "Panadol, Nurofen, Aspirin — you name it, I've got it. I never know what Trevor might need."

Fleur shook her head. "No thanks. I've taken something."

This was the guy who had been injured in the accident at the track. He was older than them, but not by much, maybe early thirties.

"Do you need any help getting the track ready for the night race?" Trevor asked.

"Not really," Fleur answered. "We'll need to put a fair bit of water on the track if it continues to be sunny, but the rain the other day would have helped."

"That's good. Nicole and I can't wait."

"Mum, can we have an ice cream?" one of the kids asked.

"Not today. We'll have to wait for pay day."

"Oh, let me treat them." Fleur dug some money out of her wallet and handed it to Nicole. "I'll see you on the weekend." She crossed the road to the park, tension radiating from her body.

Will followed and slid an arm around her waist. "Are you all right?"

She shook her head, glanced back to where Trevor and Nicole were buying their own ice creams. "Trevor wants to ride again. His brother modified a bike and the committee allowed him to test it last weekend."

"Is that safe?"

"It worked fine. I can't believe he wants to."

He tugged her closer. "It's not your problem. If your committee are happy with him riding, you need to let him."

She buried her head in his chest and squeezed him. "I know."

She felt so right there, with her head close to his heart. He wanted to make everything OK for her. "It was nice of you to buy those kids ice cream."

"It's the least I can do. Trevor can't work because of me."

His ice cream dripped down his hand and he let her go. "Come on. Let's keep walking."

A lot of people were milling around the town oval when Will pulled up that afternoon. Some had spread blankets on the grass ready to watch the game, but most of them wore the white polo shirt and pants of cricket players, and gathered in a couple of groups. How would he find Kim? He should have got his number or arranged somewhere to meet.

"Come on," Elijah said as he got out of the car.

Elijah was right. He just needed to do this. Walking towards the group of people, he scanned faces to find Kim.

"Will!" Kim gestured him over. "Glad you could make it."

"I didn't have any whites." His white T-shirt had a graphic on it and he was wearing his work cargo pants.

"That's fine. If you join us on a more regular basis, you can get some."

Will introduced Elijah.

"Hey, if you play, the other team is down a guy too," Kim said.

Elijah grinned. "I haven't played cricket in years, but I'll give it a go."

They both followed Kim over to the group of men and Kim made the introductions. He couldn't remember so many names all at once. Luckily he could fall back on 'mate'.

The game began, and his team was fielding first so he took his position and waited. It was a warm day, but not too hot and the sun was nice on his skin. It was also kind of relaxing. The nearest other fielder was a good twenty metres away, not close enough to have to worry about conversation, but he was still part of the team.

When it was their turn to bat, he took a seat on the boundary next to Kim.

"Glad to see you're feeling better," Kim said. "You looked pretty rotten at the restaurant the other night."

He'd forgotten about the migraine and that Kim had seen him throw up. His face flushed.

"Fleur got you home all right?"

"Yeah, she did."

"Good. Fleur's a great woman." The admiration was clear

on his face.

Was he interested in Fleur? "She is. We went out again yesterday."

Kim chuckled. "Relax, mate. I had a massive crush on Fleur when I was in high school, but that's in the past. She and the rest of the musketeers are like my sisters."

Will shouldn't be jealous. There were probably a few guys here who had the hots for Fleur. But she was interested in him. "They're a close group."

"They are." Kim agreed.

"Many a man has tried to infiltrate the musketeers," a guy on his right piped up.

"Who shot you down, Jeremy?" another guy asked.

"All of them."

The guys laughed.

"The options are decreasing, what with Mai engaged and Hannah dating the cop."

"And Will's dating Fleur," Kim said.

All eyes turned towards Will and he flushed.

"Good one, mate," Jeremy congratulated him.

Will nodded, uncomfortable about the way they were talking about the musketeers as if they were commodities, but it was kind of nice to be part of the conversation.

The small crowd cheered and Kim stood up. "Looks like I'm up."

At the end of the day, Will's team won. "We're going to the pub to celebrate," Kim told him. "You coming?"

He waited for Elijah to confirm he was in. "Sure."

He'd had fun chatting with the guys on his team while they'd waited for their turn to bat. Jeremy worked with Mai as a volunteer fire-fighter, Adam was a constable at the police station, and Jamie was a teacher and also Lincoln's brother.

He listened to town gossip, and while he didn't know the people being talked about, what made it to the grapevine was interesting. For the first time since he'd moved here, he actually felt part of the community.

And that felt amazing.

He drove the short distance to the pub and joined the

others inside. It wasn't as terrifying walking into the building as it had been the last time. Now he had some idea what he was in for.

He ordered a soft drink and sat next to Jamie at the long wooden table.

"Not drinking, mate?" Jamie asked.

He hesitated a moment and tapped his thigh. "Don't much like beer."

Jamie nodded. "It can be an acquired taste."

Will let out a breath. No ridicule.

"So, you're dating Fleur?" Jamie asked.

"We've been on a couple of dates."

Jamie grinned. "Then that constitutes dating," he said. "Fleur would cut you off after one if she wasn't interested."

Will raised his eyebrows. How did this guy know? "Have you dated her before?"

"Hell no." Jamie laughed. "I'm an honorary musketeer. I know stuff." He tapped his nose with his finger.

"Fleur said no guys were allowed."

"They made an exception for me when we were kids because I was always hanging around Kit's place, though now we're adults and I've been away so long, my invites keep getting lost in the mail."

That's right, Fleur had mentioned him when they'd been at Kit's farm. Will studied him. "Do you want to go?"

"Maybe." He sipped his beer. "There are some things only the girls understand."

Jamie didn't seem inclined to share, so Will didn't ask. Maybe he should mention it to Fleur, even if it wasn't any of his business.

Will was content to listen to the conversation around him and answer the occasional question when it was directed at him. No one cared he wasn't talking.

Elijah was at the other end of the table, holding court with the guys down there, laughing regularly.

"Do you know who that guy is?" Jamie asked, nodding his head towards Elijah.

"That's my roommate, Elijah. He went to school with Kit." Which he assumed meant he went to school with Jamie.

"Elijah Johnson?"

"Yeah."

"He looks a lot different from the last time I saw him." Jamie smiled, his eyes still on Elijah.

"Were you friends?"

"Not really. He went to the ag school with Kit. He was a weedy-looking kid back then. I'm not sure he had many friends."

He couldn't imagine Elijah ever not having friends. He'd have to ask him about it later.

The evening grew late and then a few started talking about heading home. Elijah was happily chatting down the other end, but Will had an early start in the morning.

He said his goodbyes and Elijah asked, "You making a move?"

Will nodded.

"All right. I'll come with you."

They walked out into the cool evening and over to the car.

"That was Jamie Zanetti sitting next to you, wasn't it?" Elijah asked as he climbed in.

"Yeah."

Elijah sighed. "He's still as good-looking as I remember. I had a massive crush on him at high school."

Will smiled. "He remembers you."

"Really?" Elijah grinned and then swore. "No, that's not a good thing. I wasn't at my best at high school."

"What were you like?"

"Being gay in a small town, especially going to the ag school where it was mostly males, and trouble makers at that, wasn't easy. Many of them were worried the gayness would rub off on them." He sighed. "I was still figuring things out and Kit was one of the only ones who was nice to me."

Will wasn't the only one who'd had trouble fitting in, but he never would have guessed it from the confident, out there man who sat next to him now. "How did that change?"

"The second I was old enough, I got out of town, got right out of the country. I went to London to work and discovered a whole culture to be explored. It was safe to be who I wanted to be because no one knew me, there were no expectations."

He laughed. "I loved it."

Will smiled as he pulled into his driveway and got out. He'd never been brave enough to do that.

"I spent a number of years in Europe, travelling, learning who I was, who I wanted to be and came home at Christmas."

"Why come home, if you loved it so much over there?" He followed Elijah inside the house.

"My last job was working on a hops farm in Germany," he said. "It reminded me of how much I love farming, and when it came down to it, the only place I wanted to put down roots was here. Australia's in my blood."

Will understood that.

"Blackbridge is much more inclusive than it used to be," Elijah continued. He poured himself a glass of water and drank it. "I'll have to show you pictures of the dweeb I was some time."

"I'd like that."

Elijah grinned at him. "I'm going to bed. See you tomorrow."

Will checked the doors were locked and flicked off the lights. This weekend had been the best he'd had in such a long time and Kim had invited him to join the team permanently, which he'd accepted.

Maybe Blackbridge could be his Europe — the place where he discovered who he was and who he could be.

Maybe.

Chapter 12

Will caught himself whistling the next day as he strode along the banks of the river that ran through the national park. It was such a happy, merry tune that he smiled. It had been a long time since he'd truly been happy or merry about anything, even if he wouldn't see Fleur until the weekend. He'd driven past her house this morning on his way to work, in case she happened to be out the front and he could stop and say hi.

He hadn't felt this positive in a long time.

That was a little sad.

He'd been living a half-life, too scared of stuffing up to take a chance. But no one he'd spoken to over the weekend had cared whether he'd said anything, or just listened. They were pleased he'd been part of the team.

It was such a fantastic feeling.

And today was a glorious day. The gum trees shaded him from the warm sun as he picked his way around the riverbank, keeping his eyes open for rare orchids and checking the river was flowing freely. He'd been told that occasionally a farmer's runoff would cause algal blooms, or sometimes branches would fall, damming up the streams that ran off the river.

So far, so good. He'd walk up to the next visitor car park, and then return to his car via a different path through the bush.

A couple of blue wrens flittered through the branches, chirping at him, and he noted some rosellas sitting in the branches of one of the tall gums. As he moved around a dense grove of trees he came across some grey kangaroos lounging next to the river. They kept their eyes on him, so he slowed his pace and took a wide circle around them to avoid scaring them off.

He brushed his fingers over the leaves of the grevillea, enjoying its smooth texture and then inhaled deeply, the earthy scent grounding him.

Would Fleur love it as much as he did? He would have to bring her out here sometime, show her all of the things he loved.

Continuing along the riverbank, something bright yellow caught his eye, hidden by the paperbarks next to the river. He changed direction and picked his way down the bank.

A bulk-sized plastic container floated on the edge.

Anger stirred as he noted another plastic container caught by the trees on the other side of the river. They had to be sealed and empty, otherwise they would have sunk, so hopefully they hadn't contaminated the water. But someone hadn't wanted to pay the tip fee to dispose of them correctly. They could have come from anywhere up river.

He took off his boots and socks, tested the depth of the river, then stripped off his pants. The water was cold, and the sand soft, creeping between his toes as he carefully waded along until he could seize the container.

Will frowned. The label said it was caustic soda. That was the same chemical he'd found dumped at the motocross track.

He should call the police.

He left the other barrel where it was and waded back to shore to call the station.

"If the containers aren't leaking, leave them where they are," Ryan told him. "We'll come and take a look."

"I'll meet you at the car park," Will said.

It would take the police at least half an hour to get there, so he took some photos for his own report and made some notes, allowing his legs to dry in the sun before getting dressed again and heading for the meeting place.

This was the third dumping in a little over a month. If it was drug related, the person was getting sloppy. Or perhaps it was because the police had managed to keep the news from the public. The first lot of chemicals had been kitchen cleaner and they'd been found closer to town by the river. Lincoln had sworn Mai and Nicholas to secrecy, just like he'd asked Fleur to keep quiet about the containers at the track.

Had they come from the lab he'd discovered? Or were there more labs around? Perhaps he should set up a search.

As he walked along the river, he kept his eyes peeled for more containers, taking pictures and water samples as he went. He'd need to borrow the PAWS dinghy to clean up the mess. He counted another five yellow containers caught by overhanging tree branches before one floated past him down the river.

Had something pried it free, or was someone dumping the containers now?

He pulled out his map. Where were the access points to the river? The car park up ahead was the only place within ten kilometres.

Maybe he could catch whoever was doing it.

He chose his footing carefully, avoiding the plants which were dry and brittle. As he neared the car park, something splashed into the water and moments later another barrel floated past.

Someone was definitely there.

His heart raced as he slid his phone out of his pocket and switched on the camera. He needed to keep low and out of sight. Around this grove of trees was the car park.

Inching closer he peered around the branches. A white four-wheel drive was parked in reverse in the carpark, its back door open, but with no one in sight. He snapped a photo, but he was still too far away. He needed to get closer.

Will checked the time. The police wouldn't be here anytime soon. Visions of Nicholas and Mai bloodied and bruised flashed into his head. If this person was involved with the man who'd kidnapped Mai and beaten up Nicholas, then they were likely dangerous. He had to be careful.

A door slammed and he flinched, glancing back at the car.

The back door was closed and a person was getting into the driver's seat. They wore a wide-brimmed hat which shaded their face and the seats blocked the view further. It could have been a man or a woman.

The engine roared to life.

It was now or never. He needed to get a number plate at least.

Lunging forward, he stumbled over a bush and the car roared away, the thick dust obscuring the number plate.

Damn it!

He dialled the police station and reported what he'd seen, pulling out his map. The road branched threeways, so it was possible the police wouldn't pass the vehicle coming in.

Hurrying to the river, he was in time to see a white container being pushed downstream by the current. He swore, took a photo, and then called the office to arrange to use the dinghy as soon as possible. Perching himself on one of the sleepers framing the car park, he waited for the police to arrive.

Twenty minutes later Adam and Ryan pulled up.

"Did you see the four-wheel drive?"

Ryan shook his head. "No, there was no one on the road in."

If they hadn't taken the most direct route back to town, maybe they weren't local. They could have been from Mount Barker, or Walpole or any of the small towns in the area.

Will showed them the photos he'd taken and where the vehicle had been parked. The gravel in the car park was dry and hard packed, but Adam searched for a tyre tread they could take a mould of while Will took Ryan to the river to see where the containers had been thrown in.

"You couldn't see the driver?"

He shook his head. "Tall and slim," he said. "The wide-brimmed hat was straw, the kind you'd find in any store. The dark polo shirt might have been a work shirt, but I didn't see a logo or anything."

"Thanks."

Will hesitated then said, "I need to get those containers out of the river as soon as possible. I can get the PAWS dinghy this afternoon."

"Good. I'll come with you."

Will did his own checks on the car park and surrounding area and then waited until they had finished their investigation to get a lift back to where he'd left his car.

He needed to find who was doing this. Dumping rubbish on the ground was one thing, but if the chemicals got into the river it would spread even further and contaminate the animals and plants along the banks. But how could he stop it? The national park was massive, he couldn't search it all. It was a pure fluke he'd come across the meth lab the other day.

He didn't know what to do.

But he couldn't do nothing.

Fleur's lungs burned as she jogged along the beach early on Wednesday morning. The day was overcast, the clouds blocking in the heat and making it muggy. She'd go for a swim before she headed home. The ocean was calm, no wind stirring to lift the humidity and as she jogged, a school of fish darted through the shallows. At least they were cool.

Sweat dripped down her neck and between her breasts and she pushed herself harder. Mai wasn't here to challenge her, to push her to her limits. Right now she'd be wrist deep in some kind of dough.

Fleur loved this time of morning, the routine of jogging so she could forget everything except putting one foot in front of the other. Nothing mattered outside of that for this short while.

Her phone rang, invading her thoughts, the sharp notes ringing out from the armband she wore. It could be work calling her in early, so she slowed and retrieved the phone.

Trevor.

She didn't want to answer, didn't want to be responsible for making any decisions related to him. She'd made enough bad ones as it was. But if she didn't answer, she'd have to call back and that would be worse. She couldn't ignore any message he left, not without seeming like a complete bitch.

She hit the answer button. "Hello." Her breath was fast

and she continued to walk along the sand. She couldn't cool down too much.

"Fleur, I'm at the track. Gavin and I were going to do some more practice, but we discovered some bastard has smashed holes in the water tank."

She stopped walking. "What?" He couldn't possibly be serious.

"There's water everywhere and the tank is empty."

Fleur swore. The tank had cost an absolute fortune and they needed the water for the night race next weekend. "I'll call Lincoln and be out as soon as I can."

"Do you need us to stay here?"

She'd prefer they didn't, but, "Lincoln might want to talk to you." She hung up and called the police station.

When Sue answered, Fleur repeated what Trevor had told her.

"I'll send someone out. Can you meet us there?"

"Yeah. I'll be a while, I'm about halfway through my jog."

"See you then."

Fleur hung up and jogged down the beach, pushing herself harder as she went. This was the second act of vandalism this month — third if she counted the dumped waste. Why had someone taken a dislike to the club? They hadn't had any complaints recently. The off-season was generally quiet. It was usually the beginning of the season, after the first race that the usual people complained again about the noise and the pollution. Not that the track was actually close to any of the complainants' houses — they just didn't like motorbikes.

Would the tank be repairable? Without any water the track would become a dust bowl which would make it too dangerous to race on. She'd need to source some elsewhere.

But first she needed to find out how bad the situation was.

She reached the path up to the car park and followed it, giving the ocean one last glance. It would have been lovely to cool off before she went to the track, but it could take time to sort out this mess and she needed to be at work in a few hours. When she reached her house, she dashed inside for her car keys and a bottle of water and then headed to the track.

The police car was already there, parked next to Gavin's

sedan. Fleur pulled in next to it and got out, heading to where they all sat on the spectator seating.

"Sorry I took so long." She nodded a greeting to them all. After the musketeers meeting she'd decided she had to admit the truth about the accident to Trevor in order to work through the guilt. She needed to get it off her chest.

"No problem," Ryan replied. "We've only just got here. Gavin was telling us what he found."

"Can you show them the tank?" Trevor asked. "I need to get back. Nicole's at work and the neighbour could only have the kids for a couple of hours."

"Sure." The conversation could wait until she could get him alone. "This way."

"When was the last time you were out here?" Ryan asked, falling into step with her.

"Last week when the clubhouse was broken into."

"You're having a run of bad luck," Adam said. "Any thoughts on who might have a grudge against the club?"

She shook her head and then paused.

"Who?"

Grimacing she said, "Maybe Paul. He was pretty mad we've banned him from the track for a year for racing modern bikes, but this isn't like him."

Ryan made a note as Fleur opened the gate that led out to where the water tank was. The dirt here was damp and there were clear paths of sand where the water had flooded. The big rain water tank perched on flat ground away from the track, so it wouldn't be an obstacle. Deep gullies were gouged out of the flat ground where the water had washed the dirt away. Dozens of jagged holes had pierced the tank like someone had taken a pick axe to it. They couldn't effectively patch them, and the club didn't have enough funds to buy a new tank outright.

She squeezed her eyes closed. She didn't need the extra work.

"They've been thorough." Adam touched one of the holes.

Ryan nodded. "They definitely wanted to leave you with nothing."

Fleur sighed. "What do you need from me?"

"We've got most of the information from the break in. Nothing's changed since then?" Ryan asked.

"No."

"Did you install those cameras?"

"Not yet." It was an expense she had to run past the committee at the next meeting.

"Leave it to us then."

She might as well try to remove the graffiti while the police did their investigation. That way she'd be on site if they needed her. "I'll be in the clubhouse."

Taking a few photos of the damage before she left, she headed back. Trevor and Gavin had already gone. It was one less issue she had to deal with.

She sighed as she walked into the clubhouse. The graffiti artist couldn't have made a more thorough mess if they'd painted the whole place. Every wall had been tagged, as had the kitchen cupboards, the fridges and some of the tables and chairs

Hopefully the graffiti removal spray she'd bought would be effective. Spraying the first cupboard, she got to work.

It was some time later when Ryan and Adam returned to the clubhouse.

"You've made good progress," Adam said.

She put down her rag and wiped her forehead. "Thanks." The furniture and fridges had responded well to the spray, but the doors had been harder, and the smell of the chemical was starting to give her a headache. "Did you find anything?" She checked the time. She'd need to leave soon.

"A footprint in the mud," Ryan said. "It might not lead to anything though. I'll send you a copy of the police report when it's done."

"Thanks." She hadn't bothered claiming the insurance for the broken tables and graffiti, but she would have to for the tank. She wasn't sure if vandalism was covered though.

Fleur walked them to their car and then cleaned up. Hopefully today's shift would be a light one, because she was already tired.

Her phone beeped as she unlocked the front door of her house. Digging it out, she smiled. It was Will.

Having a good day?

She debated lying to him.

No. What about you?

What happened?

Water tank at the track was vandalised.

Her phone rang seconds later.

"That sounds serious," Will said.

"It's seriously annoying." She took some vegetables out of the fridge to make a salad. "We have no water for our race meeting next weekend."

"What did they do?"

"Smashed about a million holes in the sides." She didn't want to think about it at the moment. "How's your day?"

"Much better than yours. I'm having lunch at one of the park's picnic spots and thought of you."

Her heart warmed. "Have I ruined picnics for you?"

He chuckled. "No. They're my most favourite thing in the world now."

She laughed. "Then maybe we should plan one for the weekend."

"Name the time and day."

She tucked the phone between her shoulder and her ear as she chopped up her salad ingredients. "I'm free all day Saturday and Sunday."

"I've got cricket Sunday afternoon."

She raised her eyebrows. "They asked you back?"

"Yeah, it was… fun. I met a couple of nice guys." He sounded a little surprised.

"Who's on your team?"

"Aside from Kim, there's Jeremy and Jamie. Jamie mentioned he's an honorary musketeer."

She grinned. "He is." And if anyone could make Will comfortable and bring him out of his shell around others, it would be Jamie.

"So, he knows the secrets of the musketeer meetings?"

"Well he hasn't been to one in years. He only moved back to Blackbridge at Christmas." The musketeers had been girls

132

only for so long, but maybe it was time they brought him back into the fold. He'd needed them as much as they'd needed each other, especially when he'd realised he was attracted to both men and women.

"Maybe you could, you know, invite him then." Will was hesitant.

"Did he say something to you?"

"Not in so many words, but he was kind of sad when he mentioned it."

"I'll talk to the girls." She should have thought of it herself.

Drizzling the dressing on the salad, she said, "I've got to get ready for work. We'll talk about Saturday later, OK?"

"I'll organise something," Will said. "Have a good night."

"You too." She hung up, already feeling better about her day.

Chapter 13

The moment the offer to organise their next date slipped out of Will's mouth he wanted to stuff it back in. But it was too late. Fleur had already agreed.

What was he going to do?

They'd been on a picnic twice and while he'd enjoyed it, going on another one would be lame, would make him seem like he had no original ideas.

Which he didn't.

But Fleur didn't need to know that.

He got to his feet, walking away from the picnic table where he was having lunch.

Think.

What had she said she enjoyed doing?

She jogged and did motocross, but that ruled out things they could do together.

So what else?

They hadn't talked about movies, or hobbies, or anything normal.

Why hadn't they?

This was ridiculous. The musketeers would know exactly what to plan for her.

He stopped pacing.

Maybe that was the answer. Maybe he should call Jamie, ask him what he'd recommend.

Would that be cheating?

It probably was, but he didn't want to stuff this up.

His phone rang, and he fished it out of his pocket. "Department of Parks and Wildlife Services, Will speaking."

"It's Kit. I found some more of those banksias. A whole patch of them in some bushland I don't get to often."

His heart rate increased.

He walked over to his backpack and pulled out his notepad. "That's great. Can I come out?"

"When?"

"How about this afternoon?" He could drop by before he went home.

"Yeah, all right. I'll meet you at the farmhouse at three-thirty."

"Sure." Will hung up and gathered his things together. He'd finish his patrols out here and then head over.

Maybe he should ask Kit what he should do on the date. Though the woman was a little bit scary. She didn't suffer fools — or people who were shy.

But it was his best chance to arrange something awesome for Fleur and he wanted to impress her.

It was exactly three-thirty as he pulled into Kit's long drive and his phone rang.

"Are you coming?" Kit asked.

He rolled his eyes. "Almost there."

She hung up. She was about as sparse with words as he was. He could appreciate that.

Kit was waiting outside the farmhouse, her arms crossed and one foot tapping.

Geez.

He pulled up, swallowing hard, but before he could wind down his window, she'd crossed to the passenger side and got in.

"It's this way." She pointed.

Not even a greeting. Was she annoyed with him? He hadn't done anything wrong.

His heart thumped uncomfortably in his chest as the silence between them grew. He wanted to make a good impression. She was one of Fleur's best friends.

"How are you, Kit?"

"Angry and frustrated." Her foot tapped a rapid beat on the floor.

"About the banksias?"

"No, not about the banksias," she huffed and ran a hand through her hair. "Sorry, give me a second." She took a couple of deep breaths. "Let me start again. Hey, Will. How's it going?" She smiled at him.

The tightness in his chest eased. "Pretty good. You want to talk about why you're so mad?"

"It's my farmhand. I had to talk to him, tell him he wasn't pulling his weight," she said. "He's a friend, you know?" She waited until he nodded. "I thought he'd apologise and promise to improve, but all he did was tell me he had shit happening in his life and I should chill. Then he left." She swore. "So now instead of being able to leave before the milking to get to the Zanettis' for dinner, I've had to call Mrs Z and tell her I'll be late."

"Can't you do the milking early?"

She shook her head. "The cows know what time to come. I don't want to mess with their routine."

"That sucks."

She nodded. "I can't manage a farm with two hundred cows by myself. People suck." Her voice was bitter.

"Not all of them."

"Most of them."

It was a dire point of view to have. Even he didn't think that. "You've got great friends."

She sighed. "You're right. Speaking of which, are you being good to Fleur?" She gave him a sideways look.

His face flushed. "I think so."

"You better be sure. My girl is too kind-hearted for her own good."

Maybe this was a good opportunity to ask Kit what to do on their date. "Actually, I wanted to ask you something…"

"Yes, Fleur likes to dominate and she's got a strap-on she'd like to use on you."

It took a second for her words to sink in and then his

mouth dropped open. Kit's expression was completely serious.

She had to be kidding.

No one talked about that kind of thing.

Did they?

Did Fleur have a fetish?

He glanced at Kit again and she cracked up laughing, holding her sides, cackling like a kookaburra. "Oh my God! You should have seen your face!" She gasped. "That was priceless." She chuckled and finally stopped laughing. "Sorry. I needed that. Thank you."

Relief flooded him as his muscles relaxed. "Good one." He deserved it for being so gullible. Still if it made her smile, he was happy to help.

"What did you want to ask?" she prompted.

"We're going out on Saturday."

"Where to?"

He braced himself for the ridicule. "I'm not sure."

"All right. Hit me with your ideas."

Crap. "There are boat cruises out of Albany, but her dad has a boat."

"Yeah, we've all done that kind of thing, and it's nicer on her dad's boat where you don't have to put up with annoying tourists."

OK, so that was off the list. "The museums seemed kind of lame."

"Yep."

He chuckled. At least she was forthright. "There's a lot of foody places, the cheese factory down the road, or the lavender farm."

She shook her head. "Nope. The Zanettis own the cheese factory so she's been there a hundred times and we went on a tonne of excursions to all the touristy stuff when we were in primary school."

He was at a complete loss. He hadn't explored the area enough. "What do you suggest then?"

She pursed her lips together. "Her favourite restaurant is Blue Yonder, near Albany. It serves the best lemon tart and we don't get there very often. You've got to book."

He pulled up in front of a gate and Kit jumped out to open it. When she got back in he asked, "What about a movie or ten-pin bowling, or I don't know — mini golf?"

Her eyes widened. "Ten-pin bowling — yes! She loves it and we haven't played since the time that Jamie and Lincoln came with us and we kicked Lincoln's ass." She smirked.

"And Fleur enjoyed it too?"

Kit nodded. "Totally. There's a nice walk around Mount Clarence as well. She'd like that. You sometimes see whales in the sound."

"Thanks, Kit." He could work with that. It would be casual and fun.

"No problem. It's nice you asked." She pointed to some trees on the edge of the paddock. "That way."

The sprawling banksia was indeed the Good's Banksia, and a really great sample of it. It spread out along the ground under the trees. Will took photos and added all the necessary details to his notes, while Kit went to check the fencing. When she returned, she sat on an old log. "What do you actually do?"

"Record the location, the size, the health of the plant, that kind of thing." He finished his notes and tucked his clipboard into his backpack. "I'm done."

As they drove back to the farmhouse, the cows were making their way to the milking shed, with no person or dog in sight to guide them. "Do the cows go on their own accord?"

"Usually. They know the drill. They get milked and fed at the same times each day."

He knew nothing about dairy farming.

"If you drop me off at the shed, I'll get started."

She'd been angry earlier because her farmhand had bailed on her. "Do you want a hand?"

She raised her eyebrows. "Do you know anything about milking?"

"No, but if you need an extra pair of hands so you can get to your dinner tonight..." He was finished for the day, so it wouldn't be hard to stick around.

She grinned at him. "That would be great."

He pulled up outside the big silver shed and followed Kit inside the building. It was massive, with a concrete floor and two rows of stalls. Between the stalls was a sunken area with a bunch of tubes and the milking equipment.

"All right, we'll add feed to the stalls and then I'll show you how to milk. You're not worried about getting shit on your shoes, are you?"

It wasn't his preference, but he shook his head.

Kit was an efficient bundle of energy. She flicked switches and ran around doing he had no idea what, until finally she said, "We're ready for the cows."

Pressing a button opened a gate and the first line of cows wandered in, taking their places in one row with no pushing or shoving. Kit pressed another button and the stalls were locked in place and the other row filled up. She motioned for Will to join her in the sunken area where he was face height with the udders. Above him were all of the cows' butts. Great.

"All right, we clean and then we attach. It's fairly simple." She showed him how to clean each of the teats and then attach the four-pronged suctioning thing that drew the milk out. Kit handed him a cloth. "Your turn."

He followed her instructions. The teat was warm and soft and kind of weird to touch. When he put the milking apparatus on the cow, Kit nodded in satisfaction. "You'll do. Take that side."

For the next couple of hours, he worked side by side with Kit. It was hot, smelly and messy work and he did need to dodge some excrement, but all in all, when they'd finished he was satisfied he'd done well. With the last cow milked, he helped spray down and clean the area and it was getting dark by the time they'd finished.

"Good job," Kit said. "If you ever ditch the environment, I'd give you a job."

He grinned at her. "I'll keep it in mind." He dropped her off at the farmhouse.

"Thanks, Will. I appreciate your help today."

"No problem." He was about to drive off when he remembered Elijah. He wound down his window. "Hey, Kit."

She turned around.

"Elijah's still looking for work. If your farmhand keeps giving you problems, I'm sure he'll help out."

She grinned at him. "Thanks. I'll give him a call."

He waved and drove away.

He'd done his bit for the community today.

Fleur got up early on Thursday morning, despite working late the night before. She had so much to do. She'd put a call out on social media for solutions to the water tank issue and needed to check if she had any responses. If not, she would have to arrange something else. The race meet was just over a week away. She switched on the kettle and her tablet.

A quick scroll through the comments showed members weren't happy, but no one had any suggestions. She needed to source a new tank, so she called Kit.

"Good timing, I've finished milking," Kit said as she answered. In the background cows mooed.

She measured out the tea leaves and then poured water into her teapot. "Great. I wanted to ask who you get your water tanks from."

"You want one for your place?"

"No, for the track. Didn't you see my post? Some bastard knocked holes into the tank and we've got no water." She got out a mug and inhaled the lemon myrtle scent coming from the pot.

Kit swore. "Something weird is going on. Could it be the usuals trying to stop us before the season starts?"

"I don't know. Ryan's investigating."

"Good. I'll call my contact and ask what he can do for us. I'm considering putting in another tank near the sheds, so he can probably do a deal."

Fleur breathed out. "That would be great. Thanks."

"No problem. Listen, while I've got you, I have to tell you, Will's a keeper."

She blinked. "Will Travers?"

"Yes, unless you've been shacking up with another Will."

Fleur laughed. "What's he done?"

"He helped me with the milking last night."

She poured some milk into her mug. "Why?"

"I found some more banksias, so I called him out. Then I had the conversation with Paul which went down like a lead balloon. He was a real prick about it, said he had some shit happening and I shouldn't interfere and then left me to do the milking by myself. I was still steaming about it when Will arrived, and he offered to help. He did pretty good considering he'd never done anything like that before."

The highest of praises from Kit. "I'm glad. Any of us will help you if you need it." But she was happy her friend liked Will.

"I know, but I shouldn't have to ask. I should be able to rely on the people I pay."

"What are you going to do about Paul?"

Kit sighed. "I documented the conversation last night. If he keeps it up I'm going to have to sack him and I want clear evidence as to why in case he makes a fuss."

"Do you think he will?"

She shrugged. "I wouldn't have thought he'd be so unreliable." She sounded miserable.

Poor Kit. She did as much of the work as she could but needed Paul to help her. She hated to be let down, hated to have to rely on anyone. If she could, she'd do the whole thing herself.

"Will suggested Elijah's looking for work so I might call him and see if he's available for casual work. That way if Paul flakes again I've got back up." More enthusiasm entered her voice.

"That's great, but we're still here for you." Fleur tucked her phone between her shoulder and ear and picked up the teapot and her mug, before heading for the front door.

"Thanks, Flower."

"Any time." She opened the door and stepped outside, placing her tea things on the little outdoor table on the verandah, before straightening and surveying her garden.

"Holy shit!" Her mouth dropped open and her stomach curdled as she took in the scene.

Every rose blossom in her garden had been hacked off and lay like a mass of bodies over the ground. The bushes themselves were now a dull brown/green, their leaves sagging and curled up as if someone had poured weedkiller all over them.

They were dead.

All dead.

Just like her mother.

"What's wrong?"

"Mum's roses."

Tears sprang to her eyes as a lump lodged into her throat. The smell of cloves made her wrinkle her nose.

"Fleur what the hell is going on?" Kit demanded.

"Someone's poisoned Mum's roses."

The litany of curses out of Kit's mouth made her blink. Slowly she went down the steps, scanning each and every bush. Not a single glossy green leaf on any of the plants. She wouldn't be able to save them.

"Call Lincoln," Kit told her.

"All right." She hung up, her whole mind numb. Who would do this to her?

Everyone understood what the roses meant to her. They were her one connection with her mother, she tended the flowers the way her mother had shown her.

This would devastate her father. He commented on the flowers every time he came over. They were a link to his dead wife as well.

Fleur sank down on the bottom step. She needed to call the police, but she couldn't quite believe it.

A four-wheel drive pulled into her driveway and Will got out.

"What are you doing here?"

"I was driving past." He stopped walking, his gaze on the plants. "What happened?"

"Someone poisoned Mum's roses."

"Are you all right?"

She took hold of the hand he held out and let him pull her to her feet. "No."

She wanted to close her eyes and pretend it hadn't happened. It was like losing her mother all over again. As long as they'd been alive, some part of her mother still was.

His arms came around her and he pulled her close. "I'm sorry, Fleur."

His gentle words crumbled her defences and she cried.

Will's heart ached as Fleur sobbed in his arms. Behind her the leaves on the roses were completely wilted, curled up and hanging like they'd lost their will to live. The ground was littered with flowers and the strong scent of cloves reminiscent of Christmas was completely at odds with the destruction. They must have used an organic weed killer, but there was also a hint of a stronger chemical underneath. Whoever had done it had been thorough.

Fleur shuddered, her tears wetting his shirt, the little gasps ripping a hole through him. How could anyone do this to her?

The roses were her pride and joy, her connection with her mother.

Someone needed to pay.

Another four-wheel drive pulled up behind his and Hannah jumped out, taking a quick look at the destruction before hurrying over to them. Ryan climbed out more slowly, dressed in his police uniform.

"Oh, Flower. I'm so sorry."

Fleur lifted her head and Will relaxed his hold on her, so she could hug her best friend. Hannah gave him a half smile before she wrapped her arms around Fleur.

"Ryan will find who did this. We'll sort something out."

"They're dead," Fleur said.

"Maybe they're not dead dead." Hannah cringed. "Maybe they're just mostly dead."

Will didn't want to mess up any evidence, but, "I could try to save them." He glanced at Ryan who was standing a couple of metres back looking at the garden.

"We'll need to investigate first when Lincoln arrives."

"Did Kit call you?" Fleur asked.

"Yeah. Right after she called Lincoln," Hannah said. "She and Mai can't make it until later."

"There's nothing they can do anyway." Fleur pulled away and ran her hands over her eyes.

A police car pulled up along the street. Will had seen far too much of the police over the past couple of weeks.

Lincoln swore when he saw the damage.

"Language, Sergeant," Hannah said.

He scowled at her and then turned to Fleur. "What happened?"

"I came out this morning and discovered it like this," she said. "The roses were fine when I got home from work last night."

"What time was that?" Ryan asked, pulling out his notepad.

"About ten."

"You didn't smell anything?"

She shook her head.

Will hesitated. "There's a chance we could still save some of the plants if we act fast. Could you get the samples you need and then I can work on the bushes?"

Lincoln glanced at the shrivelled plants and then back at him, his eyebrows raised.

"A small chance," Will conceded.

"All right. We'll talk to you all when we're done." Lincoln moved away to speak to Ryan.

"What do you need to save the roses?" Fleur asked.

"Sugar and water."

"Let me get it."

He and Hannah followed her into the house and she dug through her pantry until she pulled out a jar of white sugar. "Will this do?"

"Yeah."

"Do you need to get to work?"

No one would notice if he was late. "I'll call my boss. I've been putting in extra hours, so he won't mind." And this was more important to him.

She smiled. "Thanks."

Hannah put on the kettle. "Cup of tea?"

He nodded and sat at Fleur's kitchen table next to her.

"There's a pot outside on the table."

Hannah fetched the pot and made a new brew, moving around the kitchen getting the tea things ready as if she lived there herself.

Will covered Fleur's hand with his own, but he had no words of comfort for her.

She twisted her hand so it was palm up and squeezed his.

Hannah placed the teapot on the table with some mugs and milk, and then sat down next to Fleur. "Who could have done this?"

Fleur shrugged. "The only person I've pissed off recently is Paul. But he wouldn't do this."

Hannah nodded. "Not if he cared about his job."

They discussed people they'd interacted with recently, but the names meant nothing to Will. About an hour later Lincoln and Ryan came inside.

"We're done," Lincoln said.

Will stood up. "I'll work with the plants." He had to give it a go for Fleur's sake.

Ryan stopped him on the way out. "We'll need to talk to you before you leave."

"All right."

Working quickly, he examined the leaves. There was no residue on them, but the ground was wet and that clove smell was strong. Mixing the sugar and water, he poured the concoction over the plants, both roots and leaves. It might work to dig up a couple, soak their roots in the solution.

He'd attempt several things in case something worked.

About half an hour later, Lincoln and Ryan came out the front with Hannah and Fleur.

"How's it going?" Fleur asked.

"It might work."

"Thanks for trying." Her shoulders slumped as if they were too heavy to be held upright.

The sadness in her eyes killed him. Putting down his bucket, he walked over and hugged her.

"We need to ask you some questions," Ryan said.

He nodded.

"I have to go," Hannah said. "I'll see you after work." She kissed Ryan, and then Fleur walked her over to her car.

"What were you doing here this morning?" Lincoln asked.

The tone was abrupt, accusatory. He frowned. "I stopped

when I saw Fleur on her verandah. Then I noticed the roses."

"You live on the other side of town," Ryan said.

He was going to sound like a stalker. Clearing his throat, he checked Fleur was still talking to Hannah by the car. "I've been driving past on my way to work."

Lincoln raised his eyebrows. "Why?"

Will tapped his thigh. "She's been working late shifts, so I wasn't going to see her until Saturday, but if she happened to be outside when I drove past..." It was desperate and lame.

Ryan smiled at him. "Shift work can suck."

Lincoln stared at him as if he didn't believe him. Well he could believe what he liked. "Do you have any other questions?"

"Do you know of anyone who might want to hurt Fleur?" Ryan asked.

"No."

"What about an ex-girlfriend who might be unhappy about your relationship?"

He barked out a laugh. "No. No one." He checked the time. "I need to go."

Lincoln nodded.

As Hannah left, he walked over to Fleur, pulling her into his arms. He didn't want to leave her when she was so sad. "I have to get to work. Are you going to be OK?"

She sighed and then nodded. "Yeah."

Lincoln and Ryan were right there, watching and listening. "Call me if you need anything." He hugged her, brushing a kiss against her forehead.

"I'll see you Saturday."

He walked away, wishing he could stay.

Chapter 14

After Lincoln and Ryan had left, Fleur couldn't settle. She washed the tea pot and tidied the kitchen but couldn't focus on anything. Who would do this to her?

Who could be so cruel?

Her father was going to be devastated. She didn't want to worry him by calling him while he was out on the boat, but if he drove past before she'd warned him, it would be far worse. Maybe he wouldn't answer the satellite phone.

With a sigh, she dialled the number.

"What's wrong, Rose?" he barked.

"I'm fine, Dad," she soothed. "But I need to give you some bad news. Someone poisoned Mum's roses last night."

"What?" His voice cracked.

She cringed and explained the situation. "Will's trying a few things to revive them."

"If they used Roundup he doesn't have a hope," he growled. "Is he the greenie?"

"Yeah."

"He probably thinks some magic fairy dust will bring them back. Dead is dead."

She winced. She recognised the choked tone. He was holding back tears. She shouldn't have called him, should have waited until he was home, so she could hug him.

"I'm so sorry, Dad."

"It's not your fault." He paused, but she heard him inhale deeply. "Who would poison them?"

"I don't know. Lincoln's investigating."

"Good." He let out a deep sigh. "Are you all right?"

"I'm not great." She stared out the kitchen window at the backyard lemon tree full of fruit. At least something was thriving. "But in the end, they're just flowers."

"No, they're not."

He was right. "Yeah, I know. I'll talk to you later."

"Love you, Rose."

She smiled. "Love you too." She hung up, the sadness threatening to drag her down. She couldn't let it. The reason she'd got up early was because she had so many things to do before work. The remaining graffiti needed to be scrubbed off the clubhouse walls and she had the flat tyre that needed fixing.

The local mechanic might be able to fit her in now.

The streets were full of kids walking to school, their green uniforms identifying them as primary school students. She waved to a couple as she pulled into the mechanic's car park.

Inhaling the smell of oil and grease, she wandered over to where Morgan was already standing under a hoisted car.

"Morning, Morgan."

He glanced over his shoulder, his hands still working on whatever he was doing. "Fleur, how's things? Do you need more used tyres?"

"No. I've got a flat tyre in the boot. Think you can fix it for me?"

"I'll take a look."

She hefted the tyre out and rolled it over to him.

"Let's see what's caused the damage. It's probably a nail."

He lifted the tyre onto the bench and examined it, spraying a soapy liquid on it. He frowned and picked up a screwdriver and pried the rubber apart. He whistled. "This isn't a nail, Fleur. Someone's slashed your tyre."

Her heart jumped. "What?"

"Look here." He beckoned her over and pointed out the three long slits in the wheel.

Nausea swelled in her stomach. "Are you sure it was on

purpose?"

"It's on the side of the wheel, it can't be anything you ran over."

She stared at the tyre. First the roses, now this.

She shook her head. No, this came first. This happened last week when she'd been jogging with Mai. "I need to call Lincoln."

"You going to report this?"

"Yeah." She didn't want to tell him about the roses, but it would get around town sooner or later. "This isn't the only thing. Someone poisoned my roses last night."

His eyebrows disappeared into his hairline. "Shit. Who have you pissed off?"

"I don't know." Maybe everything that had happened around the track wasn't someone angry at the club, maybe it was someone angry at her. Everyone knew she was president.

But what had she done that would make someone so mad? She wasn't a bad person.

Pulling out her phone she called the police station.

The clock on the microwave had stopped working, Will was certain of it. It was an eternity before he could pick Fleur up and he didn't want to be early in case she was still getting ready.

"You need to chill out," Elijah said, placing himself between Will and the clock. "It's not going to go any faster the more you look at it."

Will grimaced. "Was I that obvious?"

Elijah laughed. "It's lucky I'm beginning to understand you, otherwise you could give me a complex."

"Sorry. I was listening."

Elijah raised an eyebrow. "Really? What was I saying?"

Crap. What had he been talking about? "Ah, Kit called you, right?"

"Yeah, that's what I was saying five minutes ago."

Will put his mug in the sink, turning on the taps to fill it. "Sorry. I'm listening now."

Elijah picked up a tea towel and dried the dishes. "She

doesn't have enough work right now to hire me permanently, but I told her to call me if Paul flakes on her again. Even if she can't pay me, I'll be first in line if she does sack him. And working with Kit would be great. We used to have fun together at the ag school."

"I'm glad." Elijah had been complaining about the work at the winery, saying the owners were pedantic about everything he did.

"Do you need me to clear out of here at any time today?"

Will shook his head. "No. We're heading into Albany and afterwards…" He wasn't sure what would happen afterwards. "We might go to her place." He put the last plate on the drying rack and pulled out the plug.

Elijah gestured to the clock. "Have fun."

It was time for him to leave.

Finally.

He grabbed his wallet and phone and headed out to his blue hatchback. It had been sitting in the driveway all week and was covered in a layer of dust. Maybe he should have washed it before he picked Fleur up. It wasn't like it was his work car, which was always covered in dirt.

Fleur wouldn't care what it looked like.

He got in, switching on the radio.

When he pulled into the driveway, the roses caught his attention. The leaves were still shrivelled with no signs they were coming back to life. He sighed. Nothing on the internet had given him another solution. They'd have to wait and see.

He knocked on her door and she yelled, "Come in."

He found her in the kitchen, wiping over her bench. "You should lock your front door." The words came out gruff and he winced.

"I knew it would be you."

"But someone is unhappy with you. You don't know what they might do."

"Other than poison my roses and slash my tyres you mean?"

What the hell? "Someone slashed your tyres?"

She nodded. "I discovered it yesterday when I went to get my flat fixed. It happened last week."

"Did you tell the police?"

"Yes, and I've had the lecture from Lincoln about being safe and being aware of my surroundings, so I don't need it from you." She ran a hand through her hair and bit her lip.

She was worried.

He stepped over to her and pulled her into his arms. "I don't mean to lecture," he said. "I want you to be safe." He kissed her gently and she sighed, melting into him.

His heart beat faster. His ego liked the way she responded to him, how she kissed him back with such passion.

But if they kept going, they wouldn't leave her house and he wanted to show her he wanted more from her than sex.

Stepping back, he asked, "Are you ready?"

"Yep." She winked at him. "And I'm also ready to go out with you." She grinned.

He smothered his smile. She was making it hard for him to leave in more than one way. "Let's go." He led the way out of the house, waiting on the verandah while she locked up, and then opened the passenger-side door for her.

"Is this your car?"

"Yes."

"Isn't it too small for you?"

He slid into the driver's side. "It's fuel economical."

"You live what you preach, don't you?" She tilted her head to the side.

"When I can. Everyone can make a difference to the environment by their choices." Was he being too preachy?

"Do you have a problem with the motocross track?"

The question took him by surprise. How should he answer? "People like to do different things."

She nodded. "They do. What's your take on the club — polluter, or sports?"

She wasn't going to let it drop. "It's not how I would choose to spend my time, but I have no problem with people riding motorbikes as long as they don't break the law." He glanced at her. "Why all the questions?"

"Lincoln thinks the attacks on me might be related to the motocross, because there's been the vandalism out there as well. He thought it might be an environmentalist."

His chest tightened as disappointment flooded him. "And you thought it could be me?"

She shook her head. "No. Not even for a moment. But I realised I hadn't asked your opinion about it, whether it could be an issue in our relationship."

He relaxed. Relationship. He liked her using that word. "Not for me, as long as you don't expect me to take part."

"Nope. I wouldn't force anyone into doing something they didn't want to do."

That was good.

"Where are we going today?"

"Albany."

She smiled at him. "That doesn't narrow it down a whole lot."

"Kit mentioned you have a favourite restaurant."

Her eyes widened. "Are we going to Blue Yonder?"

He nodded, and she squealed, clapping her hands. "Awesome!"

He'd have to thank Kit again later for suggesting it. "I hear there's a nice walk around Mount Clarence."

"There is. Sometimes Mai and I drive into town and jog it for a change of scenery. There's also all of the war memorial stuff, have you been there?"

He shook his head. "I haven't spent much time in Albany, so you might need to direct me."

"I can do that." She settled back in her seat. "This is going to be fun."

They parked at Middleton Beach, bought a couple of take-away coffees and wandered the trail hugging King George Sound. The view was spectacular. Several rocky islands, both large and small, dotted the harbour amongst the deep blue ocean. A gentle breeze wafted the salt air towards them, adding a touch of cool to the warm day. Fleur gave him a history lesson, telling him about the ANZAC ships that had left for World War 1 from there, and filling him in on local legends. When they headed back to the car, she took him over the mount, up to the ANZAC museum and past the massive guns that had once protected the port.

He breathed deeply as they followed a bike trail through the bush, inhaling the rich eucalypt fragrance. Fleur was the perfect companion and he held her hand, enjoying the connection, content to be by her side.

"This is lovely," Fleur said. "It's nice to get away from Blackbridge sometimes."

He preferred it most of the time. The trail ended near the beach where they'd left the car. It was close to midday, but they still had another half an hour before their reservation. "Is there anywhere else you'd like to go?" He started the car.

She pursed her lips. "There's a heritage cottage not far from here. Could we stop there on the way to the restaurant?"

"Sure." He followed her directions until he pulled into a car park. The old farm building had to be more than a hundred and fifty years old.

Fleur got out and walked over to the cottage garden, her hands trailing over the leaves of some hydrangeas. She was silent, staring at the plants, looking a little lost.

Will put his arm around her waist.

"Mum used to be a gardener here," she said. "She nurtured some of these plants."

Her sadness made sense. "Do you want to walk around?"

She sighed. "There's no real point. She's not here."

"It might make you feel better."

After a moment's hesitation, she nodded. "All right."

He went inside to pay the entrance fee and found her in the garden when he returned.

"I remember sitting under that tree chatting to her while she pruned those bushes there," Fleur said. "I must have been about six, and I guess it was school holidays or something. She showed me what to do and even let me try, though the branches were too thick for me to cut then."

He slipped his hand into hers and squeezed it.

She smiled and together they walked down the path. "She'd collect the seeds of all the different plants and take them home, recreating the garden in our backyard, though it was never quite as epic as this. It was too much for Dad and me to manage on our own — I didn't know enough then, and he didn't like the reminder that she was gone."

His heart ached for her. "It must have been hard for both of you."

"It was. I lost Dad for a while after she died. He was always working and so incredibly sad. Not long after, Hannah moved to town. Her mother had just died as well, and we comforted each other."

It explained one of the reasons they were so close.

They looped through the garden and when they reached the car, he pulled her into his arms. "I'm sorry." He wasn't sure what he was apologising for, the fact she'd lost her mother, that her roses had been poisoned, that she was sad — perhaps all of it.

She hugged him back. "Me too." She sighed. "I've finished being morbid for the day. Let's have some lunch."

He kissed her, a gentle brush of their lips to show he cared, and then opened the car door for her. "Your chariot awaits."

Fleur needed to snap out of it. She shouldn't have stopped at the farm today, not when they'd been having a lovely time. Usually the memories cheered her up, but today they reminded her of everything she'd lost.

Amazingly, Will hadn't minded. He'd been sweet, giving her comfort, being there for her like any of the musketeers would have. With him there was more though. A different kind of comfort, a different affection.

But she shouldn't get too attached. Not if he was planning to move back to Goldwyer the moment he had the chance. He'd been so adamant about it, though maybe now he was becoming part of the community, he'd change his mind.

Maybe their relationship was doomed from the beginning. His family was up there, and her father didn't like environmentalists. She needed to be careful. He was the type of guy she could really fall for.

Her stomach rumbled and she injected some enthusiasm into her voice. "I'm starving."

"Great. We'll be there soon."

She had to get their date back on track. "How has your

week been?"

"Pretty good. The park is recovering well from the fire and I've been able to survey more areas."

"Were many animals injured?"

He nodded, his expression grim. "The local wildlife carers have been pretty busy."

"At least they caught who started the fire." And he'd be going to jail for that and a bunch of other crimes he'd committed.

They pulled into the restaurant car park. The view out over the sound was breathtakingly beautiful. The ocean stretched out to the horizon, a deep, dark blue with a smattering of whitecaps like coconut sprinkled on the top of a cake.

"Wow." Will got out of the car.

"It's pretty spectacular isn't it?"

"Yeah."

The restaurant was perched near the edge of a cliff, a mixture of wood and glass. The dark brown timbers blended with the trees surrounding the car park and the garden, but walking through the back door, it was all glass and light, an uninterrupted view over the ocean.

Will gave the waiter his name and they were led across the polished floorboards to a table in the corner of the restaurant that gave them views of both the ocean and the garden full of flowers.

"This is perfect." She smiled as Will held her chair out for her. "Thank you."

He sat opposite her. "It's Kit you should be thanking. She told me about this place."

"But you thought to ask her."

His smile was small, pleased, as he read the menu. "What's good here?"

She loved how modest he was. "Everything, but the meals are large. We have to leave room for dessert."

He raised his eyebrows. "Which one?"

"The lemon tart with vanilla cream." She closed her eyes. "It's *so* good."

"Do you want to share a main then? So you have plenty of

space?"

Will's thoughtfulness was almost too good to be true. Was he trying to please her, or was he seriously this fabulous? "I'd love to. You choose what to have because you haven't been here before."

His eyes widened. "I don't know…"

She grinned. "Don't stress. I'll eat anything. What are you tossing up between?"

He named a couple of dishes.

"The fish is delicious."

He smiled as the waiter came over. "We'll get the fish to share."

After the man had left, Fleur leant forward on her forearms. "It's time to ask the serious questions."

His eyes widened.

"*Star Wars* or *Star Trek*?"

He frowned. "Huh?"

"Are you a Trekkie or a *Star Wars* fan?"

Will shifted in his seat. "Neither really."

"OK, how about Marvel or DC?"

"Ah, that's a comic book thing isn't it?"

"Yeah." Was he for real? She frowned. Hadn't he watched any movies in the last couple of years? "Let me start again. What's your favourite movie?"

He sipped his water and shrugged. "I don't watch a lot of movies."

She sat back. "What, not at all? You must have some favourite movie from your childhood at least – *Robin Hood*, or *The Princess Bride* or *Mary Poppins*?"

"Mum didn't like us watching a lot of TV and there weren't many movies available in Goldwyer."

Her mouth dropped open. "You haven't seen *The Princess Bride*?"

He shook his head. "I used to watch foreign films on SBS at uni."

It was a travesty. "I'm going to have to fix that." She'd take any excuse to watch her favourite movie. She smiled. "Let's try top five songs of all time."

"That was amazing." Fleur placed her hands on her stomach to keep it from exploding. The restaurant was now crowded with people, but it wasn't too noisy, the acoustics just right to allow conversation.

"I might never eat anywhere else again," Will said.

She laughed. "It's addictive isn't it?"

"Maybe we should have done the walk after we ate."

"Did you have anything else planned?" she asked.

He glanced out of the window. "Well, we could go ten-pin bowling, but we might need to roll ourselves down the lanes."

"I haven't been bowling in years. It's so much fun." A gorgeous walk, her favourite restaurant and now bowling. He was a keeper.

She paused. She couldn't think like that. Not until he met her dad at least. She had to slow things down. "Let's pay and walk around the gardens before we go."

"Sure."

They went up to the counter and Fleur got out her purse. Will put his hand over hers. "I'm paying."

No way. "Will, this place is expensive."

He brushed her hair back behind her ear, his thumb caressing her cheek. "I'd like to."

Holy moly. His chocolate eyes captured her and she was helpless to refuse. "All right."

"Thank you." His lips touched hers briefly and he handed over his card.

She placed a hand to her chest to slow her heart rate.

A man who asked instead of insisting. It was a rare thing.

He tucked his card back in his wallet and took her hand. "Shall we?"

She nodded and followed him out of the restaurant.

Chapter 15

Ten-pin bowling had been a blast and Fleur was surprisingly competitive. Will hadn't stood a chance. Still, as he drove them home, the smile on his face didn't fade. He'd had an amazing day. He could be himself with Fleur.

When had he got so lucky?

As they reached the outskirts of Blackbridge, he asked, "Do you want me to take you home?" It was only mid-afternoon and he'd be happy to spend the rest of the day with her.

She glanced at him. "Have you got plans?"

"Not until cricket tomorrow."

"Do you want to come to my place? We could have a movie night since you haven't seen any movie made in the twenty-first century."

He chuckled. "All right. As long as you watch one of mine too."

"Deal. We should get popcorn and ice cream too."

He pulled into the independent supermarket. Fleur grasped a basket and then his hand and together they wandered the confectionery and ice cream aisles as Fleur filled the basket with what she deemed were necessary movie foods.

Her enthusiasm was palpable as she pursed her lips and examined the chocolate. "What's your favourite?"

Chocolate had never been high on his list of must-have

foods. "I don't have one."

She grinned. "You like them all like me?"

He shook his head. "I'm not much of a chocolate fan."

Her mouth dropped opened and she stared at him like he'd told her he'd murdered someone. "You don't like chocolate?"

"It's all right." He shrugged.

"All right?" She shook her head. "That's so sad, but at least it means there's more for me." She winked and then threw a couple of blocks of chocolate into her basket. "What's your favourite treat then?"

That was a hard question. Food was normally a means of sustenance more than anything else. "I don't have much of a sweet tooth."

"What do you get from Mai's bakery?"

"Whatever looks good on the day."

"Which is everything." She sighed. "Nothing you love more than anything else?"

"The Florentines are good."

"They are." She held his hand as they lined up at the checkout and then greeted the young guy who was serving. "How are things, Trent?"

"Great, thanks, Fleur."

"Year twelve's not too hard?"

"The workload's crazy, but I'll manage."

"I'm glad you found a new job after the bakery burnt down."

He glanced around before lowering his voice. "Tell Mai I'll be back in a heartbeat when she opens again."

Will handed over his card, but Fleur brushed it aside as she grinned at Trent. "My turn to pay." She gave her card to him, then kissed Will on the lips, preventing him from arguing. Nice tactic.

His face warmed as Trent raised his eyebrows and grinned. "Have a nice day."

Fleur pulled him out of the supermarket. "Do you want to stop at your place first?"

He glanced over at her. "Why?"

"You might want a change of clothes, since it'll probably

be late by the time we get through the movies. You could stay."

His heart beat faster. She wanted him to sleep over. "OK."

Elijah's car was in the driveway when he pulled up. Should he tell his roommate he wouldn't be home tonight?

Elijah sat on the couch, laptop on his lap, frowning at the screen when they walked in. He smiled. "Hey. Did you guys have fun?"

"It was so good we're having a movie night at my place," Fleur said. "Will just stopped by to get some clothes."

Elijah grinned. "So, I have the place to myself tonight?"

Will nodded, edging towards the hallway. Maybe Elijah wanted to have his own movie night.

"Great."

"I'll be right back." Will headed to his room as Fleur asked, "What are you doing?"

That was a question he should ask himself. What was he doing with Fleur?

He'd always planned to move back to Goldwyer and it wouldn't be fair to get too involved with her. But he couldn't help himself. He wanted to.

So where did that leave his plans to go home?

He grimaced. He'd think about it later. Dragging his barrel bag out from under his bed, he dusted it off. What did he pack?

He wore boxer shorts to bed, and maybe he should throw in something comfortable for tonight. He hesitated before packing his cricket gear and then threw in his toothbrush. The bag was almost full, but he wanted to be ready for any circumstance and if he had his gear, he could go straight to the oval from Fleur's place and get to spend extra time with her in the morning.

Heading back to the living room he found Fleur perched on the armchair chatting to Elijah.

"Are you moving out?" Elijah asked, grinning.

"It's the only bag I've got."

"I'm just kidding, mate. Have fun."

Will picked a couple of his favourite movies from the bookcase and stuffed them into his bag.

"Ready?" Fleur asked.

Definitely.

As he switched off the engine at Fleur's place she gave a deep sigh, staring at the dead flowers. "They might still survive."

"Maybe."

They both knew it was highly unlikely.

She picked up the shopping and he followed her up the steps into the house.

Fleur filled the kettle and then groaned. "Sorry, seeing the roses still gets to me. I need to shake it off. Let me take your bag."

She took it into her room.

Her sadness made him ache. There had to be a way he could cheer her up. "Is there a comedy amongst the movies you want me to watch?"

"Yeah." She returned as the kettle boiled. "Cup of tea?"

"Please." He stepped into her kitchen and pulled her into his arms. "You're allowed to be upset."

Her smile was sad. "I don't want to be. Not when you're here with me and we've had a great day."

"I'll take you happy or sad." It was true. He gently squeezed her and then kissed her soft lips. "If you want to talk about it, I'll listen."

"Thank you, but I want to snap out of it." She poured the drinks and then carried them both into the living room. "You can choose which movie we watch first."

"Fine by me." As long as it made her happy. He settled on the couch and waited while Fleur brought out a couple of movies. She'd mentioned *The Princess Bride* was her favourite, so he had to go with that. He stretched his arm over the back of the sofa and his heart expanded when Fleur settled in next to him. He was doing normal couple stuff with Fleur. It blew his mind. He'd never imagined this in his wildest dreams.

The movie was surprisingly good, and he loved the ending when Westley and Buttercup finally reached their happy-ever-after. His brothers would call him a sissy.

As the credits rolled, Fleur turned to him. "What did you think?"

"It was great."

She beamed at him. "It's the perfect movie: intrigue, comedy, romance and action. Doesn't it make you feel all warm inside?"

"Yeah."

She stretched. "Are you hungry? We could order pizza before we watch the next one?"

"If that's what you want." He'd do anything to make her happy.

She frowned at him. "You didn't answer the question."

"I don't mind."

She sighed. "You're too easy going. I don't know if you're agreeing because you genuinely don't mind, or because you're too shy to stand up for yourself."

That wasn't the image he wanted to project. "If I don't want to do something, I'll tell you."

"Good. I don't want to steamroller you into anything." She stood up. "Want a drink?"

"Water would be great."

"I can open a bottle of wine if you'd like."

He hesitated. "Not for me."

"Don't you drink?"

He shook his head. "I don't like the taste."

"Fair enough." She wandered into the kitchen.

Popping noises came from there and he got up to investigate and discovered Fleur had put popcorn into the microwave and poured herself a glass of wine.

"Need a hand?"

"I've got this," she said. "Do you want to take my wine and set up your movie?"

"Let's watch another one of yours."

"No, I said I'd watch yours."

"They're both pretty sad." She'd been upset about the roses, and neither drama would help. He should have thought about it before he'd chosen them.

"I can deal."

He wanted to protest, because they were seriously heart-wrenching, but she knew her own mind. Instead he set up the movie and waited for her to return, a steaming bowl of popcorn in one hand and his water in the other. The popcorn smelled delicious.

"Help yourself."

He pressed play, then took a handful. Fleur curled up next to him, the bowl on her lap. The buttery scent mixed with her rose scent and his stomach rumbled.

"Should I order pizza now?"

His face heated. "No. Popcorn will be fine."

"All right."

The French film was full of intrigue, passion and heartbreak. At the climax when the heroine died, Fleur sniffed, silent tears running down her cheeks.

His heart stopped, and he pulled her closer to him. "Are you all right?"

She shook her head and sobs racked her body as the credits rolled. She buried her head into his chest and he rubbed her back as she cried.

"Stupid, stupid movie."

"It was." He shouldn't have brought it over. It had always made him think and feel, but he'd never cried, found the poignancy uplifting.

"It was so sad. Why couldn't they have a happy ending? She didn't need to die. It's supposed to be entertainment."

"Not everything in life has a happy ending."

She pulled back. "I know that. Hell, I've lived it. I don't need it in my movies."

Noted. "Let's not watch the other one."

Fleur sniffed. "Not if it's as sad as this one."

"It's worse," he admitted.

Shaking her head, she asked, "Why do you watch them?"

She'd feel sorry for him if he told the truth. "My television at uni only picked up SBS."

She pursed her lips. "No, that's not it. You wouldn't have bought the DVD if you didn't like it."

He winced. She was right. "It makes me feel connected."

"To the characters?"

He was such a sad sap. "No. To people." He waited for her reaction.

"You don't feel connected?"

"Not really." He'd been on the outer for so long, watching people live their lives from a distance.

"What about with your family?"

"Goldwyer is too far away to go home for the weekend and my brothers and I aren't close."

"Did you have friends at uni?"

He shook his head. "I don't socialise well and people stopped inviting me places. And I spent a lot of time volunteering at the botanical gardens."

"Well you've got me and Elijah and the cricket team now. You can connect with us and stop watching these depressing movies."

He chuckled. He was happy with that. His phone rang. He'd forgotten to call his mother today like he normally did. "Sorry. If I don't get this, Mum will worry."

Fleur smiled at him. "Go ahead."

He moved into the kitchen as he answered.

"You're alive." The relief in her voice was clear.

He winced. "Sorry for not calling earlier. I was out."

"Well that's a change. What have you been up to?"

"I went on a date." He grinned, glanced over his shoulder towards the living room.

"A date? Who with?" She sounded upset.

He blinked and tapped his thigh. "Her name's Fleur. We've been out a couple of times." A noise outside the kitchen window made him turn, peer outside but it was dark, and he couldn't see anything.

"A couple of times? Don't get too serious. She might not want to move to Goldwyer."

He frowned. That wasn't the only option. Besides, she'd been the one to encourage him to find a community here. Hadn't she meant it? "Listen, Mum, I'm out, can I call you later?"

There was a pause. "All right. We'll find you a job up here soon, I'm sure of it."

He hung up. For the first time, moving back to Goldwyer had lost its appeal. As he wandered back into the living room, Fleur looked up. "Everything all right?"

"Yeah. I forgot to call Mum earlier – she was worried."

"She must miss you."

He nodded. But he'd barely thought of her or home in the past couple of weeks.

Fleur got up and gathered the empty popcorn bowl and cups. "I don't have the energy for another movie. Do you want to head to bed?"

It was only eight o'clock. Really early. He was about to say so when he noticed Fleur's raised eyebrows.

Oh.

Bed.

Yes, please.

He'd worry about the rest later.

After Will left for cricket the next day, Fleur wandered out the back to pick some lemons. The tree was groaning under the weight and she'd promised she'd take Tim a bag.

The date yesterday had been so incredibly good — fun and relaxed with great food and company. She couldn't wait until the next one.

And the one after that.

Will had quickly become someone she wanted to spend all of her time with. She should have asked him yesterday if he still wanted to move back home. There'd been the opportunity after his mother had called, but she was afraid of the answer.

With a bag full of lemons, she headed back into the house. What else needed to be done? The grevillea under the kitchen window had a couple of broken branches.

That was odd. They hadn't had any strong winds lately.

Placing the lemons on the deck, she took her secateurs from the windowsill and went to prune it.

A deep footprint in the garden bed stopped her. She hadn't been near the bed in weeks.

Another print was on the other side of the bush as if someone had stood straddling it, peering into her kitchen window.

Chills went up her spine. She backed away and hurried

inside to call Lincoln.

After Lincoln had investigated, and left, she did as he suggested and went around the house closing the curtains.

She was locking herself in, but every creak of the floorboards had her jumpy. It was ridiculous. Normally she had no problem being home alone, enjoyed it. She called Kit, needing to hear a friendly voice.

"I've got good news," Kit said as she answered.

Fleur needed some of that right about now. "Tell me."

"I've found us a new tank for the track."

Oh, right. She'd forgotten about that. "How much?"

"Free. I spoke to Foley yesterday and he said he'd donate one. Turns out the insurance agency finally agreed to pay him out for the shed that burnt down last month. He's not rebuilding it, so he's happy to give us some of the funds."

She whistled. "That's really generous of him. I thought he was having difficulties after his wife left him."

"So did I, but he says he had a bumper crop last year and he wants to give back to the club."

"I'm not going to say no. When can we get it?"

"It won't be before the night race, but Mai's going to ask whether we can access the fire brigade water stand for the night. There's one outside the property and they might let us get water from there."

It was a good idea. "When did you discuss this?" And why had she been left out?

"Mai dropped by yesterday," Kit said. "I would have called sooner but didn't want to disturb your date with Will again."

Fleur chuckled. "I appreciate it. How are things going with Paul?"

Kit groaned. "I'm still worried. This isn't like him."

"If he doesn't open up to you, there's not a lot you can do. You can't keep killing yourself trying to cover for him."

Her friend sighed. "You're right."

Should she ask Kit whether Paul was angry enough to do all the things around the track? Maybe not over the phone. "You want to hang out this afternoon? I could bring ice cream and chocolate."

"You're not busy with Will?"

"No. He's playing cricket."

"That would be great. We don't hang out as much since Hannah and Mai hooked up. I'm going to be the old maid of the group with lots of dogs."

Fleur frowned. "No, you won't. You'll find someone nice."

"You're not denying things between you and Will are serious," Kit pointed out.

She paused. "I don't know what we are."

"How many dates have you been on?"

She counted. "Four."

"In what, two weeks? I'd say it's serious. The last guy you dated lasted two."

"I didn't realise you were counting."

"I wasn't. I'm just… envious." She sounded sad and Fleur straightened.

Kit was never interested in more than a fling. She always talked about loving them and leaving them wanting more. Something had changed. "We'll find you your perfect guy."

"My perfect guy isn't interested."

Fleur's heart twisted. Only one guy could make Kit feel like this. They needed ice cream and violent action films stat. "I'll be out at your place soon."

"Thanks, Flower."

Fleur hung up and threw a change of clothes into a bag as she called Mai. "Are you free for a musketeers' night at Kit's tonight?"

"Count me in."

"Can you call Hannah?"

"Sure."

She retrieved the chocolate and ice cream she'd bought for the movie night the day before and added them to her bag and then headed out the door. She had a friend to cheer up.

Chapter 16

Fleur lengthened her stride and pushed faster. She was going to be late. Will had been cagey about why he was dropping around, but she didn't mind. She wanted to see him. Maybe he could stay for dinner.

She focused on her breathing, her arms pumping in time with her feet. At the bottom of her hill she slowed. She wasn't a sucker for punishment and the hike up the hill would be a good cool down. She kept her paces long, waving hello to Jacob and his brothers playing in their front yard.

The sight of her roses hacked back to sticks without a single green shoot on them soured her mood. She should pull them out, but she couldn't bear to give up on them yet. There was still a tiny chance they would survive. It was the same hope she'd had when her mother had been dying — maybe some miracle would occur — but in her heart she knew the truth. The roses were dead.

She took a deep breath. No amount of anger or grief would bring her mother or the roses back. She needed to accept it and move on. Her mother lived on in her memories and in herself.

Stopping at the bottom of her stairs, she used the post to balance while she stretched her quads and hamstrings. The rumble of a car up the road had her spinning around.

Will.

He was something worth smiling about.

She brushed the loose hairs from her ponytail off her face and walked over. "Hey. How was your day?"

His smile was big, bright and a little bit smug. "Great." He pulled her close and kissed her.

Lust sparked instantly. She'd never get tired of this.

When they broke apart he said, "I've got something for you." He walked to the back of his car.

"You didn't need to get me anything."

"I wanted to." He opened the big back door and reached in, drawing out two pots, both containing a thorny twig.

Her heart sank. He'd bought her more roses. It was a nice gesture, but it wasn't the same. They weren't her mother's roses, she had no connection to them. She forced a smile. "Thank you."

"They're from the heritage farm." He carried them over to the porch. "I called the caretaker today and explained what had happened and that your mum used to work there. She remembered her and said these were some of the roses she'd planted. She let me take a few cuttings." He went to get more out of the car.

Fleur's mouth dropped open as her chest squeezed. Words failed her and the lump in her throat was too large to allow her to speak anyway. Disbelief, sorrow and joy fought for dominance and tears pricked her eyes.

He'd replaced her mother's roses.

Will frowned as he carried another two pots to the verandah. "Are you all right? Did I do the wrong thing?" He placed the pots down and Fleur flung herself at him, squeezing him hard.

"No." She gasped. "You did the right thing. Thank you." Tears poured down her cheeks. Damn, her chest was so tight she could barely breathe.

"Hey, it's all right." He stroked her back, his hands gentle. "I didn't mean to make you cry."

She nodded, unable to speak.

"We still need to make sure they root properly, and they'll need to stay in the pots for a while, but that will give us a chance to fix the soil in the front garden, check it's not contaminated."

The more he spoke, the harder she cried. He was in this with her. He wanted to help.

Love filled her heart to overflowing, there was no stopping it. Will was the most wonderful man she'd ever met. Now she understood what Hannah and Mai had.

But she couldn't tell him how she felt. Not until she found out if he was still as determined to return to Goldwyer as he'd been.

Taking a deep breath in, she pushed herself away and wiped her cheeks. "Thank you."

He examined her. "Can I get the rest out?"

She laughed. "How many did you get?"

"Two of each bush. The caretaker said we can come back and get more when they prune them in winter."

She shook her head and took his hand. "Let me help."

It didn't take long to move the pots to a spot behind the house that Will deemed had enough sun. As they washed their hands, she asked, "Do you want to stay for dinner? I'm cooking steak."

"I'd love to. Can I help with anything?"

"No. Take a seat. It'll only take me a couple of minutes to throw together a salad." She poured him an iced hibiscus tea. "What else did you get up to today?"

"Mostly monitoring work, but I was close to Albany, so I dropped by there on the way home. How about you?"

"I'm much better now that you've replaced my roses." She must look a mess. She hadn't cleaned up after jogging, but Will didn't seem to care.

She got the makings of a salad out of the fridge and chopped some tomatoes. "Have you got cricket training tomorrow afternoon?"

Will nodded. "So Kim tells me. It sounds like it's more of an excuse to go to the pub afterwards."

"Are you cool with that?"

"Yeah. They're nice guys."

Fleur was glad. He was much more comfortable in his skin now, not just around her, but with others as well. "How are things going with Elijah?"

"It's actually easy."

"I never had a problem sharing with Hannah."

"I guess it helps if you like the person, and Elijah's hard not to like."

She smiled. "That's true." With the salad made, she lit the stove for the steaks. Someone knocked on the front door and then called, "Fleur?"

Her father. "Come in, Dad." A few nerves surfaced. He hadn't met Will yet. Would he like him?

Will sat straighter in his chair and tapped his thigh.

"Don't worry. He's nice." She went to meet her father, hugging him and showing him through to the kitchen. "This is Will."

"Sorry, I thought it was Hannah's car out front." The look he gave Will was suspicious. "You're the greenie?"

Will stood up, pushing his chair back and held out his hand. "Yes. Nice to meet you, sir."

Her father snorted. "No sirs here. Call me Gary."

Will nodded.

"Do you want a drink, Dad?"

"No, I won't stay if you're about to have dinner." He ran a hand through his hair.

"You can stay if you want." She squeezed his hand, needing to share the good news. "Will got me some cuttings from the roses Mum tended at the heritage farm to replace the ones that were poisoned."

His eyes widened, a light sheen to them. "That's really nice of you."

Will shrugged. "Fleur took me there on the weekend and told me how your wife used to work there. I figured it was worth asking if we could have some."

The old Will would have stuttered a whole lot more meeting her father.

Gary cleared his throat. "That's good. Well, I'll be off. Walk your old man out, Rose?"

What did he want to say to her? "Sure." She turned down the heat on the stove and followed him to the front door.

"He really replaced your mum's roses?" His disbelief was

clear.

She nodded, a lump in her throat.

He shook his head. "Did you ask him to?"

"No. I didn't even think of it."

"Well…" It wasn't often that her father was at a loss for words. "Maybe he won't be so bad." He hugged her and then trotted down the front steps. At the bottom he turned around. "You take care of yourself. Lincoln mentioned you've been having some more trouble at the track."

Lincoln was a tell-tale. "Nothing we can't handle. Don't worry about it."

"You're my baby girl. I'll always worry." He climbed into his car.

"Thanks, Dad." She waved as he drove away and then went back inside to find Will at the stove cooking the steaks. He glanced over his shoulder. "Everything all right?"

"Yeah, he was just checking up on me."

"And checking on me?" Will asked.

"That was a bonus."

Will smiled. "It's a shame he couldn't stay for dinner. There's enough here."

"You wouldn't have minded?"

"No. I'd like to get to know him."

She placed the salad bowl and dressing on the table and got out some plates. He constantly surprised her and ticked all the boxes she hadn't realised she'd had. It was impossible not to love him. But he might want to return to Goldwyer and she couldn't imagine leaving Blackbridge.

Will carried the steaks over to the table. Sitting down, he asked, "Will you be riding this weekend?"

"No. I'm steward, which is the official for the night." And if she could get away with it, she'd be the official for each event this year. That way she didn't need to race.

"What does that entail?"

She shrugged. "It's mostly routine stuff, but someone has to do it, and I don't feel like racing at the moment."

"Because of the accident?"

"Yeah." The thought of hurting someone else gave her chills.

"Don't they say you should get straight back on the horse after you fall off?"

"I don't have a problem riding, just racing."

"What about the sidecar? You do it with Kit don't you?"

"Yeah. I'm the rider and she's the swinger." And Kit wouldn't let her make excuses for not riding.

"That must be tricky."

"It can be. The sidecar needs the swinger to turn, if they're not in the right place when you go around a corner it can get nasty." Before the accident she wouldn't have hesitated to take Will out for a ride, but now she didn't trust herself. Fleur gathered their plates, stacking the dirty dishes in the dishwasher. The evening was still warm, and she wanted to be outside, not stuck indoors. She had a bundle of excess energy. "Want to go for a swim?"

He raised his eyebrows. "OK. I'll need to stop by my house for some bathers."

"You could get an overnight bag too if you want." If he did return home, she wanted to enjoy every second she could with him.

He grinned at her. "I'd like that."

So would she. "I'll get changed."

The distinctive squawk of Will's ring tone rang from the kitchen while he was getting ready for cricket training the next evening.

"Want me to get that?" Elijah yelled.

"Yeah." It might be Fleur and he didn't want to miss talking to her. He shoved on a T-shirt and picked up his shoes and socks. As he walked down the hallway, Elijah said, "I'm his new roommate."

So not Fleur then.

"A couple of weeks." Elijah motioned for Will to come closer. "He's right here, I'll put you on." He handed the phone to Will. "Your mum."

Twice in a week was odd. He tapped his thigh. "Hi, Mum."

"You didn't mention you've got a roommate."

"I forgot."

"What's he like?"

"Elijah is nice."

Elijah blew him a kiss and turned to do the dishes.

Will chuckled.

"Nice doesn't tell me much. Can he afford his share of the rent? Is he a slob?" Her concern was obvious.

"He works at a local winery, cooks dinner for us both most nights and he's expanding my musical tastes."

"That's great." He heard the smile in her voice. "Listen, there's an environmental job going at the mine. You should apply."

Will stopped tying his shoelaces. A job close to home. It was what he'd been desperately hoping for since finishing university and a few weeks ago he would have jumped at the chance. Now though...

"Are you still there?"

"Yeah. Can you send me the details?"

"I don't have them. Aggie mentioned they're on the usual website."

"I'll take a look." This was what he'd wanted for so long so why wasn't he firing up his laptop right now? Fleur's face popped into his mind. He sighed. "How's Dad?"

"Working hard as usual."

He checked the time. "Tell him I said hi. I've got to get to cricket."

"Cricket? Since when do you play cricket?"

"Since last week. They needed an extra man."

"That's... great. I'm pleased you're making an effort." She didn't sound sincere.

He paced over to the window. "Love you, Mum. I'll call you next week." He hung up.

A job in Goldwyer. Part of him wished his mother had never told him. It would mean leaving Blackbridge, leaving a job he genuinely enjoyed, leaving Fleur.

He wasn't sure he wanted to.

He sank into the sofa. How had his life changed so significantly in such a short time?

"You OK?" Elijah walked over.

174

"Yeah."

"You look like you've had bad news."

Was it? "Mum told me about a job back home."

Elijah put his hands on the back of a chair. "Are you going to apply?"

"I don't know."

"What's it like up there?"

Lonely. He sighed. That wasn't his only memory of home. "It's a small town that revolves around the mine, but the bush is peaceful."

"Is that your mob up there?"

"No. Mum's parents were part of the stolen generation and we're not sure exactly where they're from."

Elijah sat down. "That must be hard."

It wasn't something he was comfortable talking about. "I'd better get going."

"Mind if I tag along? I need some social interaction."

"Sure." For the first time, Will understood what he meant. He was used to the contact, looked forward to it. He didn't want to go back to when he spent every night sitting at home alone eating microwave meals and working on a new craft project. He had friends now.

He would have to find new friends if he moved home. Start all over again.

"Why don't you join a team?" Will asked as they walked out to the car.

"I'm not a big fan of playing. Having a ball speeding towards me is not my idea of fun. I'd much rather watch all the lovely men." He winked.

Will grinned. "Anyone take your fancy?"

A small smile played around Elijah's mouth. "Maybe. I'm not certain if he plays for my team though. He's sending me mixed messages."

"Why don't you ask?"

"I might. I want to do a bit more reconnaissance first. I don't want to ruin any chance of friendship if he's not."

It made sense. Though now he was curious who Elijah thought was gay. He ran through the list of guys on his team. He was pretty sure Kim, Jamie, Jeremy, and Adam had been talking about women. The others were a little older, had families at home, so didn't stop at the pub afterwards for a drink.

He pulled up at the oval and Jamie and Kim were setting up the wickets in the nets. He and Elijah wandered over.

"Hey. You want to bat or bowl first?" Kim asked.

He needed to practise both. "Either."

"I'll bowl then," Jamie said, tossing a red cricket ball from hand to hand.

Will kitted up in leg pads and a helmet.

"Take it easy on him." Kim grinned. "At least at first. We don't want to scare him away."

He was used to the teasing now, enjoyed it even. It made him part of the team. He was probably one of the worst players, but they didn't care.

"You going to join us?" Jamie asked Elijah.

"I'm worse than Will. I prefer to watch." He winked.

Jamie's grin was fast. "I could teach you how."

"I'm sure you could."

The banter was fascinating, it was almost like they were flirting, but Jamie wasn't gay. At least he didn't think he was. Maybe he should ask Fleur.

Not that it was any of his business.

But Elijah was his friend and he didn't want him to be hurt. Jamie took his position at the end of the cricket pitch and called, "Ready?"

Will nodded and bent over the bat.

He'd talk to Elijah later.

Chapter 17

The next evening Will had the house to himself for the first time since Elijah had moved in. Elijah had gone to dinner with his parents, and Fleur was working. The quiet was a little unnerving. He'd quickly grown used to background music, and the sounds associated with Elijah's presence. He flicked on the radio, turned the volume low and then sat down at the kitchen table where an internet search page waited for him to enter the criteria, as it had been for the last five minutes.

No one would know he'd looked and he didn't have to apply. But this was a career opportunity, and he should explore it.

The guilt as he typed in the website address was as bad as if he was cheating on Fleur. It was ridiculous. One had nothing to do with the other.

The community website came up and the environmental officer role was the first job on the list. Clicking on the link, he waited for the information to download, and then scanned the details.

The pay was more than he was getting now, the role was varied, and he'd be able to move back to Goldwyer. But he'd be working for the mine, and that didn't thrill him.

This was the opportunity he'd been waiting for. His mother expected him to apply.

In two weeks he'd found a community here. He had Fleur

and Elijah and the cricket team. He was happy for the first time in a very long time.

But who knew how long that would last?

When the cricket season ended he might not be invited to join a football team. Fleur could dump him. Elijah might find a better place to stay.

Should he put all his happiness on people who might leave, might find better things to do?

Goldwyer would at least offer him a place with his parents and one of his brothers.

His chest tightened.

Be rational about this. It was likely to be several weeks, maybe even months before he heard back from the recruitment company, and that would give him time to discover whether what he had here was a temporary anomaly, or whether it would be something that lasted.

Applying for the job would give him options.

It was the sensible thing to do.

Yet the tension in his chest didn't ease as he got to work.

The day of the night meeting had finally arrived. Fleur and Will were the first ones at the track Saturday afternoon. The ground was damp from the light rain they'd had the night before, and the sky was overcast. If they were lucky it would rain steadily all day and they wouldn't need to put down as much water on the track.

Opening the clubhouse, Fleur winced at the traces of graffiti still on the cupboards. Maybe she could find a local artist who was willing to paint a mural to liven them up.

"What needs to be done?" Will asked.

She handed him the checklist that hung by the door. "All of this." She'd done it enough times she didn't need to read it anymore. Switching on the fridges, she closed their doors and unlocked the truck shed.

They worked side-by-side as they prepared for the race meet, sweeping the toilets and putting out toilet rolls first and then Will carried the fire extinguishers out while she carried the start line items.

"Where do you want them?" he asked.

Fleur placed one of the start line posts and boards into position. "One can go just here, and the other can go to the pit entrance." She attached the rubber band but didn't stretch it out yet. It could wait until they were just about to start. She placed the rest of the posts into position and then Hannah and Mai drove in together with Kit not far behind.

"What do you need, Madam President?" Kit asked.

"You can grade the track, while Hannah and Mai help Will set up the tables and chairs."

"Usual shortened track?" Kit asked.

"Yeah." She glanced at her watch. "The lights should be here by now." She'd call if they hadn't arrived by the time she'd set out the markers.

Kit toed the dirt, scraping off the top damp layer and then glancing at the clouds. "It's going to be dusty if we don't get any more rain."

Fleur sighed. "I know. We've got the water truck."

"I'll dump some water before I start." Kit headed for the shed.

Fleur walked the track putting out the cones that marked the shortened route. It was just as well she was steward tonight. Racing under lights was different, thrilling, made the race feel that much more special and she wouldn't be able to resist the call to ride hard. And that was dangerous.

At least she'd get one ride when she checked the placement of the lights. Speaking of which, they should have arrived by now. Fleur called the hire company as she walked back to the clubhouse.

"That order was cancelled during the week," the man said.

Her pulse spiked. What? She did *not* need this now. "Who by?"

Papers rustled. "Doesn't say."

"They shouldn't have been cancelled. Can you still deliver them?" She crossed her fingers.

"Mate, we shut at two today. All my guys are heading home."

"Give me a second." She put her hand over the microphone and turned to Hannah and Mai who were sitting out on the verandah. "The order was cancelled and they're closing. Is there anyone in the club who could transport them?"

"What about Jeremy?" Mai said. "He has a truck."

Of course. "If I can get one of our members to pick up the lights in the next half an hour, will you wait?"

He sighed. "All right. There's some paperwork I could do."

"Thanks. I'll call you back in a minute."

She hung up and called Jeremy, explaining the situation.

"I was about to head out now anyway. I'll drop by the hire place on the way."

"Thanks."

After she'd called the hire place back, she sank into a chair next to Will. "Who would cancel the lights?"

"Probably the same person who vandalised the clubhouse and water tank," Hannah said.

She was right. Someone wanted the club to fail. Or for her to fail.

But she couldn't worry about that now. She needed to put out the paperwork for the signup and go through her checklist. Fleur groaned as she got back to her feet. Then she'd help put out the lights.

As dusk fell, Fleur opened the sign-up for riders. People came in dribs and drabs to register and pay, and Fleur sat at one of the tables with a cup of tea to help the race secretary if she had any issues. Will sat next to her.

"This all runs smoothly," he said.

She nodded. "Thanks for your help."

"My pleasure."

Trevor wheeled himself into the club room with Gavin and Nicole by his side.

She still needed to talk to him alone. "How's it going?"

"Great." Trevor beamed. "I can't wait to ride. The short track is just what I need."

She glanced at Nicole to gauge her reaction. "Here to watch?"

"I could hardly miss his first race back." She smiled. "Plus, the kids always have a ball playing with the other children."

"Have fun."

The next person who wandered in to sign-up made her scowl. "Paul, what are you doing here?"

"Signing up."

She raised her eyebrows. "Did you forget about your ban?"

"Come on, Fleur. It's not even an official event."

Her race secretary answered for her. "The ban was for the whole year. You're not riding today."

Paul swore. "Be reasonable."

"Sorry, Paul. The club voted on your punishment. You'll have to wear it." How many times did he have to be told?

"You don't know anything." He strode out, pushing past Lincoln in the doorway.

"What was that about?" Lincoln asked.

"He wanted to ride."

"Ah. Maybe he won't tear up the track next time." He handed over his rider's fee.

"Maybe." She got to her feet. "I'd better get those lights going. We'll be ready to start soon." She glanced at Will. "Want to come?"

"Yeah."

The evening was cool, and the light was fading as she found Jeremy in the pits talking to Paul.

"Ready to light the generators?" Jeremy asked, interrupting a rant from Paul.

"Yeah."

"I'll help," Paul said. "I've got nothing else to do out here."

It wouldn't hurt. She had no problem with him helping, or watching the race, he just couldn't take part. "Thanks." Hopefully he would calm down by the time he finished.

Someone grabbed her arm. "Fleur, can you do me a favour?" Nicole asked.

She had so much to do, but she could hardly say no. "Sure."

"I forgot to bring the salad for dinner. I need to dash home to get it. Can you keep an eye on the kids for me?" She sighed. "I'd ask Trevor but when he's talking bikes he forgets everything else."

"Of course." She glanced around and spotted the three children playing with Felix and Jacob over by the clubhouse.

"Thanks. Back soon." Nicole hurried off.

"I'll help Jeremy and Paul," Will said. "You stay here."

She kissed him. "Thank you."

Each light was attached to a generator, and the rumble as they started spoilt the quiet of the evening. Will flinched. If he disliked that he was going to hate the roar of the bikes off the start line.

Keeping an eye on the kids, she walked over to the start line and hooked up the lackey band. Not long now and the night would begin.

And she'd be standing on the sidelines.

She grimaced. Maybe she could try racing at the next meeting. She didn't have to take the sidecar out and if she kept at the back of the pack, she wouldn't have to worry about the other riders.

Maybe.

A child's shriek caught her attention and she turned as Nicole's middle boy shoved the younger one to the ground.

Damn.

She climbed over the spectator fence and jogged over as the little boy, who was about three, dissolved into tears.

"Hey, kiddo. Did you hurt yourself?" She crouched down and helped him to his feet.

"He pushed me!" The accusatory finger pointed at his brother. "He won't let me play with them!"

"That's tough." She glanced at the older brother. "Any reason why not?"

He crossed his arms. "He's too little. He ruins everything!"

She swallowed a smile.

"He can play with me." Felix held out a hand. "We were going to have running races."

The little boy's face brightened, and he grabbed Felix's hand. "OK."

"Thanks, Felix, that's nice of you." Ryan had raised a kind son.

She watched a minute longer as the kids discussed the rules of the race and marked out a start and finish line. They would be fine.

With the crisis averted, she scanned the track. Most of the lights were on, but it looked like Paul was having difficulty with the generator on the hill.

She found Will and was about to point him over, when the generator started and the light blinked on.

The positioning of all the floodlights looked about right, but she'd ride the track when Nicole got back to make sure.

She called the ten minutes to riders' brief announcement over the PA. Excitement hummed in her veins.

Maybe she should talk to Trevor now while Nicole was gone, clear the air, admit her lie. Her chest squeezed, but she'd never work through her guilt if she didn't. She glanced around and found him alone in the pits checking his bike.

She hurried over. "Trevor, could I have a word?"

He wheeled around to face her. "Sure. What's up?"

Hell, this was going to be hard. "It's about the accident."

"What about it?"

She swallowed hard. "I lied when I said my throttle stuck. The truth is I wanted to beat you for once, so I didn't shut off when I could have." She blinked rapidly to clear the moisture welling up in her eyes.

His expression was sober. "If we're going to be honest, I could have slowed down too, but I wasn't going to let a chick beat me." He flushed. "Stupid, I know. I was trying to psych you out by riding so close and you held your line like a champion." He smiled, reached out and squeezed her hand.

"I…" She didn't know what to say. His admission made her see the whole accident in a new light. Fleur huffed out a breath and the tension in her chest dissolved.

"It's *not* your fault."

She sniffed. "I'm still so sorry."

He nodded. "If anyone's to blame it's me. Don't let it stop you from racing again. You're damn good."

"Thanks." She walked away, needing time to process this. She'd never considered the race from his point of view, never thought he would purposefully try and put her off her race.

It changed everything.

She glanced out at the track. Maybe next race she *could* be at the start line.

She checked on the kids, who were running along the spectator fence just as Nicole drove in. She waved at Fleur and went over to her kids.

Great. Now she could get started. She walked over to where Will, Jeremy and Paul were standing on the track, examining the lights. Will seemed totally comfortable there, no fidgeting or tapping his thigh. She smiled. "They look about right, don't they?"

Jeremy nodded. "My only concern is the ones on the top of the hill."

"I'll check them now." She gestured for Will to follow her over to the pits where Kit was chatting to Hannah and Mai. "Can I borrow a bike?"

"Sure. You reviewing the track?" Kit handed her a helmet.

"Yeah. I need to make sure there's enough light." She kissed Will. "I won't be long."

She strapped on the helmet and slid her hands into the gloves Kit gave her. Pushing the bike away from where the others were standing, she kick-started it and the engine's throaty rumble pierced the air. Her skin tightened, and her heartbeat increased as it always did. Having an engine between her legs made her hyper-aware and this was her only chance tonight to ride. She wouldn't deny she missed it.

Pressing down the gear lever, she moved off.

The pits were well-lit, as was the return chute. She rode around the start line and twisted the throttle.

The bike roared under her, jumping forward and she changed up gears heading for the first corner. The cool air brushed her skin and her focus narrowed to the track ahead as she hugged the bend, keeping up the speed so she could make it up the hill. So far the whole track was well lit.

The bike left the ground at the top of the hill, landing with a jolt, and she slowed for the tighter curve. Accelerating out of it, she saw a flash of silver and then something hit her across the chest. The force was so great that she let go of the handlebars, pain whipping through her as her head flung back. Almost in slow motion, her body left the bike.

This was going to hurt.

As much as Will didn't like the roar of the motorbike, it was incredibly sexy watching Fleur kick-start it and then ride off, her butt moulding to the seat of the bike. She was totally badass.

"Pretty cool, huh?" Hannah said.

He nodded and brought his gaze back to the group to find them all grinning at him. His face heated. OK, so he might have been staring after his girlfriend, but that was allowed.

"Are you all riding tonight?"

They nodded. "I've conned Jamie into riding the sidecar with me as well," Kit said. "At least until I can convince Fleur to race again. I know she misses it."

The sidecar was a huge beast, but he wanted Fleur to find her confidence again.

Suddenly a high-pitched whine split the air and as he turned, Kit's bike tumbled down the first hill, without Fleur.

His heart leapt to his throat and he ran towards the hill.

Where was she? Had she been hurt? Heart pounding hard in his chest, he scanned the hill for movement.

Nothing.

The bike engine cut out, leaving only the rumble of the generators. Behind him people shouted, but he didn't stop.

Couldn't.

He cut across the track, taking the shortest path to the top. His lungs burned.

Still no Fleur.

Where the hell was she?

Finally, he reached the top and his heart stopped. Fleur was sprawled flat on her back and as he fell to his knees beside her, a dark red stain spread across her chest. "Fleur!"

He shook her gently and she groaned.

Relief flooded him. She was alive.

"Don't move her," Mai ordered as she knelt next to him. "Where does it hurt?" She glanced at Fleur's chest and then away, taking a deep breath.

"Back. Chest. Head," she rasped.

More footsteps and Kit swore. "What happened?"

"Hit something."

"I'll call an ambulance and get the other first aiders." Hannah ran back towards the clubhouse shouting.

Thank God her friends were there.

How badly had she been hurt? Carefully he lifted her top.

Fleur hissed.

"I need to see how bad it is," he told her. The cut ran horizontally the whole way across the top of her breasts and she was grazed up to her neck. It was still bleeding, but it could have been a lot worse.

"Can you feel your legs?" Mai asked as Jeremy, Hannah and Lincoln drove up in a van that had ambulance written on the side. They jumped out and Jeremy grabbed the stretcher and a first aid kit from the back.

"I can feel everything."

Will held her hand, squeezing it gently as relief flooded him. Maybe the cut on her chest was the worst of it.

"I've called the paramedics," Hannah said.

Mai glanced up. "Good. Jeremy, you can help me. Will, I need you to move out of the way."

He didn't want to, but they were trained. He shifted away to see what Fleur could have hit. Nothing. Just as he moved, a shimmer caught his eye. He squinted. "What's that?"

The words out of Kit's mouth would have made a sailor blush. "Someone's hung wire across the track."

His mouth dropped open. That could have killed her. If it had got her neck and not her chest...

Lincoln's vocabulary matched Kit's. "Hannah, can you get Ryan up here?" he said. "We're cancelling the meeting. We've got to question people, so get Jamie and Nicholas to stop anyone leaving."

Hannah hurried away.

Anger replaced the fear. This wasn't an accident. But anyone could have been caught in the wire.

"Lincoln, no. I'm fine," Fleur said. "We don't have to cancel the meeting."

Her eyes were open, and she was a lot more coherent, but

she grimaced as Jeremy applied a dressing to her chest.

"Not your choice, Flower. This is a crime scene now." His voice was hard.

Will walked over to Lincoln who was examining the wire. It was a thick gauge and tied on to the two tyre walls in front of the trees on either side of the track.

Lincoln kept his voice low. "I need you to go with Fleur to the hospital," he said. "Don't let her out of your sight. This could have killed her."

Fear lodged in his stomach. "Anyone could have been hit."

Lincoln shook his head. "The steward always does a lap of the track before racing starts, and Fleur always does it on a bike. It's faster than walking." His lips formed into a thin, unhappy line. "Put that together with the roses, the slashed tyre and even her allergic reaction a few weeks back and she's the clear target."

"Wasn't that an accident?"

"I'm still waiting for forensics to come back. I took her bottle to be tested."

His blood ran cold. Who could possibly want Fleur dead?

"Who started the generators out here?"

"Paul." He clenched his fists, resisting the urge to find him and put his fist through his face. He wasn't leaving Fleur's side. "He was mad Fleur wouldn't let him ride."

"I'll question him first."

And when Will was certain Fleur was all right, he would have some words with him as well.

Will hovered at the end of Fleur's hospital bed, unable to stand still. She was lying flat on her back, her face a little pale and wearing a blue hospital gown.

"Will, sit down. I'm fine." The smile Fleur gave him was like the sun peeking out from behind the clouds.

He took hold of her hand, needing to touch her. "How are you really?"

She looked at him for a long moment and then sighed, her eyes clouding over. "*Really* sore. The ground was hard and the wire..." She touched her chest lightly. "I don't know who I've upset." Her eyes watered.

His heart pinched at her pain. "Lincoln will figure out who it was."

"I hope so."

He needed to distract her. "Do you want me to call your dad?"

"No!" Fleur's eyes widened. "Wait until we get the results of the x-ray. He'll worry otherwise."

"He'll worry regardless." Wasn't that what parents did?

"No. He hates hospitals and he'll come. Then I'll be stressed about him being uncomfortable."

She made a convincing argument. He wasn't going to do anything that made her feel worse than she already did. "All right."

It was half an hour before the radiographer arrived. Will wanted to stay by her side while she was x-rayed, but it wasn't possible. He clenched his hands as she was wheeled away. He didn't like having her out of his sight. He got to his feet, unable to sit still, as his phone rang.

"How is she?" It was Kit.

"She's just been taken for x-rays."

"OK, call me with the results."

"I will. What's happening out there? Does Lincoln know who did it?"

"The police are questioning a whole bunch of people and the committee is dealing with complaints about the race being cancelled and people not being allowed to leave. People are such douches."

Her disgust made him smile. "Yeah, they can be."

"No *can* about it. They're a bunch of selfish, self-important bastards who don't care about anyone else but themselves." The bitterness was clear.

Will didn't comment. This wasn't the first time she'd seemed angry at the world. He'd have to talk to Fleur about it, ask if this was normal for Kit. He liked her despite her brash personality. He wouldn't mention Paul was the one to start the generators. That could end badly. "I'll call you when we get the results."

"Thanks."

He paced the emergency room. A mother sat with her vomiting child, and from the conversation he overheard, the other guy was in for cutting his hand while juggling knives.

"Will, take it easy. She's going to be fine." Tim moved in front of him. "If something is broken, she might need surgery, but more likely she'll be in a brace for a couple of months which will drive her and everyone else crazy. But she's not going to die." He slapped him on the back.

Tim didn't know about all of the other incidents. "Sorry. I'll stay in the cubicle."

The nurse laughed. "Pace if it helps, as long as you don't get in our way. But there's nothing to worry about."

Will spun around at the rattle of wheels on the floor. Fleur was back, and she was sitting up.

Relief washed through him.

"Nothing broken," she said. "I'm good to go."

"Don't get up yet," Tim told her. "You still need the doctor to confirm,"

Fleur pouted, but it was cute on her. He waited until the bed was back in position and the orderly had left before he pulled her into his arms, inhaling the scent of her. "I'm so glad."

"Ow." She gently pushed him away. "Nothing broken, but plenty bruised."

He winced. "Sorry." He reached for his phone. "I'll call Kit."

After he spoke to her, he handed his phone to Fleur. "You should call your dad. If he hears about it from anyone else, he'll be upset."

She sighed. "You're right."

Will heard Fleur's father's voice coming through the phone, insisting he was coming to the hospital.

"Dad, there's no need. We're heading home soon."

Will touched her arm. "We'll need a lift to your place."

She nodded. "How about you pick us up when I'm done?"

She hung up. "I forgot about the car situation."

"We'll pick yours up tomorrow," Will said.

She took his hand and squeezed it. "Thanks for being here."

"There's nowhere else I'd rather be." It was true. He was happier with Fleur than he'd ever been. But was that a bad thing? Did he need to learn to be happy by himself, not let someone else affect how happy he was? Perhaps she was just the catalyst to him coming out of his shell. He had found Elijah and the cricket team on his own and they made him happy too.

He'd been so damn lonely before Fleur, but now she was at the centre of everything good in his life. So why had he even applied for the job in Goldwyer?

Fear. Fear of missing out, of making a mistake. Even now the thought of calling up and removing his application from the pool felt wrong. He had to give himself the chance, and make a rational, logical decision — not an emotional one.

But right now, his only thought was to make Fleur feel better.

Chapter 18

Fleur shifted in bed, wincing as she did so. She would have some killer bruises tomorrow, but the painkillers had taken the edge off the pain.

Will squeezed her hand. "Can I get you anything?"

She shook her head. "I must look a mess."

"You look gorgeous as always." He handed her his phone with the camera on and pointed at her. "See?"

Staring back at her, pale skin, pastel blue hospital gown, wincing in pain was someone who could have been her mother.

The world lurched and suddenly she was eight years old and sitting by the hospital bed, holding her mother's hand, telling her she would feel better soon.

"Fleur?" Will squeezed her hand.

She blinked, coming back to the present day and thrust his phone back at him.

"Are you all right?"

No, she needed to get the hell out of here. "I'm ready to leave. Can you call Dad back?" She didn't want to be here as a patient. She didn't want to be reminded of her mortality. She wanted to be back at the track figuring out who had put the wire across it.

Will shook his head. "Not until you're discharged."

"I can check myself out."

"Please, Fleur. I need to know you're OK." His touch was light on her arm, but the worry in his eyes was enough to temper her impatience.

It must have given him a fright seeing her flat on her back like that. "All right." The accident played back through her mind, rounding the corner, the flash of silver, before the whip of pain and the hard impact. How could she have missed the wire? She should have been riding at walking pace. Then she might have noticed it and had time to stop.

Instead the meeting had been cancelled and some people were going to be annoyed that they'd travelled down for nothing. All that extra work, and now she would have to smooth some ruffled feathers. Not what she needed right now.

She pressed the call button to get Tim's attention.

"What are you doing?" Will asked.

"Getting out of here." She winked at him and sat up, swinging her legs over the side.

"What's up, Fleur?" Tim asked as he came into the cubicle.

"I'm ready to go."

"Hon, you know how this works. You're no longer the priority which, yay, means you're not going to die, but, boo, you have to wait longer."

Fleur hissed out a breath. She needed to get to the track.

"I can get you a couple of magazines from the waiting room."

"No, it's fine."

"Good. It won't be too long." Tim left.

"What's really wrong?" Will asked. "Why are you in such a hurry to get out of here?"

It was ridiculous and she couldn't tell him the truth. "I need to get back to the track to manage things."

He shook his head. "No, you don't. Kit and the others have it under control."

She tapped her hand on the bed. "But I'm president. I need to be there."

"No, you don't. What you need is to go straight home to bed."

"Will, there's a whole heap that needs to be done. People are going to complain and they're going to want to talk to me."

"Tough. You were almost killed, Fleur. Everyone will understand."

"It wasn't that bad."

Will stared at her. "It could have been."

She didn't have to respond as Marian walked into the cubicle with her x-rays.

"What did you do, Fleur?" She held them up to the light.

"Fell off my motorbike." If she went into detail she'd never get out of here.

"Well you got lucky. A bit of bruising, but your spine is fine. I'll give you a doctor's certificate, so you can rest for the next couple of days — no riding, no heavy lifting."

"Sure." As long as she got out of here she'd agree to anything. She took the medical certificate Marian handed her, and after the doctor left, she went over to the nurses' station and picked up her file.

"What are you doing?" Will protested.

"Paperwork." She filled out the discharge paper, signed it and then took the file over to Tim to sign.

"In a bit of a hurry, are we?" He grinned and signed the paper.

"Thanks. I'll see you in a couple of days." She walked out of the hospital and took a deep breath of fresh air. Moths fluttered around the outside lights, but she wanted darkness. The little garden by the entrance was a perfect spot to sit to wait for her father and the sweet honeysuckle fragrance was a comfort.

Will sat next to her on the bench seat. "Your dad won't be long. Want to tell me what that was about?"

"What?"

"Your rush to get out of there."

"I told you, to get to the track."

He raised his eyebrow and said nothing.

His silence was a powerful tool. She squirmed. "It's weird being taken care of by my colleagues." Hesitating, she added, "And I got a real flashback to Mum being in hospital and it freaked me out a little."

He gently wrapped his arm around her. "That makes total sense." He brushed a kiss on her forehead. "Are you hungry?"

She nodded. His presence, his simple comfort, soothed her.

"We'll pick something up on the way to your house. What do you want?"

She wanted a bucket of ice cream and a spoon, but the supermarket would be closed by now. "How about Vietnamese?"

They ordered the food while they waited for her dad to arrive. He pulled into the hospital drive and jumped out of the car. "How is she?" he asked Will.

Fleur raised her eyebrows. "I'm right here."

"But you won't tell me the truth." He hugged her tightly and she gritted her teeth at the pain.

"The doctor says she needs to rest for a couple of days, but nothing is broken," Will told him.

"Good. What happened?"

"I fell off, is all." She stared at Will, willing him to keep quiet.

Her father glanced between the two of them. "What aren't you telling me?"

Damn it. He was going to freak out.

"Will?"

"That's for Fleur to say."

She swore. "Let's get home first. Have you eaten? We need to pick up some take-away and you can join us if you like."

"All right, but we'd better hurry. I've got some caramel macadamia nut icecream in the car and I don't want it to melt."

She smiled. Her father always knew what made her feel better.

"Thanks Dad."

By the time they got back to her place Fleur was flagging. Her body ached, and she wanted to crawl into bed, but she couldn't show it, or her father would worry. And he'd worry enough after she told him about the wire.

"Take a seat." Will placed the bag of take-away on the kitchen table and then got out plates and cutlery.

Her father raised an eyebrow but didn't say anything about Will's familiarity with her kitchen. When they were eating, he asked, "What happened?"

She stuck to the facts, downplaying the cut on her chest and the aches in her body.

"Who the hell would do that?"

"Lincoln's questioning everyone at the track." Some of the members wouldn't like it at all. She was almost glad she wasn't there to deal with their complaints.

"Good. It could have killed someone."

Will cleared his throat. "Lincoln thinks Fleur was the target."

Her heart jumped. "What?" When did he say that?

"He said the steward always does a lap of the track before the racing starts and you always ride it."

He was right, but that didn't mean someone wanted to kill her. There'd been a few nasty pranks, but this was next level stuff.

"Who would want to hurt Fleur?" her father asked.

"No one. It must have been a prank, like the roses and the slashed tyre."

"What slashed tyre?" he growled.

Crap. Now she would have to explain everything. "It was nothing."

He stared at her, the no-nonsense glare that had always been able to break her when she was a kid.

She sighed. He wasn't going to like this. "Let me start at the beginning."

When she was finished, he said, "That's not nothing, that's a shit-tonne of stuff directed at you." He turned to Will. "Did you know about all of this?"

Will nodded. "Lincoln thinks your allergic reaction is related too, Fleur. He sent your bottle to be tested and is waiting on the lab results."

Fleur's whole body went cold.

Her father swore. "That could have killed her. Next time

something happens, you call me. You've got my number, right? I want to know the instant it happens."

"Dad, I'm not a child," Fleur protested. "Don't fuss." Still, it would have been easy to slip a couple of aspirin tablets into her water bottle. And if that was the case, someone had been targeting her for weeks. Someone wanted her dead, someone who knew she was allergic to aspirin.

"You will always be my child," he snapped. "And I will protect you. You should move in with me until they find who is doing this."

That was the last thing she needed. "No, Dad. I don't need to be taken care of." She stood up, wincing a little and cleared their plates.

"It's not safe for you to be alone."

She'd survived so far when she'd had no idea she was the target. "I'll be fine."

"What about the musketeers? One of them can stay with you at all times, like you did when Hannah was being stalked."

She wouldn't be a burden to them. "Dad, they all have their own lives."

"I can stay." Will gave her a half-smile. "If you don't mind that is. With it being a long weekend, I have the next two days off and depending on your roster, you could come to work with me after that, keep me company."

"Great idea!" her father said.

Fleur bit back her retort. Her desire to be independent clashed with the lovely idea of spending so much more time with Will. "I don't want to put you out."

"I'd enjoy it."

It wasn't an argument she wanted to win. "OK." She yawned widely.

"Good." Her father hesitated. "You're staying the night?"
Will nodded.

"All right." He stood up. "I'd better head off, let you get some sleep. You take good care of my daughter," he said to Will. "Remember, if anything happens, I want to know,"

"Yes, sir."

Great, now they were ganging up on her.

"It's Gary." They shook hands.

At least they were getting along. Fleur walked her father to the door.

"Thanks, Dad." She kissed his cheek.

"You take care of yourself, Rose. I like having you around."

She smiled. "Ditto."

She waited at the door until he drove away and then returned to the kitchen. Will had done their dishes and was standing at the freezer. "Ice cream?"

"Yes, please." She could do with some comfort food right about now.

He dished up generous bowls and brought them over to the sofa. "I hope you don't mind me offering to stay. You could always get one of the musketeers instead."

"I'd like to spend more time with you."

His smile was beautiful. "I'm glad." He sat next to her and put his arm around her, pulling her close. "I'll take care of you."

She didn't want to be taken care of, she wanted to be loved.

But it would do for now.

The sharp ring of Fleur's mobile phone woke Will. Daylight seeped into the room through the gaps in the venetian blinds and as he turned over he found the bed next to him empty.

He sat up, heart thumping as Fleur hurried into the room wearing nothing but a singlet and underpants.

"Sorry, I was in the bathroom." She answered her phone, moving back out into the corridor. "Hey, Lincoln."

Will threw on his jeans and followed her into the kitchen. Whatever Lincoln was saying, he wanted to hear it.

Fleur was silent, listening.

"Can you put it on speaker?"

She screwed up her nose and then said, "Hang on, Slinky. Will wants to hear this too." She pressed a button. "Go for it."

"Hey, Will, I was just telling Fleur we've interviewed everyone who was at the track, except for Paul who left before the incident. I'm going to chase him down today. A couple of people were seen out on the track, but they all had legitimate reasons for it. I'll send the wire to the lab on Tuesday, but it's common fencing wire so I'm not expecting much."

"Do you really think it was meant for me?" The vulnerability in her tone ripped into him.

Will put his arms around her waist and rested his head on her shoulder, kissing her cheek. She leaned into him and his heart sang.

"With all that's going on, I'd say it's likely, Flower. I want you to be vigilant."

"Will's going to spend the next couple of days with me."

"I knew I liked him."

Will grinned. "I won't let her out of my sight."

"Good. Can I drop by later to interview you both?"

"Sure. Come for lunch." Fleur hung up. She ran a hand through her hair. "I should go out to the track and check how everyone is."

"Do you need to?"

"I'd feel better if I did."

He could understand that. Her sense of what was right was one thing he liked about her. "All right. I'll make you breakfast and then I'll call Elijah and ask him to drop my car around."

She smiled. "I can make my own breakfast."

"Yeah, but I'd like to. You scared me to death when you fell off last night." He moved away to fill the kettle. He wanted to wrap her in cotton wool and keep her from harm, but she didn't need him to do that. "How are you this morning?"

"Sore. My chest itches."

"Do you want me to get you any painkillers?"

"Already taken some."

"Pancakes?"

She nodded.

He got out the ingredients and mixed them together.

"Didn't you say you weren't much of a cook?"

"Pancakes are easy. One batter, no other things that need

coordinating." And he'd asked Elijah to teach him, so he could make them for her. While the pan heated, he got out the jam, yoghurt and some strawberries. He liked Fleur's kitchen, the warm, homey feel, liked the woman sitting at the table, staring off into space, deep in thought.

"Penny for them." He placed a cup of tea in front of her.

"Sorry, what?"

"Penny for your thoughts. You were off in your own place."

She sipped her tea and gave an appreciative sigh. "I'm trying to figure out who might want to hurt me."

"Any takers?"

"Not really. I mean Paul's annoyed with me because he's been banned from the club, but that was a whole committee decision, and I don't think he'd ever hurt me. He's a nice guy usually."

"He's the guy who works for Kit? The one she's been having trouble with."

"Yeah, so something must be up, but it can't be the ban from racing, the season doesn't begin in earnest until April."

He tested the heat of the pan with a dollop of batter and it sizzled nicely. He glanced back at her. It was a touchy subject, but it needed asking. "What about Trevor?"

She shook her head. "He would have struggled tying the wire at the height it was at and we spoke yesterday. He doesn't blame me, said he could have slowed down."

Her shoulders weren't tense like they normally were when she spoke about the accident. "What about someone close to him?"

"I chatted with Nicole and Gavin yesterday. They were both excited about him riding."

Excitement could be faked, and Fleur was too trusting. She wouldn't suspect anyone. "What about at the hospital – a patient maybe?"

"No. I've gone through everyone and still nothing." She hesitated. "Back when the track was being vandalised, I thought maybe the creepy guy Mai had seen with Gordon before he died last month could be involved. He was a man for hire."

He didn't like the sound of that. "What do you mean?"

"She saw him a couple of times, and he threatened to burn down Mai's bakery if she went to the police. I haven't seen anyone who fits the description though."

"Maybe you should call a musketeers meeting," he suggested. The more heads they had working on this, the better. And they would be a lot less biased than Fleur.

"You trying to get rid of me already?"

"No!" He chuckled when he realised she was teasing. "I want to solve this."

"You and me both. I'll call them now."

Which meant he had to go. He hadn't thought about that. "Tell me when you need me to leave."

She frowned at him. "You don't have to leave."

He smiled. "Musketeers meetings are no boys allowed."

She grinned. "You listened. Normally they are, but I was going to suggest Ryan, Lincoln, Jamie and Nicholas come too. I could do with their input and Lincoln wants to interview us anyway."

He sighed in relief, placing the cooked pancake on a plate and sliding it in front of Fleur while she chatted to Hannah. She seemed a little perkier than she had before.

After they'd eaten, Elijah insisted on dropping them at the track. Some caravans were still set up, people wandered across the grounds and a couple of bikes roared around the track.

So many people had camped overnight, a real community. Except someone wanted to hurt Fleur. Any of these people could be harbouring a secret grudge, could be planning to try again.

She was quickly surrounded by people wanting to know how she was, and Will stuck by her side, ensuring they gave her space. Did that guy's smile seem forced? Was there something in that woman's pocket? He twitched at the slightest abrupt movement. He had to get a grip.

"Are you taking good care of my girl?" Kit asked as she strolled up to them.

"Of course." He didn't know why he'd been so nervous around her.

"He made me pancakes this morning."

A brief look of wistfulness crossed Kit's face, but it was gone in seconds. "That's great. You can make me pancakes anytime, Captain Planet."

"Captain Planet?"

Kit frowned. "You're right, it's too long. Captain it is." She turned to Fleur. "Lunch at yours, right?"

"Yeah."

"See you then." She strode off.

Fleur chuckled. "Congratulations, you made the grade."

What was she talking about?

"Kit doesn't give nicknames to anyone she doesn't like."

A warmth spread through him. His first nickname. He grinned.

As they made the rounds, Will's respect for Fleur grew. She was so patient. Some people wanted a chat, others wanted to complain about being questioned by police or the race being cancelled, but she was pleasant to everyone. She could also end a rant and move on to the next person with ease. They'd been there about half an hour when Fleur started to flag.

"You need to rest," he said.

"We're almost done."

"No, we're not. Let's go back to the clubhouse, you can have a cuppa and rest. If there's anyone who desperately wants to see you, they'll come to you."

She sighed. "You're right."

They walked back, and Fleur sank into one of the chairs while he made her a cup of tea, white, no sugar. He liked taking care of her, particularly when she was caring for everyone else. A few people sat down to chat and he kept an eye on them. Both times she'd almost died had been here when she had been surrounded by people. Anyone could slip aspirin into her drink again. Did she have her EpiPen with her? He had no idea. Maybe he should ask, but he didn't want to interrupt. Didn't want to give anyone any ideas.

His stomach squirmed as the image of Fleur choking, unable to breathe, flashed through his head. It was worse now than it had been at the time. Now he had come to care for her.

He didn't want to go through that again.

By the time she'd finished her tea, Fleur had slumped in her chair and every movement came with a wince of pain.

"It's time we went home," he murmured in her ear.

She nodded, relief on her face.

He stood up and smiled at the woman talking to her. "Fleur needs to rest."

"Of course. I hope you feel better soon."

He helped Fleur to her feet and, keeping a supporting arm around her waist, walked her to the car. "Do you need to talk to the musketeers?"

"No. They've already gone. They're arranging lunch."

"Do we need to pick up anything?"

She shook her head. "Mai's bringing quiche, bread and some kind of delicacy. She always does."

He grinned. "It must be nice having her to bake for you."

"Yep. She's the best."

Fleur's driveway was full of cars when he pulled up. "Looks like everyone is here."

"Yeah, everyone but Slinky."

As she said it, Lincoln pulled in behind them. "Full house," he said as he got out.

They walked inside and the kitchen bench was covered in food; breads, cheeses, meats and salads, the oven was on and a lovely aroma wafted from it and several frozen pink drinks were on the table. Jamie and Nicholas were moving the kitchen chairs into the lounge room around the couches, Ryan was cutting bread, Mai was making drinks and Hannah and Kit were putting the finishing touches on the salad. The musketeers hadn't just arrived, they'd prepared everything.

It was sweet.

"We're eating in the lounge." Mai handed Fleur a frozen drink. "Yours is non-alcoholic."

"Thanks." Fleur raised the glass with a smile.

Mai turned to Will. "Frozen strawberry daiquiri, beer, or wine?"

He wanted to keep his wits about him this afternoon. "Water's fine."

As they ate, they swapped news as if they hadn't seen each other yesterday. Everyone wanted to hear what the doctor had said and what Lincoln and Ryan had discovered at the track.

"It's an ongoing investigation," Lincoln said. "You know we can't discuss it."

Kit put her hand on her hips. "Someone tried to kill Fleur. We have a right to know."

Will was on Kit's side.

Fleur placed a hand on Kit's knee. "Lincoln will tell us what he can, when he can."

Kit huffed and took a bite of her bread laden with meat and cheese.

"Speaking of which, we still need to interview you both," Lincoln said. "We should do it before we start discussing particulars."

Will nodded. "Happy to."

"How about now?" Lincoln glanced over at Ryan.

"We're still eating," Fleur protested.

"I'm finished." Will wanted to talk to Lincoln alone and wanted information in return. He took his plate to the sink and washed it. "Where do you want to talk?"

"Out the back?" Lincoln said.

The day was pleasantly warm and he took a seat at the outdoor table. Ryan and Lincoln sat across from him.

"You arrived at the track with Fleur, didn't you?" Ryan asked.

He nodded.

"Can you take us through yesterday from when you arrived?"

It took a while to go through everything, particularly with them asking questions — had he seen anyone on the track, had anyone acted strangely? He wasn't much help to them as he didn't know many of the people there.

"Do you know of anyone who might be unhappy with Fleur?"

"Aside from Paul, maybe someone in Trevor's family."

"Trevor?" Lincoln asked, his gaze sharp.

"Because of the accident last year. Fleur blames herself and maybe his wife or brother blame her too. She's sure neither of them would though."

Ryan made a note.

"And Fleur mentioned a creepy guy last night. Someone who threatened Mai? She said she hadn't seen him, but he could be still around."

Lincoln scowled. "I'll talk to her about it." He flipped his notebook closed. "Have you noticed anything else strange around the national park lately?"

Will frowned. That was some segue. "Like the dumping?"

"Anything that seems out of place."

He shook his head. "No. It's been quiet since I saw the four-wheel drive, but it's a big park. I'm moving into a new area next week. I'll let you know if I find anything."

He wanted the person stopped as much as Lincoln did. Not only was cleaning up those chemicals time-consuming, but also the risk of contamination was high.

"Thanks. Can you send Fleur out here?"

"Wait. What did Paul say when you questioned him?"

"We haven't been able to get in touch with him," Ryan said.

Will's eyes widened. "What?"

"It seems like he left the track and decided to go camping for the rest of the weekend."

That sounded dodgy. "Did Kit give him leave?"

Lincoln frowned. "No. She knows to tell us when he rocks up to work again."

"What happens now?" He wanted some answers.

"We're waiting on forensic results and we're treating this seriously."

He scowled. "That's the best you can do?"

"We know you're worried," Ryan said. "We'll tell you whatever we can."

He would have to be satisfied with that. "Thanks." He headed back inside to where Fleur was chatting to Jamie. "Your turn." He helped her to her feet, kissed her.

"We should get going." Jamie stood. "We're already late."

"Late?"

"For cricket. I called to tell Kim and he was going to get us to bat first."

Shit. He'd forgotten all about it. He was supposed to be spending the next couple of days with Fleur. He glanced at her.

"I'll be fine. The musketeers are staying until you get back."

"Kit's giving me a lift home," Jamie added. "I've got my gear in her ute."

Will didn't want to go but he'd made a commitment to the team. "All right." He shook his head. He'd never thought he'd have too many things he wanted to do.

"Take my car," Fleur said. "The keys are on the bench."

"Thanks."

He grabbed them and met Jamie at the front door. "Let's go."

The sooner he left, the sooner he could return.

Chapter 19

Staring at the long laceration across her chest, Fleur's stomach sank. Would it scar, a forever reminder someone had wanted to hurt her? She touched it lightly, wincing at the pain before covering it again with a waterproof bandage.

"Fleur, are you all right?" Will knocked lightly on the bathroom door.

"Be right out." She'd asked him to give her a bit of space while she changed the dressing and he had. She didn't want him seeing her like this, even though he'd seen it when it had happened. He wasn't going to suddenly reject her because she'd been scarred. But for her it was proof she was fallible, that life could end in an instant and she hadn't been able to shake the general unease all weekend long even while they'd lazed about talking.

She pulled her T-shirt on and taking a deep breath, she opened the door. "I'm ready."

He gave her a long look. "Great. Shall we go?"

"Sure." She picked up the backpack containing their lunches off the kitchen bench and followed Will out to his work vehicle.

It was weird to be going to work with her boyfriend, but Lincoln had been adamant that she wasn't left alone, and she was curious to see what Will did. Tomorrow she'd be back at work and the musketeers had organised an after-hours roster between them.

She hated that she'd put her friends out like this, that she wasn't safe in her own home. Now she knew how Hannah had felt when she'd been stalked.

"What's on today's schedule?" she asked as Will drove out of town.

"There's a section of the park I haven't been to in a while," he answered. "I need to check the roads and the tourist areas. My predecessor wrote notes about a different orchid population there and I want to take a look at them."

There was a lot more to being a park ranger than she'd expected. She settled back in the seat and closed her eyes. She hadn't slept well over the past couple of nights, the aches and pains in her body waking her whenever she moved. She lifted her face up to the sun coming through her window.

"How are you feeling?" Will asked.

"A little tired." She glanced at him. "And though I'm enjoying all the time with you, I don't like being baby-sat."

He chuckled. "I'm pleased you need me. Does that make me a bad person?"

"Not at all." Her heart smiled. She didn't want to jinx it by asking him how long he was planning to stay though.

They drove in silence, entering the national park and on to an unsealed road that was in good condition. It was quite far from town. "Are we on the edge of the park here?"

"No, it's about the middle," Will answered, pulling into a picnic spot.

"I didn't realise it was so big." She got out and wandered over to the wooden picnic table while Will got his pack out of the car. He took a clipboard from it and started ticking something.

"What are you doing?"

"General checks," he replied, pressing on the table. "I need to ensure the equipment is still in good condition, that the area is free of rubbish and general weeds and there's nothing that might harm a tourist."

He squatted down next to a round concrete fire pit not far from the table and picked something up from the ground. "The barbecue's been used recently."

Fleur walked over. Grey and black ashes were spread out in the bottom of the pit. "How do you know?"

"We always clear them out at the beginning of the fire season," he said. "My notes say they were all cleared, but this one has ashes in it."

"Maybe they didn't read the signs."

"More likely they didn't care." Will threw the charcoal back into the pit in disgust. "People don't realise how quickly a fire can spread. All it takes is a stray spark."

"You don't need to tell me," she said. "I've had that lecture from Mai a dozen times or more."

He stepped back and sighed. "Sorry. It bugs me when people are so selfish."

She kissed his cheek. "I like that you're so passionate about your job." She gingerly perched herself on top of the picnic table, wincing from the muscle aches, as he continued. He was so thorough, touching everything to make certain it was sturdy, not just relying on his eyes to make the assessment. He walked further into the bush, circling the whole area. His intensity was so damned sexy. Was it any wonder that she loved him?

"I'm done," Will said as he came back.

She wasn't. Not nearly. And they were all alone out here, nothing but the birds and bees around them. Perhaps she could convince him to show her how intense he could be.

Fleur ran a hand over his chest, and around the back of his neck. She pulled him close for a kiss.

He smiled against her mouth. "Are you trying to distract me, Miss Lockhart?"

"Absolutely. Is it working? We're all alone out here."

In the distance, the low rumble of a car reached them. Will stepped back and sighed. "Not as alone as I'd like." He listened and then frowned. "I need to check my map." He spread it out on the table. Fleur hopped down so she could look at it.

"We're here." He pointed. "There aren't any other roads around us, only a fire track. No one should be using that."

"Maybe someone got lost."

"Maybe." He folded up the map and took his phone out

of his pocket. He hesitated.

"Who do you want to call?"

"Lincoln. He said to call if I saw anything odd after I discovered more barrels being dumped by the river."

Fleur's heart rate sped up. When was that? "You don't know it's related. It could be a joy-rider. There are lots of people with four-wheel drives who enjoy taking them off-road."

He nodded. "Yeah, but I'll call it in anyway. Come on." He headed back to the car, dialling as he did so.

With all that had been happening, she'd forgotten about the dumped chemicals, but Lincoln had been super alert about them. If the car they'd heard was related, it could be dangerous, especially if it was the creepy guy. She didn't want Will to be hurt. She slid into the front seat.

"I'll call if I find anything," Will said and then hung up. "Lincoln wants me to keep him posted."

"Do you think it's unsafe?"

"No, but I need to check it out." He drove out of the picnic area and then turned on to a fire track. Dust floated in the air, proving someone had come this way recently.

The track was a lot bumpier, soft sand rather than compacted gravel and they had to go slow. She held the seatbelt away from her chest, so it didn't rub.

"Where does this lead?" Fleur asked.

"It joins up with one of the other roads through the park." He wound down his window and leaned out to listen. "It could be someone taking a short cut."

"Hear anything?"

"No." His hands clenched the wheel.

Did that mean they'd stopped? They could be waiting around a bend. Her chest tightened. At least she was here with him and he wasn't facing whoever it was by himself.

They rounded a curve in the track and Will slammed on the brakes, swearing.

Fleur braced herself, gritting her teeth as the seat belt dug into her laceration and they hit one of the big plastic containers in the middle of the track. The container bounced out of the way and came to rest in the bush as the car stopped.

"Are you all right?"

Her pulse raced, and her chest now throbbed. "Yeah. You?"

He nodded. "These must have just been dumped." In the distance was the rumble of another car driving away.

Will growled. "Call Lincoln." He drove around the other containers and accelerated.

"Shouldn't we wait here?"

"Not if I can get a number plate."

She understood his irritation, but the creepy guy who had threatened Mai wasn't someone to be messed with. She dialled Lincoln's number, told him what they'd discovered and where.

"I'll send someone out as soon as I can," he said. "Did you see anyone?"

"Not yet. Will's trying to catch them."

Lincoln swore. "That's not a good idea. Let them go."

If Lincoln was concerned, the matter *was* serious. She pressed the speaker button. "Do you want to repeat that so Will can hear?"

"Will, let it go."

"I'm not going to confront them. I want a number plate," Will answered, not slowing.

"Damn it. I don't want either of you hurt."

"We won't be."

Will's face was set. She wouldn't change his mind. "I'll call you if we catch them." She hung up. Was there anything she could use as a weapon in the car? Nope.

Keeping her eyes glued on the track in front of them, she braced herself for anything. They reached a T-junction and the gravel road split into two directions. A faint cloud of dust floated to the right. Will followed it.

At least now they were on a main road it wouldn't be so obvious that they were following. The trail of dust grew thicker and thicker. They were gaining on whoever it was. Rounding the next bend in the road, a white four-wheel drive appeared ahead.

"Same car as last time," Will said.

"What now?" Fleur asked. Would the driver get alarmed and attack them?

"I'll pass them," Will said. "You write down the number plate and see who's driving."

This was a very bad idea. "Will, the road isn't wide enough to pass safely and you're already going too fast." She gripped the armrest even as she opened the notes app on her phone. They were gaining on the car, and the driver didn't increase speed.

The whole back of the four-wheel drive was covered in dirt and there were a couple of stickers on the back windscreen, but it was hard to make them out. The number plate was also hidden by the thick red dust.

"We're coming up to a T-junction," Will said. "We might be able to pass on the new road."

Fleur's skin prickled.

The four-wheel drive slowed and indicated left. As they drove up behind it, the dust settled and a stick figure family of five with a dog was on the back windscreen.

Suddenly Fleur was flung to the side as the car fishtailed. Will swore as he pulled to a stop. The white four-wheel drive accelerated down the road. "Did you get a look at the driver?"

She shook her head. "Let's call Lincoln, tell him which way it's gone." She winced as she touched her throbbing chest.

"Are you all right?" He squeezed her hand, expression concerned.

"All the braking hasn't helped."

Will swore. "Sorry, I forgot. Let's head back to the containers."

Fleur breathed out a sigh of relief. "Thanks." She didn't want either of them to get hurt.

They drove back towards the fire track where Ryan and Adam were meeting them. Will's phone rang, coming loud through the stereo in the car.

"Hello?"

"Is this William Travers?"

She smiled. It was weird hearing him being called William. "Yes."

"This is Jenny Loveday from Big Sky Mining. We've read your job application and we'd like to interview you as soon as possible."

Job interview? Where?

"Ah, thanks." He glanced at Fleur. "When?"

"Are you available for an initial video interview today?"

There were no mines near Blackbridge, so it had to be a fair distance away, particularly if they were doing a video interview. She frowned.

"Late this afternoon would be best — four o'clock?" He pulled to a stop before the dumped containers and shifted in his seat.

"That's great. I'll email you a link."

Will hung up and got out of the car.

He wasn't even going to acknowledge the call? Fleur slammed the door, tried to keep her voice casual while her stomach fluttered. Didn't he want her to know about it? Maybe he wasn't sticking around. "What's the job?"

"Environmental officer." He didn't look at her. It was like he'd reverted to his original shy self. She didn't like it.

"Where?"

"Goldwyer."

Her heart clenched. A million miles away, but it was his home. Maybe he'd applied weeks ago, before they'd met. "When did the job come up?"

"Mum told me about it last week."

Last week. She swallowed hard. OK, so not so long ago. Her heart squeezed. She needed to be rational. They'd only been dating three weeks. It was too soon for him to be serious about her, and she'd known this was a possibility.

But damn did it hurt.

He hadn't even mentioned it to her, which meant she wasn't a factor in whether he took it or not. But she wouldn't say anything, wouldn't make it hard on him. She didn't want to hold him back from something he really wanted. It was her own fault she'd fallen for him too hard and too fast.

She forced a smile. "That's great. Good luck with it." If Will cared about her, he would offer her some words of explanation.

The police car drove up the track and she went to meet it. Will said nothing.

Will ran a hand over his face and suppressed a groan. He'd completely stuffed that up. The call had thrown him, turned him mute.

And Fleur had been right to question him. They were dating and he hadn't mentioned he'd applied for a job that would take him thousands of kilometres away. And despite the fact she'd wished him well, he hadn't seen her posture this stiff since they'd run into Trevor and Nicole at the ice cream shop.

Maybe he would have figured out a way to explain if the police hadn't arrived.

Or knowing his track record, maybe not.

After the police left, he'd explain to Fleur that he'd felt like he'd had to apply, that he didn't know if he wanted the job.

And hope she'd understand.

Ryan and Adam were thorough in their investigation, though Ryan had been irritated that Will had gone after the vehicle, therefore obliterating any tyre tread tracks they could have got.

He hadn't thought about that.

When they were finished, Fleur asked Ryan, "Can I get a lift back into town?"

She wanted to leave? "You shouldn't be alone."

She barely looked at him. "I'll visit Hannah."

"Sure," Ryan said.

"I'll call you later." She smiled, but it wasn't a Fleur smile. It was the kind of smile she'd given the more annoying members of the club when they'd complained about the meeting being cancelled, the I'll-pretend-I-agree-with-you-but-I-actually-think-you're-an-arse smile.

Crap. It had to be about the interview. There was nothing else it could be.

Did she not want him to move?

Or was it because he hadn't told her about it?

Was he meant to share his whole life with her?

Though this was an important step, so yeah, he should have given her the heads up. But in his defence, he hadn't expected the call when she was in the car with him.

Great. Now he was debating with himself.

Will sighed and waved as they backed down the fire track. He checked the surroundings, made sure nothing had spilt and then went back to his checklists.

He'd figure out what to say to her and call her tonight.

That afternoon, Will arrived home early. He would call Fleur as soon as he'd finished the interview. He connected his laptop directly to the modem to ensure it didn't drop out and settled at the kitchen table, his stomach a dust storm of nerves.

Jenny called at four on the dot and introduced the two other people on the call. They were both older males, Tony whose skin was so pale it looked like he never saw the sun, and Andrew with the brown, weathered skin of someone who was never in an office.

He could do this. He'd had a lot of practice talking to people now. Smiling, he said, "Nice to meet you."

The interview itself was fairly standard. They asked him about his qualifications, his experience and whether moving to a small town in the middle of nowhere would be a problem.

"I grew up in Goldwyer," he said.

"Are you Brian's son?" Tony asked.

Will nodded.

The man smiled. "Great guy your dad."

"Thanks."

"We're done here," Jenny said. "We'll call you by the end of the week."

Tony interrupted. "I think it's safe to say Will's made the shortlist."

Hell.

Andrew nodded, while Jenny's eyes widened, and she scrambled for a piece of paper.

"Let's get him to fly up and take a look at the place."

Will stared at the screen. He should say something. "Sure. When?"

"As soon as possible. I want that position filled. I'll leave Jenny to arrange the details." He disconnected.

Andrew smiled. "You'd be good up here. I'll look forward to meeting you in person." He hung up.

Jenny cleared her throat. "Right. Well, that's not the normal way we do things here," she said. "But we do have a FIFO flight coming up tomorrow. Can you get to Perth for it?"

So soon? He wasn't even certain he wanted the job. But at least he'd be able to make a decision quickly. And Fleur was back at work tomorrow. "Yeah." His boss wouldn't mind if he took a couple of days off. "Can you send me the details?"

"I'll do it right now."

The flight was at six which meant he'd need to leave in the middle of the night to make it or drive up tonight. He needed to talk to Fleur.

He needed some fresh air. He went outside into the garden, ran his hand over the soft leaves of the woolly bush.

They were keen to have him. Was he the only person who'd applied?

Had his father asked them to interview him?

He'd been so focused on getting back to Goldwyer, he hadn't cared what kind of environmental job it was, but now he had connections here, friends here, Fleur. He hadn't told his mother how settled he was.

"Hey, Will. You're home early." Elijah slammed the back door behind him as he came outside.

"Had a job interview."

"Where?" He took a sip from his beer.

"Goldwyer."

Elijah's jaw dropped. "You applied?"

Will nodded.

"What about Fleur?"

He shrugged. "I don't know what I'm going to do. They're flying me up tomorrow to look at the mine, to explain the job and show me where I'd be living."

"Wow, that's quick." He tilted his head to the side. "You

don't seem too happy about it."

"A month ago I would have been ecstatic…"

Elijah nodded. "But now you have me. I get it mate, really I do, but I can't hold you back from your dreams."

Will opened his mouth, but no words came out.

Elijah cracked up. "I'm kidding."

"It's partially true." Will smiled as Elijah's jaw dropped open. "I mean, before you moved in and I met Fleur, my life was empty. Now I have friends, a quirky roommate and an amazing girlfriend."

"I'll take quirky." Elijah walked over to the back steps and sat down. "So what does Goldwyer have?"

"My family."

"You're close to them?"

Was he? When was the last time anyone other than his mother had called? His brothers never did — though that could be a general brother thing. "How do you tell? Are you close with yours?"

Elijah pursed his lips. "My sister's a hoot and we call each other regularly, and I love my parents, but they don't get me. They support who I am without understanding it."

"My parents are the same. They supported me going to university, but I'm the first one in the family to go."

"Do you miss the town? Do you have a connection to the land up there?"

"In part. It's what called to me, made me study environmental science at uni."

"Do you have the same connection down here?"

He shrugged. "I haven't been here very long."

"Sounds like the best thing to do is go back, see how you feel when you get there." He stood up. "You just need to tell Fleur."

He winced. "She already knows. She was in the car when I got the call about the interview."

"How did she take it?"

"She wasn't happy." He stood up. "I should call her."

Fleur answered on the second ring. "How was the interview?"

"Good. They want me to fly up tomorrow for another

one."

She was silent for a second before she said, "That's great."

Her tone was off. He wanted to see her, explain in person, hold her. "What are you up to tonight?"

"Hannah and I are at the movies in Albany. It's about to start."

She wouldn't be back for a few hours and he needed to get to Perth for his flight. "Is someone staying with you?"

"Yeah. Hannah's staying the night at my place and then I'm working a morning shift tomorrow. I'll be fine."

She didn't sound fine. She sounded not exactly cold, but not her normal warm self. "About the job—"

"Listen Will, I'm sorry I've got to go. The movie's starting."

He sighed. "I'll call you when I get back."

"All right."

He hung up. Fleur was still upset.

Hopefully he'd know how to fix it when he returned.

Chapter 20

The plane touched down on the runway in Goldwyer, the rumble of the wheels on the tarmac surprisingly loud. Will braced himself as he peered out the window at the blue sky, red dirt and the small airport terminal building across the way. The moment the plane doors opened, the dry, scorching heat would flood in.

Welcome to summer in the Pilbara.

Will waited for the rush of passengers to disembark and then hefted his duffel bag over one shoulder and walked down the steps of the plane, closing his eyes for a second to embrace the heat. A year since he'd been home. The heat still evaporated every bit of moisture from his skin almost before he had a chance to sweat.

It wasn't something he'd missed.

He followed the FIFO workers in the direction of the airport building. He'd never flown up to Goldwyer, so the airport wasn't a building he was familiar with. People milled about under a shaded verandah waiting for their luggage to be unloaded, and a couple of people held signs with names on them. He spotted Jenny.

"Did you have a good flight?"

He nodded.

"The car's this way." She led the way through the building to a white ute with Big Sky Mining written on the side. "We'll introduce you to the team and do the second interview first," she said, backing out of the car park. "Then Andrew will take you out to show you the mine and tell you about the type of monitoring work you'll be required to do." She glanced at him. "But you're pretty familiar with it, aren't you?"

"Yeah. My parents have both worked there."

She grinned. "Sounds like you're the perfect person for this job."

Maybe he was.

It was a short drive into town. The rich red dirt and small pale green shrubs that spread out over the plain had been his playground. So why wasn't he excited about being home?

"You've organised your own accommodation for tonight, haven't you?" Jenny asked.

"I'm staying with my parents." His mother had been ecstatic when he'd called to tell her.

"Great. I'll get the address from you and pick you up at seven-thirty tomorrow to take you back to the airport for the flight home." She was efficient and friendly. They passed the big blue sign announcing Goldwyer and then turned right to head into town. "I'll take you for a quick tour through the town before we go out to the mine — though I know you're familiar with it."

For most of his life, this was all he'd known, the extent of his existence. There was the hospital he'd gone to when he'd broken his arm playing with his older brothers, and the primary school was down there.

He didn't recognise any faces on the streets, but this was a mining town and people came and left according to their jobs. There wouldn't be much of a town if the mine wasn't right next door.

After the short tour, Jenny headed out of town to the mine office. His muscles tensed the closer they got. He needed to relax, needed to interview well in case he chose to stay.

Sitting at the reception desk was a face he knew well.

"Aggie, what are you doing here?" The last time he'd seen his neighbour, she'd been working as a wildlife rescue officer.

"Will, it's great to see you." She stood and hugged him.

He'd spent many an afternoon at her place, helping her take care of the injured animals. She'd nurtured his love for the outdoors.

"I'm getting old, and those hourly feeds for some of the babies were getting too much. I've passed the baton to Enid and got a job here."

"And she's a gem," Jenny said. "The meeting room is this way."

He'd never thought Aggie would give up caring for wildlife, but she was a lot older now. Circumstances changed. He followed Jenny into a meeting room without windows. All it contained was a long oval table surrounded by six chairs.

"Can I get you a drink?"

"A glass of water would be nice." He needed to focus on why he was here. He had to decide whether he wanted the job, whether he wanted to move back.

Andrew walked in.

This was it. They could take him as he was, or not at all. The nerves dropped away as he shook Andrew's hand.

"Nice to meet you."

By the time the interview was over and he'd toured the mine, it was close to four o'clock. "Where can I drop you?" Andrew asked.

"In town would be great." He wanted to walk through, find out whether it felt like home.

The tour of the mine had been interesting. He'd been there several times at community open days, but this was the first time he'd been told in depth about what environmental monitoring was required. It depressed him to watch the big haul trucks moving ore and the way the mine cut into the environment. There would be no rehabilitation until the mining had finished.

Andrew pulled up in front of the supermarket. "Will this do?"

"Yeah, thanks." He shook the man's hand.

"Thank you for coming up on such short notice."

Will hadn't asked how many people they were interviewing; how many were flying in for a second interview.

He almost didn't want to know. Slinging his duffel bag over his shoulder, he wandered down what accounted for the main street, taking in the atmosphere. It was still thirty-six degrees and sweat ran down the back of his shirt. It was dry and the land was flat, the buildings low to the ground. He'd forgotten how hot it could be and how the buildings were all the same. There weren't even any friends here in town that he could visit. How tragic was that?

He continued to the small brick and tile house where his parents lived. Inside his nieces and nephews yelled playfully. His mother had retired and now cared for his brother's kids after school while their parents worked. He knocked loudly on the door and before he could open it, feet thundered towards him and then the door swung open wide and he was faced with a collection of kids ranging from three to twelve. "Hey."

"Will!" Alyse, the oldest, said.

Her brother turned and yelled, "Nanna! Will's here."

"Well, let him in," she called.

Alyse gestured Will in and he found his mother in the kitchen cooking dinner. Her long dark hair had more grey in it and her face had an extra line or two, but the hug she smothered him in was just as he remembered. He squeezed her back. He'd missed this comfort of home.

"How did the interview go?"

He stepped back, poured himself a glass of water. "Not bad. Andrew seems OK."

"He is, isn't he?" She squinted at him. "Did you get the job?"

"I don't know yet." He hesitated. Should he admit he wasn't certain if he wanted to return to Goldwyer? She would be upset.

"I'm fairly sure you will." She smiled.

He winced and sipped his water.

She pursed her lips. "Something's wrong."

He wished she couldn't read him so well. "What do you mean?"

"You don't want to move back home?" Hurt flashed across her face.

Will swallowed hard. "The job's not exactly what I want." It was the truth. He wanted to be proactive in protecting the environment, not part of a company who destroyed it. His job would entail monitoring and reporting and justifying that the mine was complying with all the environmental regulations.

"At one stage you didn't care what environmental job it was as long as it got you back here."

Living in the city had sucked his soul. Now though…

"It's Fleur isn't it?"

His heart jumped. "What?"

"She doesn't want you moving home."

"She hasn't said either way."

His mother frowned. "Then she doesn't love you. You shouldn't give up your chance to come home for her."

How dare she judge Fleur? She hadn't met her. Will stepped back and folded his arms. "We haven't talked about it yet."

"I'm telling you if she cared, she would have told you not to go to the interview."

"Or maybe she just wants the best for me," he snapped.

Her eyes widened and she put a hand over her mouth.

Crap. He'd never spoken to his mother like that before. "I'm sorry, Mum."

She scowled, pursed her lips together. "You can put your things in your old room." She opened the pantry door.

He winced and turned to go. No. He couldn't leave it like this. "Mum, I know you're upset, but a lot has changed for me in the last few weeks and it's not just Fleur. I've got friends now and I love being a park ranger. I'd hate the environmental monitoring at the mine."

"What about me and your father?" She pointed out the door to where the kids were playing. "You're missing out on your nieces and nephews growing up."

He raised an eyebrow. "I have other nieces and nephews that don't live in Goldwyer."

She frowned and then put down her spoon and walked over to him, examining him. "You really have changed," she said, tears glistening in her eyes. "You never would have stood up to me before."

She was right, and he was happier for it. Fleur had brought laughter and friendship into his life. She'd helped him come out of his shell and encouraged him to be the best version of himself. He touched her arm. "I still love you though."

She hugged him, squeezing him tight. "I love you too. It's hard seeing my last baby grow his wings and leave the nest." She sniffed and pushed him away. "Go put your things away. I need time to adjust." She wiped her eyes.

He kissed her cheek. Everything was going to be fine between them. He wandered down the corridor to his room. It hadn't changed since he'd left. He'd slept on the bottom bunk while his two brothers had the single bed and the top bunk. Still hardly enough room to move. It was one reason why he'd spent more of his time outdoors, in the bush. He dumped his bag on the single bed and checked the time. Fleur would be at work, but Elijah should be home. His finger hovered above the call button.

Here he was, back in Goldwyer, back where he'd been wanting to be since he'd left high school, but the people he wanted to be with were home in Blackbridge.

Home.

Was that what it was?

He had friends, a place of his own and most importantly he had Fleur. He'd make a home wherever she was.

He rocked back on his heels.

Did he care for her that much?

Yeah, he did. He wanted to be with her, to protect her, to love her.

So what the hell was he doing all the way up here?

The urge to return immediately was overwhelming, but he had no car, and even if he had, it would be quicker to wait for his flight in the morning.

Blackbridge wasn't going anywhere, and Fleur was protected. She was staying with Hannah tonight.

He smiled. Now he knew what he wanted. And she was close to two thousand kilometres away in Blackbridge.

He couldn't wait to get home.

Tim walked Fleur out to her car after she finished work. She scanned the car park looking for anything out of place, but it was empty. This edgy feeling that made her jumpy was unwelcome. She wanted to catch whoever was after her as soon as possible, but would they even try if she was constantly surrounded?

"Thanks, Tim, but you really didn't have to."

He laughed. "Kit told me in minute detail what she would do to me if I let you go by yourself," he said. "We all want to make sure you're safe."

Maybe not everyone. She hadn't heard from Will since he'd left. He hadn't even sent a text message. Blocking the pain, she hugged Tim and got into her car. "I'll see you tomorrow." She drove out of the car park and towards Kit's farm.

Perhaps foolishly she wanted Will to be the one to contact her, to show that he missed her, that he cared.

But maybe he didn't.

Or maybe he'd been busy catching up with his family.

It didn't take more than a minute to send a text.

She was so stupid. How could she fall in love with someone when she'd known he might not stay? She should have been like Kit and kept things casual. Then her heart might not hurt so much.

She shook her head as she turned onto the highway. She had to stop obsessing. She needed something else to think about.

Her phone rang.

"Fleur, it's Nicole. I left my salad bowl out at the track on the weekend and I really need it back. Any chance you're heading out that way?"

Fleur slowed and pulled over on to the side of the road. Kit would be pissed if she was late. "I'm on my way out to Kit's."

"*Please*, Fleur. I've got Trevor's parents coming for dinner tonight and it's the only bowl big enough to feed the horde."

She squirmed in her seat. She shouldn't go out to the track by herself, not when someone was trying to hurt her, but no one else with the clubhouse key would be able to do it. And

Nicole had been working hard since the accident. "All right. I'll drop it around shortly."

She made a U-turn and headed towards the track. She needed to call Kit.

"What's wrong?" Kit demanded.

"Nothing. I'm calling to let you know I'll be a little late. I need to stop by the track to pick up something Nicole left in the clubhouse on the weekend."

"You shouldn't go out there by yourself. Can you pick up Mai?"

"She was heading into Albany with Nicholas this afternoon," Fleur said. "Don't worry, I'll be careful. Only Nicole knows I'm going out there."

"She could be the psycho trying to kill you."

Fleur flinched. Kit was right. "OK. Can you call Lincoln for me? Get him to meet me out there?"

"I'll do it right now."

She hung up. Could Nicole be the person who was trying to hurt her? She shook her head. No, it was more than likely Paul, who had finally turned up and proclaimed to not know anything about the wire. Nicole wouldn't have had time with her two jobs and taking care of the family. She drove through the open gates of the track. Seriously, how difficult was it to stop for a second and latch them?

Annoyed, she drove a loop around the clubhouse before pulling up outside it. No one else was here, the grounds were free of rubbish and the cockatoos squawked to each other as they sat in the branches of the gum trees. Still Kit's warning made her shoulder blades itch.

She would be quick.

She got out, sorting through the keys to find the one for the door. It opened easily, and light filtered through the open door, so she didn't bother switching on the power.

Where was the bowl?

She should have asked Nicole where she'd left it. The tables and bench tops were clear. Normally the fridges were cleaned out because it could be weeks before anyone was back, but Fleur opened them anyway.

Nothing.

She glanced towards the open door, her unease mounting. She'd be trapped in here if someone did want to hurt her. She'd check the cupboard under the bench where all the miscellaneous crockery was kept and then head back to the car.

The cupboard was stuffed full of mismatched plates, and bowls of every variety; plastic, glass, big, small. Any one of them could be Nicole's.

She squatted down to get a better look. Nope. She would have to call Nicole back, but she'd do that from the safety of her car.

A noise behind her had her twisting around.

There was a blur of metal, then piercing pain, and nothing.

The big green sign proclaiming 'Welcome to Blackbridge' made Will smile. After a two-hour flight and then a four-and-a-half-hour drive, he was finally home. He drove straight to Fleur's place, needing to see her, to tell her he was staying in Blackbridge. Her car wasn't out the front, but he knocked on the door anyway.

No answer.

She would be with one of the musketeers. He dialled her mobile. It rang and then went to voice mail.

Was she ignoring him?

Nerves fluttered over his skin. She couldn't still be mad at him, could she? He tried Kit next.

"Is Fleur with you?"

"She should be," Kit growled. "I just hung up from her and she was heading out to the track to pick up something Nicole left behind."

His gut clenched. "By herself?"

"Yes."

What was she thinking? "Did Nicole ask her to?"

"I guess so. Fleur asked me to call Lincoln and I was just about to."

He climbed back into his car. "I'll head out there too." His phone connected to the car as he backed out. Though she seemed to have resolved things with Trevor, Fleur would do almost anything to help them.

He frowned as the thought resonated with him, the image of the sticker family on the back of the vehicle they'd seen flashed through his mind. Trevor had three kids. "What kind of car does Nicole drive?"

"It's a white four-wheel drive like Hannah's."

Damn it. Every instinct in his body went on high alert. He accelerated out of town. "You'd better call Lincoln."

"You think it is Nicole?" Kit asked.

"I think she might be the person dumping the waste. If Nicole thought Fleur had seen her, she could be in real trouble. Get him out there." He disconnected. If he was wrong, and overly paranoid, he'd apologise when Lincoln arrived.

Will drove as fast as he dared. He was overreacting. Fleur would be perfectly fine, and he'd probably pass her on the way out. And if he wasn't, then he'd pick Fleur to win in any fight against Nicole — unless Nicole was armed.

He pressed the accelerator closer to the floor.

When he hit the gravel road, he was forced to slow. Almost there.

He would be ridiculously relieved when he arrived, and Fleur wandered out from the clubhouse. He'd forgive her for not answering her phone.

The gates were wide open, and he drove through, pulling up next to Fleur's car. He grabbed his phone and jumped out, jogging to the clubhouse.

His heart lurched.

Empty. But what was that on the floor by the sink? He moved closer and nausea rose in his stomach.

Blood.

Something had happened to her. But where was she?

The toilet keys still hung on the hook on the wall, but that didn't mean Fleur didn't have an extra set.

He jogged over to the toilet block. It was locked. There were no other buildings that she could be in.

He scanned the whole area, looking for a flash of colour which would prove to be Fleur doing something out on the track.

Nothing.

His heart beat rapidly in his chest.

Think.

He needed to check the whole track before he indulged in any kidnapping scenarios. There were only a few places where the track couldn't be seen from the clubhouse. His feet drew him in the direction of where they'd first discovered the waste. It was hidden from view and if Nicole was involved she knew about it.

He called Lincoln.

"Did you find Fleur?"

"No." He kept his voice low as he scanned the whole track. "Her car's here, but she's not and there's blood on the floor of the clubhouse. I'm heading for where we found those chemicals."

"We're about five minutes away. Be careful."

Will hung up and switched his phone to silent. He needed to watch where he trod so that he didn't make any noise. If Fleur was in trouble, he didn't want to alert her attacker.

And had to hope she was still alive.

Chapter 21

A sharp impact jolted Fleur awake. Pain shot through her body and she groaned. What was going on? She raised a hand to her throbbing head and blinked to clear her vision. Why was she lying in a hole in the ground?

An acrid smell filled her nose and as she shifted, her hand brushed a plastic container. More chemicals. She gingerly sat up. She was in the hollow where they'd found the original containers. She frowned. They'd cleaned those up.

"Fuck, why won't you die?" The pissed off voice came from her right where Nicole stood at the top of the depression with a wheelbarrow.

Nicole.

Looking for her bowl.

Being hit over the head.

Was Nicole behind all of the attacks? "What are you doing?"

Nicole's laugh was brittle. "You're so dense." Gone was the usual polite and friendly woman Fleur had thought she knew. In her place was a person whose movements were jerky as she loaded the wheelbarrow into the back of her car. Nicole retrieved a shovel from the boot. "This is all your fault." She strode down to her. "You and those stupid, fucking motorbikes. You paralysed my husband."

Fleur winced. "I never meant to hurt Trevor." Obviously

Trevor hadn't told her about their conversation. It *had* been an accident — a horrible, tragic accident, but an accident nonetheless — no one was at fault. She cautiously tried to rise.

Nicole pushed her back down with the tip of the shovel. "You're not going anywhere." Real fury shone in her eyes.

Fleur's pulse raced. Nicole could do real damage with the shovel. Slowly she shuffled into a more comfortable seated position, keeping her eyes fixed on the crazy woman above her.

"You ruined my life. I loved being there for my kids. And then you fucked it up."

Fleur didn't dare speak. Nothing she said would calm Nicole's anger. There had to be a way to get away from her, but she was at a distinct disadvantage in the ditch. She needed to get to her feet.

"You can't even comprehend how hard it's been. We were suddenly without any income and he was in hospital in Perth for *months*. I couldn't afford to stay up there to be with him, I had to find a job." She stabbed the shovel on the ground.

Fleur flinched. It was too close to her.

"The pay barely covers our mortgage, so I had to get a second job. I've been slaving my guts out for months to provide for my family." She paced away. "I can't even afford to buy the kids ice cream when they want it."

Fleur scrambled to her feet, her head spinning. She blinked rapidly, trying to clear her vision. "I didn't realise it was so bad."

Nicole whirled back around. "That's because you didn't ask," she snarled. "You prance around with your stupid friends as if you own the town, but don't lift a finger to help anyone not in your inner circle."

Her words hit Fleur right in the chest. Had she been that selfish, that self-absorbed? It had been guilt and fear that had stopped her from reaching out to Nicole, but that wasn't a good enough excuse. "Is that why you turned to this?" She gestured to the containers.

Nicole laughed. "This pays my bills and groceries," she said. "I can't afford to say no to any opportunity and they pay me well to dispose of some extra waste."

Fleur's stomach swirled. She had assumed Nicole had friends and family to help her.

"Then I discovered that behind my back Trevor and his stupid brother were making plans for him to ride again. Like it wasn't dangerous enough when he was fully able! And *you* said yes." She stepped forward, raised the shovel high over her shoulder like a baseball bat. "And Trevor thinks you're so damned saintly for letting him. *He* feels bad because you feel guilty."

The determination in her eyes froze Fleur's blood. She stepped back and tripped, falling back into the hole. Her head spun, and Nicole split into two figures as her vision blurred.

"You didn't have the decency to die when I slipped aspirin into your water, or strung the wire across the track, but you won't escape this time."

Nicole swung the shovel, aiming for Fleur's head.

Fleur had time to blink as she raised her hands to protect her head. Her forearms blocked the metal handle of the shovel, the jolt of the impact numbing her hands. She needed to grab it before Nicole swung again.

She wasn't ready to die.

She had so much to live for, so much she still wanted to experience.

But Nicole had the advantage, standing over her, and she ripped the shovel away to swing again.

She had to get to her feet. Had to stop the spinning in her head. She got her legs under her into a squatting position as Nicole brought the shovel down again.

"No!" The bellow distracted Fleur and a figure launched himself at Nicole.

Will.

He tackled Nicole, but the shovel hit Fleur anyway, pain exploding through her side as she was knocked to the ground again.

Gravel bit into her palms as she pushed herself up. Blurred shapes rolled on the ground in front of her.

She had to help Will.

Scrambling to her knees, nausea welled up in her. She

didn't have time to be sick, she needed to protect Will, she couldn't let Nicole hurt him.

"Calm down!" he yelled. "It's over."

Fleur's vision cleared. Will had Nicole pinned under him, his hands on her wrists, his body weight on her chest.

Nicole bucked under him. "No. You can't stop me. She has to die." She wrestled a hand loose and punched Will in the face.

Fleur crawled towards them.

"The police are on their way, Nicole. You won't get away with this."

Her eyes widened. "The police?"

Fleur hoped Will was telling the truth. Her strength was failing her.

"No, no, no." Nicole cried. "They can't arrest me. No one was supposed to know. I'm all my family have. I can't go to jail." She spat at Will, struggling under him.

Tears blurred Fleur's vision even further. This had all started from Nicole's desire to protect her family.

"Too bad," Will said.

She had no idea what he was doing there, how he'd known where to find her, but she was glad he was.

"Will! Fleur!" It was Lincoln. Fleur sank back to the ground, relief flooding her.

"Over here!" Will yelled back.

Nicole renewed her struggle, tears pouring down her face, but Will didn't move.

Lincoln appeared at the top of the hollow and swore, Ryan right behind him.

Lincoln made a bee line to Fleur, while Ryan went to help Will. "Are you all right, Flower?"

She shook her head and the stars appeared again. "Help Will."

He glanced over. "Ryan's got that sorted. What happened?"

It was hard to form words. "Nicole ... shovel ... hit."

"Nicole hit you with the shovel?"

"Yes."

"We'll get you to the hospital, get you checked out." He

spoke into his radio.

"No ambulance."

She didn't need to arrive at work for the third time in an ambulance. She leaned against him, his shoulder solid.

Then Will pulled her into his arms and everything was that much better.

She was safe. Will was there.

"What happened, Will?" Lincoln asked.

Fleur didn't listen to his explanation. It was too hard to focus. All she wanted to concentrate on was that Will was here.

She closed her eyes.

Fleur was warm in his arms and Will wanted to hold her forever, but she needed medical attention. The side of her face was covered in blood and her whole body was limp. He pushed her gently away. Her eyes were closed.

"Fleur."

She murmured, but her eyes didn't open.

His heart jumped. "Stay with me, Fleur."

Lincoln was already on the phone calling an ambulance.

"Look at me," he ordered, and her eyelids fluttered. "That's it."

"What happened?" Ryan asked. Nicole sat handcuffed on the ground, sobbing. All fight had left her.

"I found them both here. Nicole attacked Fleur with the shovel and I tried to stop it." His wrist ached from hitting the ground hard, but Nicole's body had cushioned most of the impact. She had to be hurting too. "She said she'd slipped aspirin into Fleur's water bottle and hung the wire at the track. She's been trying to kill her since she discovered Fleur agreed to Trevor racing again."

He'd bet she was responsible for all of the other things too including dumping the waste.

Will brushed a kiss over Fleur's forehead. "She needs to get to the hospital."

Lincoln nodded. "Ambulance is on the way."

Fleur's eyes were closed again.

"Come on, Sweetheart, keep your eyes open," Will murmured, his heart pounding. "You know what to do."

"Hurt. Sick."

"I know, but I've got you. You'll be all right." He refused to contemplate anything else. He knew little about head injuries, but the fact she was having trouble focusing couldn't be a good thing.

His chest squeezed. He wouldn't lose her. Not now, not ever. He loved her. He wanted to spend the rest of his life with her. He wouldn't let Nicole take her away from him.

Where was the damn ambulance?

Finally he heard the sirens and Ryan went to meet it.

"We'll need to interview you both later," Lincoln told him as the paramedics appeared at the top of the hollow with a stretcher.

"As soon as I know Fleur's all right." No way was he leaving her alone.

"OK."

Will was forced to move out of the way as the paramedics examined Fleur. She was a bit more lucid, answering their questions, so perhaps the worst was over.

As he waited, he called Gary and left him a message.

Eventually the paramedics were satisfied, and they helped Fleur into the ambulance. He climbed in with them.

"The clubhouse is open," Fleur said.

Only Fleur would be worried about something like that while her brain had been scrambled. "Lincoln will see to it." They needed to get to the hospital.

It was several hours before Fleur was discharged with a mild case of concussion. She'd been taken to the Albany hospital to have a CT scan and Will had stayed by her side the whole time. He'd called Kit and the musketeers had rallied around, and now they were all back at Fleur's place.

He wanted to be alone with her, to hold her in his arms and tell her he loved her, but her friends needed to fuss around her as well, making sure she was comfortable.

Gary had arrived, still smelling of fish and all in a panic

until Fleur had assured him she was fine.

Will understood the panic. He couldn't bear the thought of losing her either.

Which meant he needed to make sure he didn't.

But was it too soon for declarations of love? She probably needed time to process everything that had happened to her first. He should give her a couple of weeks at least.

But he didn't want to. He wanted to tell her he was in for the long haul, if she'd have him.

It was getting late and Fleur was hiding her yawns behind her hand.

"Do you want to go to sleep?" he murmured.

"Yes."

He stood up, interrupting Kit's conversation about Paul. "You need to go."

"What?" Kit said, bristling.

Crap. That didn't come out the way he meant. "Fleur needs to get some rest."

"But that doesn't mean we have to go. She shouldn't be alone."

"I'm staying." He met Kit's stare, daring her to disagree with him.

"Listen here, Captain. Don't think you can boss us around. We love her, and she almost died." There was real concern in Kit's eyes and her voice broke on the last word.

"I love her too."

It wasn't until the room went deathly silent and all three musketeers stared at him with their mouths open that he realised what he'd said.

Hell. That wasn't how he'd meant it to go. But there was no changing it now.

"What did you say?" Fleur whispered.

He crouched in front of her, brushed the hair gently off the bruised side of her face. He swallowed hard. "I love you."

"But you're going home to Goldwyer."

He shook his head. "No, I'm not. I had to go back there to realise that it's not my home anymore. Blackbridge is. No, that's not right. Anywhere that you are is home for me."

Behind him one of the girls gave a heartfelt sigh.

She stared at him. Maybe he'd said too much. "I don't expect you to feel the same way, it's all happened so fast, but I'm patient. I want to be right here next to you for the rest of my life." He glanced up at Lincoln. "But not in a stalker way."

Lincoln grinned.

She was still silent. He might have made a real mess of this. "Maybe I should go." He turned, and she grabbed his arm.

"No!" Her eyes sparkled. She tugged him closer and he sat next to her on the couch. She cupped his cheek. "I love you too, Will Travers."

His mouth dropped open. She loved him. The grin that spread across his face couldn't be controlled and his heart beat so fast he was afraid it would burst out of his chest.

"Well, that's a relief."

Laughter rang out behind him and he winced. He might never completely cure his foot in mouth disease, but that didn't matter.

This was Fleur.

And he had nothing to hide from her.

Epilogue

Every muscle in Fleur's body still ached three days later, but the bruise on her face had lost that angry purple colour and was moving towards mauve. She'd been given the weekend off work to recover and she'd spent it with Will.

"Should we eat outside?" Will asked. "It's a lovely evening and we could move the kitchen table out on the deck to make room for everyone."

She smiled. "Great idea. I'll help you move it."

He shook his head. "No, let's wait for the musketeers to arrive. One of them can help me."

"I'm not going to break if I lift a table, Will." He'd been fussing over her all weekend, which had been nice at first, but now she was ready to get back to her normal life. She'd be working tomorrow, and she needed to stretch and exercise.

He drew her close to him, brushed a kiss against her lips. "You're precious to me, and I keep seeing Nicole swinging that shovel at you." He shuddered.

"I'm fine, thanks to you." She would never get tired of being held in his arms. "Now why don't you get that end and I'll get the other?"

A loud knock on the door followed by a yelled, "Is it safe to come in?" made them both grin.

Kit.

"I'll get it." Will headed for the front door.

He was just as comfortable in her house as the musketeers were. She liked that, liked the confident man he'd become.

Kit and Jamie had arrived together, quickly followed by the rest of the musketeers and their partners. Lincoln was the last to arrive.

Jamie and Will had carried the kitchen furniture out to the deck while Mai and Hannah made drinks and Kit ordered the pizza. It wasn't until the food had arrived and they were all sitting around the tables outside that Kit asked, "So what's the latest with Nicole?"

It was a question she'd been dying to know the answer to. Certain parts of the investigation would take time to get answers and she hadn't wanted to think about what Trevor and his family were going through. Lincoln had strongly suggested she stay away from them until all the evidence was collated, but she'd sent Mai and Hannah around to see how they were getting on.

Everyone had been in shock.

"We can't comment on an active investigation," Lincoln said, his cop face on.

"That's bullshit, Lincoln. Fleur has a right to know," Kit said.

He ignored her.

Fleur didn't want them arguing. "What we do know is she was responsible for dumping all the waste around town. From what she told me, it sounds like she was getting paid by the drug manufacturers to dispose of it." She hated that Nicole had been so desperate, but she was past the guilt. Nicole could have asked for help.

Will squeezed her hand. "She also admitted to three attempts to kill Fleur: putting aspirin in her water bottle, the wire and then the attack at the track."

Hannah shook her head. "I had no idea. I spoke to her about Trevor riding again and she seemed perfectly fine with it."

It was comforting to know she wasn't the only one who had been fooled.

"Did she admit to the roses and the tyre?" Mai asked.

Fleur glanced at Lincoln, but he said nothing. "I can't

imagine it would be anyone else."

"We can tell you the finger prints and blood found at the clubhouse were a match for Nicole, and she has shoes that match the footprint we found near the water tank," Ryan said.

"What's going to happen to her now?" Hannah asked.

"She's been charged with a number of offences including attempted murder and vandalism."

Fleur closed her eyes. "Has Trevor been to see her?"

"Yeah, he visited her at Albany station. She's not going to be granted bail."

"Poor Trevor." Nicole's whole life was over. She was barely going to see her kids or her husband and Trevor would need to manage on his own. "Maybe we should see if Trevor needs a hand."

"Are you kidding me?" Kit said. "His wife tried to kill you."

Fleur winced. "Kit, part of this happened because no one asked if they needed help after Trevor's accident."

Kit rolled her eyes. "Which wasn't your fault."

"I know, I realise that now." She would still do what she could to help Trevor, but the guilt was no longer there.

"Fleur wouldn't be Fleur if she didn't care for everyone." Will pulled her close and kissed her.

She smiled, drawing comfort from his nearness. She liked this demonstrative side of him. Her friends smiled back at them, except for Kit who scowled and turned to Lincoln. "You need to catch this drug cartel before anything else goes wrong. I'm tired of my best friends getting attacked."

His stare was hard. "We're working on it."

Fleur squeezed Kit's leg. There was more than one reason why Kit was taking her frustration out on Lincoln. She'd have to talk to her later, when they were alone. "I'm sure Nicole will tell them more when she calms down." She let out a deep breath. There was nothing she could do about Nicole or the drug cartel making Blackbridge their base of operations and she needed to reduce the tension between her friends.

"Does anyone want another strawberry daiquiri?" Hannah stood up.

Fleur wanted to celebrate being alive and having her

friends around her. Celebrate being in love. "Make mine a virgin." The painkillers wouldn't mix well with alcohol.

Next to her Will chuckled. "Not anymore," he murmured.

She laughed. "I love you just the way you are."

Thank you for reading!

I hope you enjoyed the book. It would be super awesome if you could leave a review wherever you bought it, because I love to hear what you thought of the story (yes, even if you didn't like it!)

Acknowledgements

As always there are so many people to thank for helping with this book. I had many people help me with my research so first of all to Matt Hartfield who continues to help me with all the policing details. Any mistakes are my own and for the good of the story. Also to Gary and Frank who helped me with the night race and vintage motocross information, Ian Anderson for giving me an insight on being a park ranger, Stephanie from Yates for answering my questions about poisons and roses and Jennifer Maughan for the dairy details. The information you gave me was invaluable.

I also need to thank my cousins, Scott and Marian Leggett for being my sensitivity readers for this story.

And finally thank you to those people who helped me see this book into print: thanks to Lana Pecherczyk for the awesome cover, Ann Harth for her structural edits, and Teena Raffa-Mulligan for her copy-edits.

Nothing to Lose

The Blackbridge Series #4

Kit's story is coming early 2019.
http://www.claireboston.com/NothingToLose